PAIN IN PALMYRA

PAIN IN PALMYRA

BRUCE ALTERMAN

Columbus, Ohio

Pain in Palmyra

Published by Gatekeeper Press
2167 Stringtown Rd, Suite 109
Columbus, OH 43123-2989
www.GatekeeperPress.com

ISBN (hardcover): 9781642372991
ISBN (paperback): 9781642372984
eISBN: 9781642372977

Printed in the United States of America

ACKNOWLEDGEMENTS

SPECIAL THANKS TO Scarsdale, New York, Police Detective Richard Fatigate, for his expert research and technical assistance. This book would not have been possible without his contribution.

Tremendous gratitude goes to Port Neches, Texas, physician John H. Lee, DO, for his broad insight and physiological mastery, regarding medical facts in this book.

I would like to thank my wife, Dawn, for her invaluable editorial expertise and style recommendations.

Distinguished Boston, Massachusetts, attorney Marc Estrich, generously brought his gifted mind to this book for consultations concerning prose and inherent legal issues

CONTENTS

THE HOUSE ON CANAL

"The world is a dangerous place to live, not because of the people who are evil but because of the people who don't do anything about it."

—**Albert Einstein**

THE CEMENT-BLOCK ROOM was lit with a string of bulbs on an extension cord, a wire hanging from one wall, up across the ceiling, to the other wall. Muscular men, bare arms, biceps bulging, laughed loudly as they tossed turkey drumsticks back and forth. Heavy sputum dripped down their chins. Large white teeth jutted out from their open mouths behind long bushy beards as they bit down on the barbecued poultry. Noisy floor fans blew hot, stale air through the basement. The artificial breeze was the only escape from the oppressive heat in the concrete room.

Two teenage girls sat on wooden chairs, silent and still. Another young woman lay asleep on a mattress in the corner. They did not move and did not scream. They were in shock, too scared to do anything, their slight builds in stark contrast to the behemoths who were reading books or practice fighting with huge knives. Some of the bearded long-haired men were sparring, circling each other, and then striking out. One would block a punch followed by another punch that would get through. Other large muscular men with cutoff sleeves, and exposed veined biceps lifted weights and grunted during heavy squats with sandbags across their backs. Two of the men sat on a couch at the far end of the room. Their combined girth filled up the space on the small, orange cushioned couch. Both wore sleeveless denim jackets, exposing their bulging arms. They spoke in hushed tones.

"We need just one more girl to complete the quota for the chosen seed masters."

"Where are we going this time? Albany or New York City?"

"We're going to New York City this time. The Albany police might start thinking that there's a pattern if we go there again. We better get down to New York City tomorrow because I'm itching to get back to Zion. Where are Brothers Walton and Elijah at?"

"They're upstairs, in prayer and reading scripture."

"Let's get 'em down here 'cause they got to be ready to go tomorrow morning."

One of the men on the couch yelled to the group in the middle of the room.

"Somebody go get Elder Elijah and Elder Walton down here! I need to talk to 'em!"

One of the larger men walked up the basement steps and went out through a rickety door. A few moments passed before the basement door opened again. The light from upstairs shined down onto the small stairway from the door's threshold. Two crisp clean-shaven young men walked down the narrow basement steps. They had fresh short haircuts parted on the side and looked early twenties in age. Their short-sleeved white shirts were starched stiff, and their neckties had flawless full Windsor knots around neatly-buttoned collars.

The clean-cut young men presented a conservative appearance juxtaposed to the unsavory Neanderthal group who occupied the basement. An outsider would never see the oddly constructed faction all together.

The two Caucasian young men unfolded metal chairs and sat in front of the two large, long-haired characters, who made the three-cushioned orange couch look small.

The two girls sitting in the chairs started to cry.

"When are we getting out of here, Walton?" a girl asked.

"Two more days, my sweet sister, and then we will travel to Zion. Your salvation awaits you in just a few days. Be patient, my sister, Zion is just hours away," Walton said.

"But you told us that we would be in Zion two days ago, and we're still stuck here in this basement. Can you take us for a walk along the canal again?"

"I'm sorry, my sister, but we cannot leave our basement chapel until we are ready to ride to Zion. I imagine it will be just another two days. Then you will see the warm glory and the red rocks of our Promised Land. You will pray to Jesus and our Heavenly Father that Zion exists and it was worth this waiting. It is prudent at this time that you read the scriptures that we have provided you. True salvation and happiness with God is just a moment's time away. Read and pray for now. We will be in Zion before you know it," Walton said.

"But I want to see the sunshine. We've been down here too long," the other girl said.

"If Satan can get us thinking that our time should be preoccupied with TV programs or overcrowded schedules or caught up in some other aspect of the press of modern life so that we do not have prayer, he has effectively won on that point. We must use this time for prayer. Satan doesn't care how he stops us . . . just so he stops us. Ask yourself, how many times have you prayed this last week? Who is winning in your soul? What's the score? Don't let the evil one win. You can overcome him with God's help," Walton said.

"You boys ready for another mission into New York City?" The big man's voice was gravelly loud.

"Yes, Elder Jessop, they will be His, and He will save those who need saving. Heavenly Father, we pray and ask that You watch over our endeavors. May our Heavenly Father bless this place where we stand now, the holy land, oh the Sacred Grove. We have been there now. We have blessed the sister wives in its glory," Elijah said.

"Uh, well yes, purity is now achieved through the prayer inside the Sacred Grove. Yes, bless the prophet and all who follow him," Jessop said.

"Regarding the potential fourth sister wife, we were able to teach her some of the commandments this week during a lesson. She is doing great, but it is tough to be able to meet with her. She also is so young, so sometimes she isn't as serious, but we are trying to help her. She is a little confused right now, as she doesn't know what to do. So we have focused a lot on prayer, and trying to help her pray, as God answers our prayers. We were able to visit her two times and basically taught her the same things both times, as she didn't understand, really. It's much harder to teach the doctrine to a nineteen-year-old than a forty-year-old person who is familiar with the gospel terms. We shared a lesson on obedience and shared a scripture! So we were talking to her about baptism. She is totally ready but just needs to make a leap of faith with the decision. We think that her desire to be baptized has increased this week, and we will be working really hard with her on that. We are going to try to baptize her this week!" Elijah said.

"If the Spirit is within us for the task, then it shall happen with the grace of God," said another large man.

"When are we traveling to New York City? Do you need me to fill up the van with gas?" Walton asked.

"Yes, good thinking, Elder Walton. Yes, fill up with gas. God directs this work. Following the Spirit is of the utmost importance. And we should always be attentive. Let us spend the night in New York City so that you missionaries may complete your work on the fourth sister wife for the seed master," Jessop said.

"I was also wondering if this is the last sister wife that is required for the prophet before we head back? Will our mission finish once we select the fourth sister?" asked Elijah, his narrow head tilted.

"We are complete upon connecting the fourth sister wife with the seed master. We leave tomorrow. You and Walton, ride up front in the van as usual. I will sit in the back seat of the van on the way down and back up. Hershel and Dunlap will be riding with Brother Barlow in front and behind you."

The two young men stood up.

"Walton and I had better get upstairs for some rest. Praise Jesus Christ and the prophet, and let's pray for our safe return to Zion," said Elijah.

"Yes! You boys get on upstairs and get your beauty sleep. We'll be here waiting for you in eight hours. May the Spirit be with us," Jessop said.

"Good morning, elders, rise and shine. We have a big day in front of us."

Jessop was up early to make sure everything went well with today's operation. In the early hours of the next morning, on a mild summer day, the young men were dressed impeccably in their stiff white shirts and perfectly creased dark slacks. They arrived back from the gas station with the large white van and parked in front of the scraggly, paint-chipped house. Elijah and Walton entered the small house, sat down on the couch, and prayed to God that their mission would be successful and that they may return to the Promised Land of Zion. Silence reigned through the house, cloaking the misery and fears of the three teenage girls who were seated in chairs in the concrete basement. They showed obedience, only raising their hands when they either were hungry or had to go to the bathroom. A few mattresses were on the floor in case they wanted to lie down and go to sleep. All three girls had books on their laps and were required to read the scriptures. Their white dresses were spotless, and they didn't look like they were being mistreated. However, they were essentially prisoners, as expressed by the grim looks on their faces.

No more than a few motorcycles would leave the barn at one time. The most anyone else in the neighborhood might see would be two well-dressed young men leaving the front entrance. The heavyweight-sounding Harleys would ride out just once in a while. The white panel van parked out front was of no concern to anyone. It was innocuous enough, and the only drivers were the two young men.

Elijah was the real brains of the good-looking twenty-something duo. However, Walker was not stupid; he was just not as smart as Elijah. Walker had very good looks, a square jaw, blond hair, blue eyes, chiseled cheekbones, and a thin waist. His broad shoulders framed his perfect head, kind of what people might describe as a "Ken doll." Elijah was plainly handsome, having wavy dark hair, evenly apportioned features, and brown eyes that could look into another's eyes and pierce their souls while also pushing their personal buttons. People found it difficult to look away from his magnetic stare.

"The van is gassed up. We're ready to go anytime you guys are," Elijah said.

Jessop stood up from the couch and turned to the three girls, who were now sitting in wooden chairs. His sheathed Bowie knife and heavy motorcycle boots made him look extra ominous. The girls pretended to read their books and were too scared to look up. Jessop towered over them. His wide girth, long black hair, bushy beard, and over six-and-a-half-foot height made him appear like a giant warrior from another time.

"You sisters, keep to your studying of the scriptures and continue your prayers. We'll be back tomorrow. Then it will be on to Zion, and you will finally be in the Promised Land to fulfill your promise to Jesus Christ and the Heavenly Father. We pray that the Spirit will keep us on our path to salvation and glory . . . our souls live forever."

"Can we get something else to eat besides barbecued turkey, beans, and bread? Do you have any salad upstairs?" a girl asked.

"Of course, sisters, I'll make sure one of the elders goes out this morning so you may enjoy your salads for lunch. How does that sound?"

The girl looked down at her book.

"Good, I guess?"

"I'm going on a short mission with Elijah and Walton, and you girls, all study your scriptures now. Anything you need, just speak up and these elders here will get it for you. Remember, my sisters, soon to be saints in Zion, we are all children of God. He loves us and knows our needs, and He wants us to communicate with Him through prayer. We should pray to Him and no one else. The Lord Jesus Christ commanded, 'Ye must always pray unto the Father in my name.' As we make a habit of approaching God in prayer, we will come to know Him and draw ever nearer to Him. Our desires will become more like His. We will be able to secure for ourselves and for others blessings that He is ready to give if we will but ask in faith."

Jessop walked up the basement stairs and closed the top

door behind him. The time had arrived for their final mission before returning to Zion.

Three motorcycles rode from the driveway, made a left turn, and disappeared, their rumble fading in the distance. The white van pulled out from the backyard of the house. Their arrival in New York City was a mere six hours' time ahead.

SAVE HIM

"It is not the healthy who need a doctor, but the sick. I have not come to call the righteous, but sinners to repentance."

—Jesus of Nazareth

H E OPENED HIS eyes and looked up. The light from the bright-blue sky streamed down in sparkling golden rays. Powerful white light detonated behind his eyes. His temples felt locked in a vice, squeezed by an unseen force. A constant high-pitched wailing rang in his ears, rising and falling, like an air-raid siren, echoing inside his head.

Pain coursed through his entire body. The throbbing had awakened him from a long unconsciousness. He felt agony and terror in the absence of any cogent thought. Fear ran through his soul at the uncertainty of his being. He had no idea who he was or where he was. He felt his left eyelid caked in dried blood, causing a crusty cover that only let him see through thin cracks.

Pictures flashed in his mind, but he didn't recognize those mental images. His focus was primal. An intense concentration to stay alive was his only resolve.

When he finally struggled enough to sit up, he noticed that

his left arm was limp and useless. There was an ACE bandage wrapped around his forearm, and the pale color of its elastic fabric was soaked in blood. His right arm was still strong, so he used it to drag himself a few feet and then sit up by reaching for the lower branches of a small tree.

He struggled to stand using both shaky legs, but swayed back and forth with dizziness that sent him reeling. Yet he didn't fall. Somehow he remained upright and stood in one place. All he had to do was hold on to the tree branch and try not to collapse.

The surrounding forest started to spin, which made him feel dizzy. Instinctually, he let go of the tree branch and reached up to the left side of his forehead. With his right hand, he felt a hole, a hole in his head, big enough for his index finger to fit inside a jagged rim. His finger touched the empty void in his skull. Simultaneously, he felt a bolt of pain explode in his head like white lightening. The pain flashed from the back of his neck all the way down to his right leg. He leaned forward a bit, and sharp pains stabbed from inside his body, almost crumpling him to the ground. Yet, somehow, again, he kept on his feet.

An amount of time passed before he could finally take a step forward, and after some long minutes, one foot continued to step in front of the other. He occasionally had to grab onto a branch or lean against a tree to compose himself. His heart pounded in his ears like a concert kettle drum. A constant loud ringing started in his head and continued like a deafeningly loud fire bell. The pressure in his head was pushing him to new heights of pain, a hellish consciousness usually reserved for those who experience medieval torture.

The direction he took was aimless. Walking was his only goal. He dragged his feet on the ground and stumbled forward but managed to stay upright. If he stopped, then he knew that collapse would soon follow. He grabbed onto tree branches as he made his way through the maze of forest growth.

Blood started to ooze from the hole on the left side of his forehead. It ran down his cheek and dripped from the curve of his chin. Somehow he remembered to reach into a pocket that was stitched into the left arm of his black one-piece jumpsuit. When he looked down, there in his hand was a small, orange first aid kit. He popped open the plastic latch with his thumb and saw a merciful wad of white cotton gauze, which he promptly stuck into the hole in his head. The pain was excruciating and his face twitched, but he was too weak to scream. He involuntarily squeaked out a pathetic whimper.

The forest floor was full of tree roots, rocks, and rotted logs. The strong wind whipped the leaves from the trees. His pace was slow, but he still had two good legs and a stout right arm. He walked slowly, aimlessly, unsure where he was going. A thought occurred to him that if he wanted to stay alive, he had to find a road.

If I don't go home now, I will die out here.

Overwhelming panic overtook him and produced a shot of adrenaline that coursed through his body. The trees swirled around him, and the ringing in his head coupled with uncontrolled anxiety beleaguered him. His upper body tightened and he couldn't breathe, which led him to grab his chest with his right hand. The last thing he saw was the ground fast approaching.

When he awoke, his left cheek was pressed against soft green moss. His eyes opened slowly, and the woodlands floor came into view. First he saw strands of green grass and colorful leaves. Then, resting against a small rock was a knife, propped up like it was purposely positioned in a trade show display. He recognized the knife—it was his—and he suddenly remembered everything. The icon of his Japanese-style tanto filled his head with a flood of images. His rejuvenated memory was catalyzed by the sight of the glorious ten-inch blade. Droplets of morning dew created tiny prisms that reflected a purple sparkle upon the steel. He reached out with his right hand and grabbed the handle; its form in his palm brought a rush of emotions that caused his body to tremble. His hand conformed to the familiar feeling of the knife's handle and brought on a torrent of recollections. He now remembered that he was Dom DioGuardi, also known as "La Morte," also known as "Tommy Karate," and he was in a Catskill Mountain forest. Those were his last conscious thoughts before passing out, again.

When he woke up, many hours had elapsed. He knew that it must be sometime in the afternoon because the sun was low in the western sky above the mountaintops. The leaves looked like they were turning color. Then he recalled it was autumn and the year was 1998. He remembered that his car was hidden to the west, and the setting sun would indicate the direction to take.

He stood up again. Blood continued to seep from the hole in his head, and the ACE bandage on his aching left forearm was soaked in blood. He slid the large knife into its sheath on his belt and started walking again.

The sun continued to shoot its golden rays through the trees. Step by step, he walked on. He cradled his left arm with his right hand. The pain was slowing him down. That's when he saw the human bodies sprawled on the ground. There was a wide, deep hole in the ground. One of the two bodies was decapitated, and the other man's body was pockmarked with bullet holes. He used his knife to cut the shirtsleeve off the headless body to make a sling for his left arm, tying a knot with his teeth.

As he stumbled through the forest, a sudden vision of a gun's muzzle blasting into his face made him almost fall; he had to stop. It was a most horrific memory, one that kept recurring over and over like an endless film loop. Sheer terror struck him again. The worst event that he could imagine had happened: shot in the face.

When he stepped out of the forest and onto the road, a certainty of surviving gave him confidence. Sunshine lit the comforting hard asphalt under his feet and filled his soul with warmth. He walked a bit and then removed the leafy branches covering his car. In his zippered shoulder pocket was a key, and he opened the trunk. The sight of his five-watt cell phone pack was the solution to all of his problems. But there was no cell signal, not even one bar of strength. He would have to drive up the road for a cell signal to make a call.

The pain he felt sitting behind the wheel of the car made him wonder if he would be able to stay on the road without fainting from blood loss. There were no other cars on the road, so he was able to drive slowly, his torso bent over to his right. The pain coursed through his entire body. He struggled to keep his head above the dashboard.

After driving two miles north, he drove onto a side dirt road and stopped. He curled his torso onto the steering wheel. The pain was excruciating. The pack phone on the passenger seat suddenly beeped, indicating there was cell reception. He drove farther down the side road to the top of a dirt patch under the cover of trees and made the phone call to Brooklyn.

He heard ringing, glorious ringing, twice, three times, and then "Yeah."

"Frankie, you hear me okay?"

"Sure, boss, you don't sound too good."

"Come get me now. You got to get here as quick as you can. I'm hurt real bad. Bring Joey because he's gotta drive my car back. Get a pen and write down where I'm at."

He described his location and then fell sideways onto the front passenger seat, hoping his boys would get there soon.

A DAY AT THE OFFICE

> "Choose a job you love, and you will never have to work a day in your life."
>
> **—Confucius**

THINGS WERE GOING great for Pete Baranowski. The crisp New York City air of summer, 2002, had the fresh promise of ever-increasing success. The inside of his new midtown office on West Thirty-Fifth Street was furnished with authentic art-deco guest chairs and mid-century desk lamps. Pete's maple-wood desk, bought from a SoHo antiques dealer, swooped around his high-backed leather office chair like a crescent moon. The guest chairs facing the desk were Danish blond wood with black-and-white checkered cushions, all purchased with gift money from his friends, who had suddenly struck it rich.

New insurance clients were calling daily with cases. The downtown Broadway personal injury lawyers gave him more than a few cases each week. Additionally, the marital surveillance business was providing an excellent revenue stream. Cash flowed from clients who wanted to catch their spouses cheating. Pete's young private investigators would tail the philandering spouses and obtain pictures of the commingling paramours. In fact, he was doing so well, he hired an efficient secretary to sit in a reception area out front to answer phones and conduct online research.

Pete's workday was consumed with assigning an array of insurance claims cases to his team of five field investigators and then making sure that his reports were accompanied with invoices. Occasionally, on a very important case, Pete would have to handle the matter himself, especially when a longtime client requested his personal attention. He preferred traditional PI gumshoe work over straight surveillance cases. Sitting in a surveillance minivan all day was not his idea of a good time, even though the money was great for nailing insurance claimants with an incriminating video. For Pete, it was the face-to-face, upfront-type investigation that inspired him to do great work. Whether it was obtaining a signed statement from a witness or taking pictures of an exploded boiler, Pete didn't mind the footwork as long as things went perfectly and his invoices were justified.

Undercover work wasn't Pete's thing either. Sneaking around all day, keeping secrets, and spying on the people he was working with at the client's business felt like an unpalatable way of making a living. Of course he had done his stints of undercover work, posing as a host in a restaurant when the owner wanted to know which bartender was stealing cash, or becoming a factory worker in a precious-metals plant for nine weeks, while secretly investigating who was stealing platinum. Pete had learned that the employees who weighed the platinum were hiding tiny pieces under their tongues, which didn't register on the metal detectors on their way out because the amount was so small. After a few years, the platinum thieves had amassed quite a large sum. Pete's work put the kibosh on their misdeeds.

Working an undercover case takes a certain intense dedication by the investigator, and the undercover investigation always consumes a lot of time. Pete was too busy to go undercover these days, so he always gave these cases to his investigators.

Surveillance and undercover cases are always the most profitable. By their very nature, these cases demand long periods of time spent concentrating on gathering evidence. In business terms this means that invoices to the client yield large profit margins for the PI firm. The undercover investigator always profits in a big way by double dipping. Spying on fellow workers produces not only an employee paycheck to the undercover agent from the client's business, but also a regular salary from the investigator's PI agency.

One of the most dangerous business situations to avoid is the passion that can evolve within the undercover investigator. The investigator often starts to sympathize with the people he is spying on and might even come to sincerely befriend them. This emotional attachment to his coworkers deflects the investigator's loyalty and may lead to the investigator covering up the illicit activity that he is supposed to be reporting about. It is similar to a syndrome known to affect hostages who have been kidnapped, referred to as the "Stockholm syndrome," where the hostages sympathize with their captors. In this not-too-uncommon predicament, Pete humorously referred to his investigators as acquiring the "Helsinki syndrome"—an amusing twist on the Stockholm syndrome—when the investigator started sympathizing with his surveillance targets. If the investigator appears like he or she is defending the culprits, then the undercover agent must be "exfiltrated" from the case.

A year had passed since the 9/11 tragedy, and the downtown World Trade Center dust continued to permeate structures south of Fourteenth Street, making the area practically uninhabitable as far as Pete was concerned. With his personal health a foremost consideration, he was able to move uptown with the help of a wad of money he had received from his friends. Pete moved his office from his East Village Second Street location to a posh, upscale office building on West Thirty-Fifth Street. In 1998, Pete received $100,000 from two friends he had helped during an intense case. Last year, they generously sent Pete an additional $300,000 with a cryptic note constructed of cutout newspaper print that read "We'll never forget what you did for us." He shifted his office operation into a two-room midtown PI office up on the fifth floor in an old 1930s building that had a brown brick façade with large windows. It turned out to be a great move; he found that clients seemed to take him more seriously because of his new office location. This justified Pete to raise his hourly rate.

Living in Manhattan can be a money pit, but business with the insurance companies and lawyers was good enough to support Pete's comfortable lifestyle. The occasional marital case or juicy undercover assignment added to his coffers with big heaps of cash. Pete had two young sons, and the large, upper-eighties West Side apartment made it seem like there was never enough money. It was a blessing that his wife, Cathy, had a good job as an office manager of a downtown law firm. Her salary made the occasional family vacation possible, and her connections added to Pete's private investigation business by directing personal injury cases from lower Broadway lawyers to Baranowski Investigations.

Manhattan was always Pete's hometown. Born and raised on the island, his young persona growing up was an eclectic mix of the people he connected with. Known for his sardonic attitude, he was the class clown. His pudgy frame wasn't necessarily fat—Manhattan always required a lot of walking, which burned off calories. However, the lunches and desserts had put a few pounds around the middle, and some pants had gotten too tight. He didn't care for working out, and haircuts were few and far between. His black mustache always needed trimming.

His parents brought Pete up loosely in the Jewish faith, but he never took religion seriously and thought that all religion was bordering on insane behavior. Pete's respect for the masses who believed in religion was always evident. He never outwardly voiced his disdain for religion, and inwardly, Pete was void of any prejudice. In Pete's mind—organized religion was a cause of the world's major woes for hundreds of years. However, even with all his skepticism towards religion, Pete had occasionally prayed to God and made a pact with God that acknowledged that God did exist. His prayers, in the past, had somehow saved Pete on many occasions.

Pete leaned back in his chair and put his feet up on the desk, just to take a moment to wallow in his current contentedness. That's when his intercom suddenly lit up with the voice of Vicky, his secretary in the next room. Vicky said that a man who spoke with an English accent was on the phone. The man said that he was referred to Pete by the Investigators Online Network.

The Investigators Online Network—or ION, as it was known—was an international membership of private investigators who were connected by a single office in Tempe, Arizona. The ION office accepted cases from all over the world and then matched up the nature of the case with an assigned investigator's skill set and location. Pete was an active member in the network. Since 1989, he had received many assignments from ION and had been a guest speaker at their annual Scottsdale convention. New York City was a hotbed of private investigation. The ION office was calling Pete a few times a year, with cases coming in from all over the world.

A person who spoke with an English accent on the phone was not unusual, as Pete had conversed with other investigators from South Africa and Denmark within the past few months—they needed investigations handled in New York City, and Baranowski Investigations could supply the talent to take on their cases.

During the conversation with the Englishman, it seemed to Pete that it might be some kind of hoax. The case that the Englishman described strained Pete's common-sense parameters. However, the more Pete questioned this Oxford-sounding private detective, the more Pete believed that he was authentic. Pete had been a member of the Investigators Online Network for a number of years, and this English guy was name dropping some of the investigators who spoke at the 2002 convention in Scottsdale, Arizona, just a few months ago.

The articulate voice on the long-distance call said that his name was Jonathan Edwards and that he hadn't met Pete at the convention, but did hear about him through other attendees. Jonathan Edwards continued to tell a story about his former career as a member of the MI5 spy force in England before opening up a high-tech private investigation shop in the United States, located in Pontiac, Michigan. His agency catered to millionaires in the area who were connected with big-time car manufacturers. The president of the Investigators Online Network had recommended Pete as the best man in New York City for assigning agents to cases.

Pete listened as the Englishman related a story about his client whose daughter had run away from their home in Bloomfield Hills, Michigan, to New York City, and they'd located her possible residence. They'd also located where she may be working. The daughter's name was Julia. The father, a powerful CEO, wanted his daughter back home at any cost.

When Pete asked about the daughter's age, Jonathan replied that she was only nineteen years old and that she might be staying at the Martha Washington Hotel, on Twenty-Ninth Street in New York City. He continued to say that her work situation was unique; they believed she was a prostitute in a cat-house apartment also located on Twenty-Ninth Street. Jonathan said that he didn't have anyone in New York City to physically pose as a customer and go up to the apartment to determine if she was really there. Additionally, Jonathan said that New York City was a place he didn't like to work in because it was too chaotic. Moreover, in such a situation, his people would not be able to wear a gun inside the house of prostitution. This was a problem, because his people wouldn't go anywhere without a gun. He inquired if Pete's agency had anyone who could undertake this case.

Well this is a nice undercover assignment indeed. I'll use Greg to act as a young customer to go up into that apartment. This should be a short, sweet case for a big chunk of money.

"If you can overnight me a cashier's check for three thousand dollars and make sure you include her picture in the envelope, then I can send my agent up there tomorrow," Pete said.

"The parents, my clients, are very anxious to know if she is there. They are prepared to immediately board a flight from Michigan to New York City if you can positively identify that their daughter is there. If I sent the check and her picture on an air flight to New York today, do you think that someone could go to the airport for the envelope and then go up to the apartment today?" Jonathan asked.

"Okay, Jonathan, call me when you put the envelope on the plane, and tell me when the flight is coming in. I'll have my man waiting for it at the airport."

Pete was taken by surprise at the urgency of the whole matter, but he wasn't going to turn his back on a $3,000 check.

THE BROOKLYN PATIENT

"In poverty and other misfortunes of life, true friends are a sure refuge. The young they keep out of mischief; to the old they are a comfort and aid in their weakness, and those in the prime of life they incite to noble deeds."

—Aristotle

GINO NARDONE WAS a flashy young doctor beholden to the Italian mob. He was also a respected young resident physician at Kings County Hospital, located in East Flatbush, Brooklyn. When he wasn't working, Gino lived with his new girlfriend in an expensive private brownstone located in posh Brooklyn Heights. Working on this patient in a small apartment was not his idea of an illustrious night helping humanity. The place had two undersized bedrooms, and he was in one of them with a man who was grievously shot in multiple parts of his body. The room was big enough for two small chairs and a narrow single bed. Anyone else who wanted to be in the room would have to stand. At least the room had bright lights, so he could see what was going on with this patient, who appeared to be on the verge of death.

The expenses for Dr. Nardone's lifestyle had put him in this situation, including his Mercedes-AMG sports car parked in front of the Avenue U apartment building. Gino had done what he could to help the severely mangled patient lying on the narrow bed, but it wasn't enough. The doctor's eyes went wide when he first saw the nickel-sized hole in the man's skull. He had seen many grievously injured people before, but the patient lying on the sunken thin mattress looked in fatal condition and was near total shock. The man's left forearm was shattered, with sharp splintered bone protruding from the skin. In this apartment, without anything other than a bone saw in his bag, Gino's options regarding the man's left arm were limited to sawing it off or letting him die.

The time had finally arrived. His Gravesend neighborhood acquaintances were calling in his debt. Dr. Gino Nardone was in a bad situation; he had accepted a lot of money from sketchy friends to pay off his delinquent medical school loan, except now it was time to pay that loan back. This favor was called in by the lieutenant of the Gravesend, crew: Frankie Flaco. Dr. Nardone had to do what Frankie said; otherwise, there might be an ice pick stuck in the back of his head as retribution for not fulfilling a promise.

The doctor was able to close the cranium wound by screwing down a small, round steel plate, the size of a Susan B. Anthony Silver Dollar, over the forehead hole. It appeared to Dr. Nardone that a bullet must have hit the man's head and then glanced upward, skipping off of the skull, causing a sizable hole. Thankfully, the operation to close the man's head wound was successful, but the left arm below the elbow could not be saved. The man's left forearm was practically split into two pieces, held together only by some strips of connective tissue. The arm appeared as a bloody pulp of bone and stringy sinews. He deduced that it was an injury caused by a large caliber gunshot. The bullet had shattered the forearm bones and turned the arm into an inside-out ripped mess of muscle and tendons. If the man's arm was not amputated below the elbow soon, it was apparent that the dead flesh would cause a gangrene infection and kill his patient. The man remained unconscious, and therefore, the consent to amputate usually given by the patient could not be given.

Frankie Flaco said, "Just do it!" He was calling the shots in the small second-floor Brooklyn apartment that had bars over the windows. So with great regret, Dr. Nardone took a small bone saw out of his black leather bag and proceeded to cut off the man's left arm, just below the elbow.

In Gravesend, Brooklyn, someone frequently sat by his bedside the whole time he was there. A couple of IVs were in his right arm, and his halved left arm was draped in heavy white gauze. The top of his head was also wrapped like a mummy. Whoever was scheduled to come into the apartment would change the IV bags hanging from hooks. A cold pizza was usually in the fridge and the television droned on with useless cable channels. Sometimes the room was vacant after the IV bags were changed and Dom was left in darkness for many hours, all alone, to suffer, night after night, day after day.

Dreams came to him, of Japan when he lived as a young man: beautiful flowers, fog wrapped mountains, his job in the chopstick factory, karate practice, fish, and rice. Somewhere deep in his mind, he remembered fluent Japanese and began to think in Far East Oriental symbols. He saw himself as a young man studying under his karate master. His hair was long, down to his shoulders, just like Bruce Lee. Then he was back in Tokyo, the sidewalk was bustling with people, and his gi was white with a black belt. He dreamt that he was with his revered karate master, Hiroshi Masumi, after winning a high-stakes competition. Suddenly he was in the dojo in Tokyo, where he became an expert in tonfa, nunchucks, and katanas. The traditional Japanese clothes fit him well. The dream took him to the exhibition mats when he fought opponents for the pleasure of the crowd. The cheering made him feel good; a smile crossed his face. He was Tommy Karate again, the person everyone knew and respected in Gravesend.

When he opened his eyes and saw only half his arm, he was shocked, even scared. His heart started beating fast, but then he purposely calmed himself to avoid having a heart attack. His eyes drifted around the room, but he didn't remember the names of the faces he should have recognized. He could remember generalities, like how he probably got into this room, but the details of everything escaped him.

A young face was looking over him. He didn't recognize this face at all.

"How are you? Can you hear me? How are you feeling?"

He didn't answer. He was too weak and too angry.

Then a skinny pockmarked face was close to his, looking at him from just inches away; he recognized that face. It was his trusted lieutenant who had been with him for over twenty years. They had been through many good heists before, but now Dominic knew that he would be deemed a useless liability. The upper echelon of the Gravesend mob was not going to appreciate a broken Tommy Karate. He was now a liability. There was a lesson to be learned about being greedy and going for a score all alone. Now Dominic was paying the price for not involving others in his job; whatever it was. No one knew how he ended up shot in the Catskill forest, and Dominic wasn't saying anything about what had happened.

"Frankie, I'm hurt bad," Dom whispered.

"Don't you worry, boss, the doc here has a shot of the good stuff for ya,'" Frankie said.

As the syringe emptied its viscous liquid through the hypodermic needle into his arm, he focused on Frankie's eyes. The expression from those eyes mocked Dominic; he realized that Frankie now thought of him as a pathetic bedridden anchor that wasn't good for anything.

"Frankie, Frankie, this guy, he somehow got the best of me. I don't know how he did it or what went wrong," Dom said, his voice drifting off.

"Who did it, boss? Who got the best of you? We'll take care of him for you," Frankie said.

Dom didn't answer at first. His eyes closed and slowly opened again.

"He's going to be mine . . ." Dom whispered, and his eyes closed again.

A few more days went by. There were short periods of consciousness with long hours of sleep. When he opened his eyes, there by his bedside was his number-two man. At first the elongated face of Frankie Flaco was fuzzy and out of focus. Eventually, he saw his face sharply, every detail, the prominent nose close up, hovering over him. Frankie's expression was serious, like he was about to say something bad. Dominic was powerless to do anything, physically incapacitated and mentally damaged. Depression was starting to set in, but Dominic's psychotic deep anger kept him half-sane.

"Listen, Dominic, you no longer is gonna be running jobs, so I'm taking over for a while. I just wanted to let you know it's nothing personal, only business," Frankie said.

He was expecting this, so it was not a surprise. This new life was going to take a long time to get used to. Recovery from his severe injuries was his primary goal. To be able to walk again, fight again, and think clearly again, that was going to be his main objective. After that step, things might get back to normal, maybe even better than ever. Yet, his fatigue was completely consuming, making it impossible for him to make plans for the future. All he could do was hope to get out of the apartment, and everything else would come after that.

The dreams of Japan were present throughout his slumber—different dreams but all taking place in the Land of the Rising Sun. Bonsai trees, samurai swords, breaking boards, and throwing metal shuriken became intermixed images during his sleep. A couple of weeks later, when he finally woke from a drug-induced sleep, Dominic mumbled that he wanted to fly to Japan. There he would recuperate and get strong again. His return to Brooklyn, whenever that may be, was going to be a long time away. No one would really care if he came back to Brooklyn anyway, because Dominic had no immediate family in the U.S. except his crazy institutionalized mother at an elderly care facility down in Florida.

The request to go to Japan from anyone except Dominic DioGuardi would be an odd command, especially from a capo in the Bonanno crime family. Yet, the man lying in the bed wasn't the run-of-the-mill mafioso. He was known as La Morte, or in other words, translated to English, "The Death." La Morte was better known to his associates as Dom DioGuardi, a serial killer, assassin, jewel thief, and drug dealer on a wholesale level for the Brooklyn mob. Dominic was also known as Tommy Karate by his mob compatriots. As a young man, Dom had traveled to Japan and stayed for years to become a master in Tae Kwon Do, and also became proficient in the martial arts of the ninja. To those in the mob who knew him well as a karate expert, coupled with his known love of his father's Thompson "Tommy gun", the Gravesend, Brooklyn, reputation of "Tommy Karate" became a neighborhood legend.

He had killed over sixty people in his career and was at the top of his game, with loads of money and a fleet of cars. He liked killing people, and got an extra thrill after he took their jewelry and neatly displayed it inside a lighted hidden wall compartment located at the back of his clothes closet. Dominic was never arrested by the police, not even stopped for a speeding ticket. Amazingly, he was not on any law-enforcement radar, even though he was the ruthless leader of a criminal twelve-man crew. However, things had taken a turn for the worse. He had been bested by a person who was below him, a person he now wanted to torture and kill more than anything else in the world.

The only way to become halfway whole again was to return to Japan, where he knew the ancient remedies would breathe vigor back into his broken body. If he stayed any longer in this Brooklyn apartment, he'd become a wheelchair-bound invalid for the rest of his life. If people are given enough power to make choices when they can, then they should. This thought prompted Dom to leave the apartment and get the next flight to Japan at all costs. Frankie and the crew would be glad to see him leave the country so they could take over all of his rackets.

He made a promise to himself to come back to Brooklyn after Japan. First, it was time to get back to normal, to get strong, to become what he once was, a Mafia capo and a ruthless assassin that everyone feared. The day would also come when he could hunt down the man who almost killed him, and that day would signify a reckoning that marked the end of his recovery and the start of a climb back up the criminal stairway towards greatness. Gaining respect again in Brooklyn was the most important thing in the world to Dominic, and he would eventually return from Japan more powerful than ever. Then he'd be the feared Tommy Karate in Gravesend, Brooklyn, once again.

BIG GREG

"All you need in this life is ignorance and confidence, and then success is sure."

—Mark Twain

THE CITY WAS his oyster and he was on top of the world. His leather Ike jacket matched the color of his brown belt and shoes. Everything fit perfectly, of course. He wouldn't have it any other way, because he loved it when women stared at him. The six-pack stomach and defined shoulders supported his Roman jaw of confidence coupled with a steely green-eyed gaze that emanated self-confidence. Greg was the master of his world because things had always worked out his way. In fact, he was so good at commanding his life's ambitions that referring to himself in the third person, as an entity higher than that of a mortal man, was his normal way of thinking. "Big Greg" or the "Greg Man" always knew what to do in any situation, without even having to think about it.

When Greg's cell phone rang, he was busy maneuvering through the Bronx traffic on his way to take some pictures of an uneven metal cellar door on a sidewalk. A personal injury claimant was suing the bodega because she had tripped and broken her ankle.

Pete's voice crackled over the phone. He sounded harried

as he told Greg to stop whatever he was doing and drive to LaGuardia Airport to pick up a packet. A picture and a check should be inside an envelope that was scheduled to arrive on a 1:30 p.m. flight from Detroit.

Greg was intrigued with this sudden emergency assignment. He had handled some out-of-the-ordinary cases for Pete in the past, but he couldn't imagine what kind of situation would prompt someone to send a same-day payment by jet delivery. Pete had told him that when he got the envelope, he should open it immediately. There should be a $3,000 bank check and a picture of a girl in the envelope. Then Greg was to drive directly to the midtown office for a meeting about the case.

The envelope at the airport was handed to Greg by a young female clerk who tried her best to flirt with him by tilting her head and batting her long eyelashes. Unfortunately, Greg had too much on his mind to partake in the usual repartee with the woman who desired a flirtatious interaction. He was used to women coming on to him all the time. With his athletic six-foot tall build and strong good looks, including a perfect cleft chin and deep-set green eyes, many females couldn't help but steal a glance to admire his young twenty-four-year-old handsomeness. Some girls compared his face to the Greek mythological features of Adonis.

After opening the Zip Express envelope, Greg found a $3,000 bank check and a picture of a red-haired girl with the most beautiful face he had ever seen. She had blue eyes and a bright-white smile that lit up her red rosy cheeks.

This girl looks unbelievable.

He immediately assumed that the young woman in the picture must be another one of Pete's volatile marital cases involving an insanely jealous husband who was shelling out tremendous amounts of money to find out if his pretty young wife was cheating. Greg had just finished a whole set of surveillances for one of Pete's wealthy clients, who was married but wanted his secret mistress followed everywhere. The wealthy guy gave his girlfriend two tickets to a Broadway show, hoping that his girlfriend would take a guy and get caught by Pete's agency. Greg took pictures of the girlfriend and her new guy friend walking into the theater together. Pete was inside already, sitting in a seat one row directly in front of them so he could listen to every word they said to each other. Greg ventured to think that the woman in the photograph must be a case with another hot girlfriend cheating on her rich sugar daddy.

On the way back from the airport, he stopped at his Woodside, Queens, one-bedroom apartment to pick up his laptop. It was a typical bachelor pad, with just cans of beer in the fridge and a fold-up card table with two wooden chairs. The apartment was small, but it was in a great location because he was near the Long Island Expressway, which enabled a quick drive into Manhattan. His aunt owned the small three-story brick building with six apartments and she charged Greg a mere $400-a-month rent. He was only twenty-four years old but acted like he owned the world. Greg was just two years out of Marist College, where he became a varsity letterman on the lacrosse team. Greg started working for Pete right out of college when he saw a want ad in the *New York Times* for an investigator trainee, "no experience necessary." When Greg was first interviewed by Pete, it seemed to Greg that Pete was cold to him, but Greg knew the job was sealed tight when Pete called after getting Greg's thank-you letter for granting him the interview. Working for Baranowski Investigations fit right into Greg's lifestyle of movement and action. Pete sent him all over the city, and Greg always took advantage of whatever fun there was to be had in each neighborhood, especially in Queens, the Bronx, and Westchester.

The office secretary, Vicky, greeted Greg with a happy smile. She liked it when he walked by her desk so she could steal a peek at his athletic body. He wore his usual elastic-waist brown leather bomber jacket and white collared shirt when he walked into Pete's office.

"Ah, Greg, just in time. Vicky can now get to the bank before it closes," Pete said.

"So what's the caper this time, boss?"

Greg fancied himself a man's man and liked to inflect his voice with a New York tough guy's swagger. He threw the envelope onto Pete's desk and leaned back in a guest chair.

Greg figured that this would be another one of those cases where he would wait in his car for hours and then have to react within seconds as soon as he saw the subject. Surveillance came naturally to Greg, mostly because he was mentally lazy. Doing absolutely nothing except sitting in a car didn't faze him. In fact, he reveled in the monotony. He'd park for hours, happily passing the time, consumed with the minutia of his own superfluous thoughts about pretty girls and fast cars.

"This is going to be an interesting case, Greg. I need you to go up to an apartment on Twenty-Ninth Street to see if this girl in the picture here is up there. She is supposed to be working as a prostitute inside the apartment," Pete said.

"Are you shitting me? You're saying that this girl is working as a hooker? After seeing this picture, it doesn't look like she's that kind of girl. Who's the client?" Greg asked.

"Her parents hired these ex-British spies to find her, and I spoke with one who said that he was referred to us by the Investigators Online Network. He said that they tracked her down to this location and they don't have anyone in their agency that can go up there. He also mentioned something about New York City being the only place they won't go. Her name is Julia Olsen. Of course she'll probably have a different name up there."

"So how am I supposed to get into the apartment? What's our angle?"

Pete said that he had already figured out a successful scenario within short order. Greg marveled at Pete's knack to quickly analyze any logistical problem and solve it within minutes. Greg also envied how Pete considered all the options and then arrived at the perfect solution. Case results were ninety percent successful because Pete always described the perfect setup.

Pete explained to Greg that he should act like a naïve kid, a virgin nerd, in order to dupe the house of prostitution into thinking that he was just another immature first-timer anxious to get laid.

"You have to go up there pretending to be a young, doe-eyed, first-time virgin. No doubt, there's going to be a guy who is some kind of pimp in there. Make sure you act like a total dork, someone who is clueless and nervous. Take off that leather jacket, pull up your pants, and button your top shirt button. Talk in a nasally, nervous voice. Explain that your friend, Anthony, told you about the place and it's your first time there. Hopefully the clown routine will get you in the door. Then once you're in the apartment, you'll have to spot her. Don't let them convince you to settle for just any hooker. Tell them that you want a girl about your age who has red hair. Talk to them with a stutter, like you're overly nervous and bashful. Tiptoe around a little, like you are waiting to take a bad piss. And say this is your first time having sex," Pete said.

"What should I do if I see her?" Greg asked.

"Say you want to be with her. Then you'll go back into the room with her, but when you get to her room, say to her that you're too nervous to have sex."

Pete threw five one-hundred-dollar bills on the desk.

"Show her the five hundred dollars so she knows you were serious, but only give her a hundred bucks and say you're sorry, you can't go through with it. Tell her the first time to have sex should be a holy thing because you're a devout Christian. Then just get the hell out of there."

"Okay, sounds like a plan. See you in a little while, boss. I'll walk over there right now. Keep your fingers crossed that she's up there. Otherwise, this case could be a bust," Greg said.

"And, Greg, I know you're a horn dog, so don't even think about having sex with this girl. Are we clear? Her parents are the clients. And don't forget to leave your cell phone and business cards in your car."

"Oh, don't you worry about it, boss. I got my own bunch of babes to choose from any day of the week. This girl might be beautiful and all that, but Big Greg is busy with more than enough hot chicks. So no worries, boss," Greg said, smiling.

The world was perfect for Greg. Everything was coming up roses.

What other job could I get paid $350 a day to see if a girl is there? Man! Thank you, God! What a life! Wait till I tell my buddies about this one! Cold beers, spicy wings, and hot girls, here comes Big Greg ready to lay down the Italian pipe. When it comes to the sex department, just leave everything to Big Greg.

MOUNT TAKAHATA

"It is not the mountain we conquer but ourselves."
—**Sir Edmund Hillary**

DOMINIC DETAILED TO the crew exactly where he needed to be taken in Japan—specifically, a remote retreat tucked away near Mount Takahata, about fifteen miles from Koka, Shiga Prefecture. In the ancient civilization of Japan, there is a special chapter that contains a unique historical factoid: Koka is the province known as the birthplace of Japanese ninjutsu, the martial art of spying, deception, and assassination, which developed there centuries ago. Emperors and lords used the ninja assassins to capitalize on political control by secretly killing their rivals. The specialized martial art of ninjutsu encompasses other dark activities, including poisons, the use of disguises, illegal entry, and fighting with edged weapons. The town of Koka is proud of its ninja history, shuriken throwing star designs lay on the tile floor of their local train station. Although Western culture has glamorized the role of the ninja, an essential truth remains: this so-called "martial art" is all about deception and killing. Also included in ninja training is the art of lying, lock picking, and throwing acid in someone's eyes. These abhorrent violent activities are severe criminal offenses in the modern age.

Dominic knew that he was special. Very few Mafia capos with a crew had ever been both a martial artist and a serial killer. From the time he was just seventeen years old, he shaped his body in Japan. He was supposed to be in Japan for just fifteen months on a scholarship, but then did not go back to Brooklyn until years later. The swords and the knife blades of Japan obsessed him. That's all he could think of—the edge, its chisel point, the curved steel blade, the perfect design, its power in his hand, to instantly and silently kill. The tanto knife made him complete. During his early years in Japan, Dominic supported himself by working in a chopstick factory. Towards the end of his eight years there, Dom made his money working for the Japanese crime mafia, known as the Yakuza.

As an upstart, full of energy, in his twenties, after eight years of intense training and participating in Japanese gang assassinations, he felt ready to return to his Brooklyn roots for his career as a mafia soldier. First, however, he would make a stop in Calabria, Italy, to visit relatives.

After some months working for the crime bosses in Calabria, the mention of La Morte within family circles brought on both comfort and fear—comfort in that he was family, protecting the interests of their clan, but at the same time, the family was fearful of La Morte's sadistic nature. Only after he gained a reputation as a Mafia assassin in Calabria did he return to Brooklyn, still in his twenties and ready to take on New York for money and power.

Presently, the state of his body was in horrible condition. He desperately needed to return to Japan, where he had felt so virile during the 1970s. The plan was to seek his recovery among the monks who had unique Eastern knowledge of the body, with their special understanding of how to cure all bodily ailments. Thirty years ago, as an immature martial-arts student, he was intensely trained, and he never forgot the people or the lessons he learned. He knew that the ancient Eastern medicines and physical techniques could bring his body and mind back to one hundred percent. The priests would have no mercy on him, no compassion. Their rehabilitation training was elemental, but it worked. Dominic was determined to do whatever it took in order to become his former self again.

The unalterable decision to travel to Japan was accomplished, with the help of a wheelchair. Dom was rolled onto a private jet by an extra-large four-hundred-pound crew member known as "Vinnie the Whale." The long journey towards recovery commenced.

The fourteen-hour flight was excruciatingly painful due to some jostling turbulence. The altitude of the pressurized cabin seemed to cause Dom's blood vessels to constrict, which contributed to his sheer agony.

Finally, Dominic felt well enough to open his eyes and look out the small window of the private jet. There, down below, was his love. He saw the Land of the Rising Sun, his adopted country, Japan. Bright golden streams of sunlight cut through the misty hills on the outskirts of Tokyo. For the first time since that horrendous day in the Catskill forest, Dominic had a feeling of well-being that spread over his body. Finally, the future was looking good.

The sky was dark gray with a thick cloud cover. A slight moist breeze flecked Dom's cheeks as The Whale pushed the wheelchair slowly up the cobblestone pathway to the fortress. The structures were fifty-foot-tall Japanese-style stone buildings, shrouded in mist and elevated by a forty-foot rock wall; it looked as if the entire structure were placed on an enormous gray altar.

The uneven cobblestone bumps jostled Dom, and he grimaced in pain as he sat uncomfortably in the wheelchair. He looked up and saw the familiar flared multilevel roofs of two buildings that were symbolic of oriental architecture. All the windows were covered with white vertical iron bars. In front of the larger building, at the top of fifty stone steps, there was a massive double door that was fifteen feet tall, made out of one-foot-thick iron wood reinforced by heavy, black metal strips.

The front door opened a crack, and two Japanese men dressed in blue tunics and toe shoes descended the steep stone stairway. They looked like dwarfs as they stood in front of The Whale. One of the Japanese men looked up and said something with sharp tones.

"What the fuck did he just say to me, boss?" Vinnie asked.

"It doesn't matter, just walk back out to the gate and drive away before they cut your fucking head off," Dom said.

The Japanese man then asked Dom a question, and Dom answered in perfect Japanese and bowed his head.

"But, boss, I'm supposed to just leave you here? How the fuck am I supposed to get back to Brooklyn?" Vinnie asked.

"Get the fuck out of here, now!" Dom rasped.

Vinnie the Whale turned and lumbered back down the cobblestone road as the two Japanese men lifted Dom's wheelchair and carried him up the stone stairs into the confines of the fortress.

Once the front door was closed, the complete attention of the entire compound was focused on Dominic's recovery; the ninjutsu sanctuary on Mount Takahata accepted him as a rehabilitation project. Dom would return to full health by the sanctuary's use of ancient healing herbs combined with physical therapy. The stone temple monks might take years to employ their curative techniques, but they would implement the recovery plan with a dedication that is seldom seen in the western hemisphere.

White smoke trails from burning incense and pungent juniper filled the candlelit room. Deep resonating sounds of multiple singing monks vibrated within the stone room, the vocal harmonies eerily droning in low tones as a rectangular dark-wood box was brought into the room by one of the monks. Another monk stepped over to the pedestal where the three-foot-long by one-foot-wide cherry-wood box was placed. The lid was slowly opened by one of the monks. Inside the box, surrounded by a red velvet lining, was a human-shaped black arm with a hand. Its fingers were slightly curved yet extended. From the molten forges down in the temple basement, the steel arm was crafted by expert Japanese sword makers. The hand's every detail was meticulously molded to resemble the lower left arm of a man. Tears welled up in Dom's eyes when he saw the black arm resting in the red velvet–lined box. Leather straps attached to the base of the forearm unfurled over Dom's elbow, and the straps buckled around his shoulders to hold the black steel limb in place. When the steel hand was covered by a leather glove, the gloved hand extending from a coat sleeve would not look abnormal to a casual observer.

He hadn't felt this kind of intense emotion since his mob girlfriend had died from a heroin overdose. Dom had blamed his girlfriend's best friend for buying the heroin that contrib-uted to his girlfriend's overdose. His feelings of anger over his girlfriend's death had finally been quelled, only when he shot his girlfriend's best friend in the head with two nine-millimeter slugs from a silenced pistol while she slept. He felt like he had killed everything he ever loved—his girlfriend, his dog, and his only friend was whacked by a rival. So much sorrow, too many dead to count.

The intense helplessness he'd been feeling since his arm was amputated was now absent upon the sight of the black arm. He would soon be whole again with the help of the Japanese monks at Mount Takahata.

Time passed; Dom did not know how long. There were no clocks. Much of his day was spent inside walls of misty darkness, where his body and mind were tested beyond all endurance. It felt like years, so long, never ending. He knew that one day the relentless training might stop, but only when he was strong enough, beyond tough, to another level of strength where his victims had no defense against him.

They will want me out of here. I will show them, when I hurt them.

For just a couple of seconds, the meditation bowl produced a particular penetrating sound that enveloped everyone in the room. Dom held the bowl, balanced on the palm of his steel left hand. He rubbed the wood wand around the rim of the steel bowl with his right hand. The droning sound became loud when his revolutions around the bowl were consistent. Then the resonating vibrations of the bowl suddenly stopped, and the wooden wand that was meant to circle the bowl's rim slipped from Dom's right hand and bounced off the slate floor, rolling five feet before coming to rest.

Dom screamed.

A monk in flowing black robes sprang through the air from across the room and landed with bare feet in front of Dom. The monk slapped Dom on the cheek.

Dom quietly sobbed and held his head down to the bowl, looking at it through bloodshot swollen eyes.

He screamed when he bent down and reached for the wand on the slate floor and then slowly stood back up again. This time, his concentration was even more intense. Getting slapped by his masters was a painful experience, and the acute facial sting worked as an incentive for Dom to perform flawlessly. He looked down at the bowl in his left steel hand and proceeded to move the wooden wand around the rim, once again producing a certain high-pitched vibrating tone, a droning, meditative frequency that he sustained for over a minute this time. The monk in the black robes stood up again and handed Dom a larger bowl, ordering him in guttural Japanese to support the heavier bowl with his metal hand. As he started to move the wooden wand around the rim of the bowl, Dominic grimaced in pain. The increased weight of the larger metal bowl strained his shoulder muscles and made it harder to balance.

The self-imposed torture led Dom to a state of angry reflection, inspired by pain and desperation. The harsh environment compelled Dom to believe in himself. He was once known as La Morte, The Death. He must achieve that renowned physical prowess once again! Dom must live, but so must La Morte. Psychotic anger drove him to the next level of his rehabilitation.

The steel left arm felt heavy to him. His upper-arm bicep wasn't strong enough to use his new metal arm effectively.

Dominic's therapy was physically difficult and extremely painful. Inside the Buddhist compound was the healing pavilion, an ancient rehabilitation place for wound recovery. When his masters assigned him physical tasks, they were harsh with him, especially if he did not perform. The tasks usually entailed more pain than an ordinary person could endure, except, perhaps, for those who were able to achieve a psychotic state of mind that surmounts pain. Dom's strength of will persisted, and he refused to succumb, despite his body begging him to quit.

A daily diet of rice, fish, and vegetables made his physique lean, light, and agile. No pizza, no ice cream, and definitely no lasagna ever crossed his plate as he sat cross-legged on a straw mat, eating with chopsticks, devouring whatever measly rations they gave him. He had paid the monks well, so this unwarranted mistreatment made him angry.

During recovery sessions at Mount Takahata, Dom spent long hours inside a hot eucalyptus steam room practicing slow tai chi. His body began to morph back into the physical specimen that he once was, before the awful experience he had in upstate New York.

Day after day, he pushed himself to the limit, and then his masters pushed him even further. Months passed and then years. Time flowed along some hellish line of physical brutality and meditative visions of violence. He wasn't going back to New York until he was ready. Dom wanted his revenge to be exacted the way he fantasized—so Peter Baranowski would suffer like no one had ever suffered before.

More years passed. Time flowed without much sunlight—smoky, dark, gray stone-walled rooms, the air inside filled with men chanting in strange tongues and echoes of low-throated moans. Hours of time became indiscernible space, one day after the other, melting into a single string of space and time.

He was instructed by a Japanese technical surveillance expert in the new methods of electronic eavesdropping, using the latest in cell phone and audio technology. Small-frequency receptors that fit inside his ear canal enabled him to listen to cell phone conversations.

Time flowed by, and Dom achieved a physical toughness never previously realized. Although Dom's eyesight was perpetually blurry due to the incident, he wore thick glasses to correct his permanently damaged vision.

His mind became sharp again. The merciless training that the monks put him through had finally come to fruition. Dom was ready to take on any opponent; in fact, he craved the fighting bloodlust more than ever before.

The metal arm was now an integral part of him. Its initial unfamiliar feeling of leather straps and odd weight was in the past. Dom wielded the steel appendage like a pendulum, swinging the ebony arm with enough force to break bricks with a hand chop and pulverize stone with a finger stab.

Sparring always turned out bad for Dom's opponents. He didn't want to hurt people he liked, yet the worst came out of those good people during practice matches, they'd always tried to take advantage of him because of an inner mean streak. Teenager Dom learned early while sparring in Brooklyn, when he was sixteen years old, that friends can easily become enemies. The eighteen-year-old karate "master" kicked him unfairly right in the testicles because Dom was winning the sparring match.

During the last match between Dominic and his Japanese taskmasters, the outcome of the fight left three black-robed monks writhing in pain. They were victimized with pointed body blows by the tips of Dom's steel fingers. More black-clad and blue-pajama-outfitted monks then entered the room, all wanting to challenge Dom, including one older man dressed in imperial yellow robes. They circled him. Their movements were dancelike, looking for an opening to strike a debilitating blow. This unfair onslaught by a gang of teachers angered

Dom, and once again, something snapped within him. There, in that marble room, at a point of time lost in the universe, was an irrationality born of deep rage. His emotions exploded, releasing a power that exceeded physical human limits. The crazy in him had arisen, like so many times back in Brooklyn. Here, now, in Japan, he wanted to hurt them all.

So he struck out with a blistering vengeance, fomented within a dangerously troubled mind. Rage had now consumed him, pumping blood into every fiber, making his muscles hard as ice. If a monk struck at him, he'd become water, not letting the blow have any impact. Then his frenzied mind turned his muscles back into hard ice, disseminating a force that no man could withstand. His strikes were similar to bullets hitting skin, impacting soft flesh and tearing through it. The involuntary, loud screams of Dom's psychotic anger filled the marble room with thunderous echoes that were horrifically disturbing. His high-pitched yelps were also like weapons, inducing sudden fear. Monks tried to block Dom's flailing arm but they could not. Their wrists broke and their skulls dented; patches of blood marred their scalps. Dom turned, twisted, and whirled like a ballet dancer, his metal left arm following him like a whip, snapping into the suspecting monks who could not stop his forceful chops. The disconcerting crack of their bones echoed off the stone walls. Then the room became suddenly quiet, except for the chorus of sorrowful moans. As Dominic slowed his dance of cruelty, there was no one left standing. Bodies lay unconscious on the stone floor in puddles of dark blood. The lucky ones were left writhing in pain. He had destroyed them all!

The time for his comeback had finally arrived, physically and psychotically. Dominic "Tommy Karate" DioGuardi had become more dangerous than ever before.

OPERATION IDENTIFY

"Secret operations are essential in war; upon them the army relies to make its every move."

—Sun Tzu

THE DECAYING BRICK building looked like it was built sometime during the 1940s. In front of the building lay a homeless person curled up on the sidewalk next to a steel accordion security gate stretched across a vacant store. Greg walked through the front door of the dilapidated apartment building. He noticed garbage strewn everywhere. Beer cans were in the hall along with filthy rags and frayed brown chair cushions. The hallway smelled like wet cigarette butts masked by pungent air freshener.

So here it goes. This is going to be good. If this place is for real, then Big Greg is going to be scoping some hot ladies. I hope they're all fine. I wonder if this girl is really going to be here. There's no way a girl who looks like that could be here. The girl in the picture looked totally wholesome. Ah, now's the moment of truth, there's the apartment, time for Big Greg to go to work.

Greg walked up to apartment 2B and pushed the buzzer on

the red-painted steel door. A gravelly female voice emanated from inside the apartment.

"Yes, can I help you?"

"Uh, yes, mmmm, my friend said I should come here?"

Greg thought it was fun playing the part of a nervous virgin.

A peephole opened on the door and an eye peered out.

"Oh yeah? What's your friend's name?" She asked, quizzically.

"Anthony, he said it's a good place. I don't know, uh, it's my first time," Greg said through the peephole, appearing nervous in order to make her believe his ruse.

The door opened and Greg walked in. When the door closed with a steel-sounding clang, there in front of him stood a robust middle-aged woman with a silver bouffant hairdo. She looked like the vaudeville-era actress Mae West, caked with too much makeup. A purple low-cut corset bustier presented her ample cleavage, and a translucent chamois red shawl completed the ensemble. Her hazel eyes were keenly on Greg. He noticed that she had cunning and intelligence. If he wasn't believable, she might smell a rat and close down Greg's operation. He knew that everything he did from now on would be intensely scrutinized by this zaftig woman.

"I have to tell you, I'm kind of nervous because this is my first time. Hate to say it, but I'm a virgin. Guess I was studying too many college books at Marist and never went to parties."

Greg laughed nervously.

She hugged him. Her hands went all over his body, and her breasts squeezed up against his chest. Greg knew that this was the frisk that he and Pete had talked about. The usual procedure of leaving a wallet and a cell phone in the car paid off this time, even though she was probably just checking for weapons.

"Eh, you're clean . . . ha-ha!" she laughed. "Hey, Harvey, you get a load of this cherry kid over here?"

From the shadow of the room's corner, a giant man walked out, wearing a colorful Hawaiian shirt, darkened with shadows by the single-bulb lighted vestibule room. He was big and fat, at least six foot five tall. He put his heavy arm around Greg's shoulders and made Greg feel small. Harvey smelled of heavy cologne and hot pastrami. His gaze at Greg was intense, necessitating that Greg concentrate on saying the right things while under such extreme evaluation.

"Hey, kid, don't worry. It's everyone's first time the first time. Go ahead and follow Zeva here. You pick a nice one, okay?" Harvey slapped Greg on the back.

Holy shit! That dude is big! I have to play this escapade smoothly or I'm going to have a problem with that guy and not be able to get out of here. Looks like this place is the real deal. I'll have to tell my buddies about it.

The madam took Greg's hand and led him through a series of doors until they arrived in a large living room with a red semicircular couch. She clapped her hands a few times and sat down on the puffy red cushions. Zeva motioned for Greg to sit down next to her. His body sank into the fluffy cushions. The glass coffee table in front of him had a few water bottles and a bowl of potato chips. The entire living room was draped in red velvet wallpaper. Gold rimmed large mirrors hung on the walls, and the floor was covered with a red carpet.

"Girls! Girls! Come out! There's a nice young man out here! You have to come to the lounge and see this one!"

Out walked a few women from different doorways into the center room, seven women in all: two heavy-set Hispanic women with black hair; a skinny, Caucasian, sunken-cheeked heroin addict with scraggly blonde hair; three African-American women; and a young Asian woman. But no red-haired girls were in the group. He didn't see Julia. They all walked in a circle around the living room and then stopped in front of Greg, posing with hands on their hips.

"Aren't these girls just wonderful? Look at them. Have you ever seen such pretty girls in one place? Go ahead, choose one. They're all very nice girls," Zeva said.

Julia was not in the line of women standing in front of Greg. This scenario was discussed between Pete and Greg back at the office. Pete suggested that Greg follow the script that they rehearsed together. Greg knew what he was going to say in case he did not see Julia among the other women presented in the apartment. If Julia was in the apartment, this was the only chance he had to determine if she was in the back somewhere.

"I always wanted a redhead girl for my first time. Do you have any girls with red hair?"

"Well you should have said something in the first place. Lucy! Lucy! Come out here! Someone wants to meet you!" the madam yelled.

A few long seconds passed.

Then, she appeared, standing in the wood-framed doorway. She was shoeless and scantily dressed, wearing just cherry-colored knee-high socks, pink panties, and a black lace bra. It was her brilliant smile and bountiful red hair that were unmistakable. She was the most beautiful girl Greg had ever seen. It was Julia! Her full, wavy red hair cascaded over the sides of her head and fell past her shoulders. The picture that Greg had studied did not do her justice. In real life, she was much more beautiful. She was beyond compare. Julia's blue eyes sparkled, bouncing off the light in the room, producing tiny stars that twinkled whenever she moved her head. She looked tall in height, about five feet six inches in bare feet, with a slender figure. Greg felt a natural attraction toward her, like a connecting chemistry. He anticipated that being together with her in the room was going to feel magical. The possibilities ran through Greg's mind about what could happen once they got into the room, but trying to stay true to his word with Pete, he wasn't going to take advantage of the opportunity to have sex with Julia. Besides, he didn't really feel that way about her. The moment he saw her, he felt instant love and wanted to get to know her more than anything.

"Hi, I'm Lucy. Why don't you follow me? C'mon."

Greg rose from the couch and followed her down a narrow, dark hallway. He couldn't help but marvel at her perfect lithe figure as she walked in front of him. Some doors to the rooms were closed, but others were open, single beds filled up most of the inside space.

They entered a room together and she closed the door.

"Listen, I don't know if I can do this right now. It's my first time, and also, I'm a devout Christian who believes that sex should be saved for marriage," Greg said.

"Really? You are an incredibly hot guy. I'm kind of surprised. And a good Christian too? Hey, I might get to like you. C'mon, it's okay. We can do it. I want to do it with you. You can still be a good Christian."

"Well, I'm sorry, I can't do it right now. Looking at you before me, I see a person who is smart and beautiful, someone I have a lot of respect for. But I really have to go. Maybe I'll think about it and come back another day. I'm sorry."

"Oh, that's okay. No problem. What kind of Christian are you?"

"Well, I've been a Catholic all my life, but now I might be converting to Evangelism, you know, like what you see on TV during the weekend mornings," Greg said.

"Oh, that's interesting. I'm in touch with some missionaries who are teaching me the true way of Christ and striving to live in Heavenly Father's holy realm. I know that seems a little hypocritical right now, but things are changing for me soon.

Sometime in the near future, I will embrace the Lord and all His goodness to spread the gospel for all the good people to know."

Greg gathered that Julia was not a typical prostitute. He could tell from the first time he saw her picture that she didn't belong here. He wondered what got her into this situation. Why was she working as a woman of ill repute amongst other lowlife characters? This apartment was certainly not the proper place for the likes of Julia Olsen. Greg needed to find out more about her. He wondered if she was available for any kind of real relationship.

"Yeah, well, I pray a lot, and when those preachers on TV start going off on evil Satan, that's what I like the best, when they get worked up and start talking and dancing with real gusto. Mostly, though, I go to a regular Catholic church because that's the religion I was brought up in. I pray to Saint Francis of Assisi because of the animal parade the church does every year. I like animals. Do you like animals?"

"Oh, I love animals. I love to play with them and snuggle them. I used to play with my cat all the time, but those days are gone, unfortunately. One day, I would love to live on a farm and take care of all the animals."

Julia looked down. She was trying to hide her sad face.

"God loves all animals and all people. The kindness of Jesus is something that everyone should strive for, to achieve ultimate goodness among our fellow people," Greg said.

Greg was faking it the best he could, and knew that he couldn't sustain this dialogue much longer. Moreover, he started to feel guilty about leading Julia on. He wasn't who he said he was, and this deception felt like a heinous act, mocking Julia's trust. Greg wanted to be totally honest with her right then, but of course he couldn't.

It was time to get out of there. He reached into his pocket

and took out the $500 as Pete had instructed and placed a one-hundred-dollar bill in her hand.

"Here, please, take this. I'll be back. God would want you to have it. Thank you so much. I really enjoyed our talk. You are a special lady."

"You're kind of special too. Make sure you come back so we can talk some more. I'd like that. I'm into religion big time, and I think I've almost found my way. When you come back, we can also talk about your Christianity. Okay? C'mon, I'll walk you out."

Julia led Greg back down the hallway by holding his hand the whole time. Her hand was perfect, smooth, and small. Her fingers were long and thin. The warm palm of her hand was like holding a connection of true love. Somehow, the tingly feeling of her affection was apparent through their touch. Julia squeezed Greg's hand before she led him to the madam in the living room lounge.

"We'll see you soon, okay?" Julia turned to the madam. "He'll be back. He's just feeling shy right now."

As Greg walked back to the office, he felt like a seventh grader who had just found his first girlfriend.

Man, I can't believe her. She was the hottest girl I've ever seen! I wonder if I should just go back there later on my own dime and be with her. Pete wouldn't know if I did that. I'll give it a little time, but I'm definitely going back up there to see Julia. I need to be with that girl no matter what! She is so special. I have to risk going back up there. I've fallen in love with her just from talking with her and holding her hand. Is that possible? If religion is what she wants, I'll find religion with her, no problem. Wow!

BACK IN
NEW YORK

"One can't paint New York as it is, but rather as it is felt."
—Georgia O'Keeffe

THE LONG ROAD to recovery took years to complete, and even now, Dom wasn't going to be one hundred percent fit, and perhaps he never would be. His former second-in-command, Frankie Flaco, from the old crew, was now the capo of the jobs. Word out on the Brooklyn streets was that Tommy Karate was back from Japan and was all messed up. It was going to be a hard road to recovery for Dominic. Returning to the mob and gaining back respect might be a lost cause. He knew the uphill battle to gain respect in his mob was a tough endeavor, but right now he wasn't too concerned. Sometimes jobs were better done alone—no witnesses to kill later and the loot didn't have to be split up. All Dominic could use was a second guy to stand there and watch his back when he stole from one of the drug dealers. Even though Dominic was an eighth-degree black belt, the physical presence of a partner in the room provided any opportunists pause, especially if they were thinking of getting the physical upper hand during a deal.

Gone were his more adventurous days, like the time he went

to the Bronx and told the Ching-a-Ling Latin gang to stay off his turf in Brooklyn. Whether there was a language barrier or the gang not knowing who Dominic DioGuardi was, they challenged his authority by drawing their guns. The police found the five dead gang members only after a neighbor called the police and said a cat was licking up what appeared to be blood streaming from under the door of a Bronx social club. A couple of days later, the Ching-a-Ling had a meeting at the same social club. A bomb blew up under their second-story room and killed thirteen of the eighteen members who were in attendance.

A storage locker in upstate Orange County held enough drugs to keep him in the money for years. The forty-foot shipping container sat on a one-acre lot of grass that Dominic owned through a shadow corporation, which had a bank account that automatically paid taxes on the property. A new crew to distribute the goods was all he needed to make the revenue stream flow. Dom took the one-hour drive from the city north to Orange County, to marvel, once again, at his arsenal of weapons acquired over the years. When he turned on the lights inside the shipping container, the corrugated steel walls were lined with over sixty machine guns, and at least half of them were 7.62-millimeter belt-fed machine guns. Additionally, there were pistols, samurai swords, and various knives that were displayed neatly on built in shelves. Also placed perfectly on display were two .50-caliber Browning machine guns, five high-powered sniper rifles on bipods, RPG rocket launchers, land mines, five sacks of hand grenades, pipe bombs with timers, containers of C4 high explosive, and a flamethrower rifle connected to backpack fuel canisters. Stacks of books and manuals about spying, killing, and combat were piled up in the corners. There was a three-foot safe in the back of the unit, bolted to the floor. When Dom opened it, there were two stacks of brown heroin bricks and twenty plastic bags filled with white cocaine. On the other side of the safe were columns of hundred-dollar bills. He took one plastic bag of cocaine, a brick of heroin, and five stacks of hundreds, and put everything into his deep coat pockets. He carefully placed armfuls of weapons in the trunk of his car before he left. The drive back to New York City gave him time to think about how his life used to be before he was shot. Dominic tried to imagine a promising future, but he couldn't stop thinking about the past and how painful his life was now.

Back in 1998, when Dominic was the captain of a twelve-man mafia crew, he foolishly went after a big-time score all by himself. The results were disastrous: his left arm was shattered by a bullet, and another bullet skipped off his head, causing a hole in his skull. He couldn't get medical treatment for those wounds for over a day, and that worsened his overall condition. His left arm was now made of metal, and the head wound had caused constant headaches. Recently, the throbbing was so painful that it often distracted his concentration. Yet his purpose in New York remained clear: torture and kill Peter Baranowski.

There were also a few other vendettas that he could finally take care of. It was time to get a new crew and rip off some of the cocky street drug dealers. If the competition caused too much trouble, then it would be like old times—kill them, cut them up, put the pieces in suitcases, drive out to Staten Island, and bury them in a marsh. Dominic insisted on burying the head separately in a different area. His skewed belief was that the cops wouldn't be able to identify the bodies because they didn't have a head. Decisions about killing people became a factor in Dominic's daily work schedule. If he had to kill a business rival, getting rid of the body was time consuming. From butchering to packaging body parts in suitcases to transporting the suitcases and burying them in Staten Island, the work was very intensive after a good killing.

Tommy Karate sometimes kept the heads of his victims in his home freezer and always saved the departed's jewelry. Those were the distorted actions and criminal thoughts of a mafia psycho killer. His jewelry collection included mostly watches and gold rings. His secret bounty continued to grow larger with every passing year.

New York was always as he remembered it, a fertile ground to make money, any way possible, and the city offered rich pickings for those willing to make the effort. The new millennium brought on 21st century electronic wonders for surveillance. Dom became enamored with the enhanced technology of 2002, especially the cell phone interceptor that his Japanese hosts gave him back at Mount Takahata. It was part of his kit now, along with some other surveillance/countersurveillance devices from Japan—also, lock picks, binoculars, and a Walther PP automatic pistol with a silencer and an extended thirty-round magazine of 7.65-millimeter bullets. He liked the little Walther because it was quiet and had enough bullets in the magazine to negate the need to reload. The small Walther automatic was easy to conceal when he wore a shoulder holster in a horizontal fashion so that the extended long magazine of extra bullets lay vertically along his rib cage. Although wearing the pistol in a shoulder holster made for a slower draw, it was considered to be more of his go-to offensive weapon when penetrating a secure area.

Prior to the 1998 incident, he was a zealous ninja purist and carried his large, custom Japanese-styled tanto knife as his only weapon. Back then, four long years ago, his arsenal of varied machine guns, pistols, and edged weapons was pinnacled by his crowning firearm jewel: his father's 1930s Tommy gun. He loved that Thompson machine gun, and everyone knew it. But alas, it was lost with everything else except his tanto knife, on that fateful day in the Catskills. The nickname "Tommy" stuck because the other guys in the mob knew that he was overly enamored with his father's gift. Together with his love of karate, La Morte had acquired a second nickname, Tommy Karate, which was sometimes used contemptuously behind his back. However, when Tommy walked into a bar in Gravesend, Brooklyn, invariably, the crowd became hushed. Whispers were prevalent among the patrons, and he saw furtive glances out of the corners of inquisitive eyes. Back in the eighties and all through the nineties, Dom owned a small bar called Just Us. It was a good place to make plans to rip off drug dealers or strong-arm some weak businessman into giving the crew money. If any unknowing patron showed up just to get a drink, the price for them was three times the normal cost. Of course, this chased away any real customers from the bar. Moreover, it was a great place to invite people to a meeting and then kill them. A small old-fashioned tub in back permitted Dominic to saw up his victims while he was in the tub, naked, with the dead body. A trickle of water constantly ran so the blood got washed down the drain. Other members of his crew thought that Dominic's behavior was more like a psycho serial killer than a Mafia capo.

His mind was placed firmly on revenge, and nobody was going to defeat him. If anyone got in his way, then he'd use the tanto knife first, but if things got hairy, then he'd have no choice but to use the Walther pistol. Gleeful thoughts of torturing Baranowski were vivid in his mind. The notion made Dominic's heart beat faster—if he could only get a hold of Baranowski alone somewhere to torture him forever!

Dominic's plan was simple: call Pete Baranowski's cell

phone while the frequency interceptor was in a car below his office. Then once Baranowski's phone frequency and codes were obtained, it was easy to listen in on all of his cell phone conversations. He sat in a parked van below Baranowski's office and later in another car below his apartment building. The electronic interceptors captured and recorded every conversation.

The new case with the young runaway girl was intriguing. Dom listened as Pete spoke to his investigator over the cell phone. There were times that he would have liked to surprise Pete Baranowski and kill him right on the street. It would have been easy if he had a crew or even just one more person. Yet Dom was all alone in New York now. His crew had been taken over by Frankie Flaco with the blessing of the big bosses. It wasn't easy working alone. There was no way to coordinate with a lookout or someone to drive a getaway car.

I don't need anyone else. I never needed another person to help me pull off a job. Besides, no witnesses, that's a good thing. Fuck those guys who rescued me from the Catskills. Now it's like they don't want anything to do with me. They think I'm fucked up and incapable of the work we used to do. They got another thing coming! These guys think my absence was my downfall, but it wasn't. I will show them when I'm back on top again. Then they'll be crying to me for jobs, and then I'll say, 'go find your own fucking jobs'. I won't give them anything! I'll get a whole new crew. First off, I want to dissect that fat piece of shit Baranowski, and then I'll get down to some serious business again. Respect will be mine, and those fuck-ups are going to be kissing my ass when I get the money ball rolling.

Dominic stewed and stirred uncomfortably in the surveillance van. He hated the drive back to Brooklyn at the end of the day because that was one more day that Baranowski got to live. La Morte wanted to torture him so badly. A quick kill might not satisfy his bloodlust revenge. However, the time was near. He was keying in on all of Baranowski's movements, and soon enough, if he couldn't get Baranowski in a place to torture him, then the tanto would come up from behind and slice Baranowski's head clean off from his shoulders.

Sleep did not come easily for Dominic. The maladies that affected him also kept him up at night. If he had not been in such good shape from the decades of serious exercise, the wounds he suffered that night in the Catskills would have killed him. In addition to the bodily aches and pains, his mental issues were a daily struggle. He had to contend with his conscience. Buried deeply, under his cloaks of tough guy posturing and callousness, was a pained soul. He ruminated about the murders, especially the victims he had killed slowly, like the guy he shot seven times, once in each limb, because the guy owed money. Even though killing elated him, the dead victims' former spirits' nightmarishly invaded Dominic's consciousness. Barbiturates taken in hefty doses offered Dominic the sleep that his body yearned for.

The closer they get to the light, the closer I get to the darkness. My shadow grows like dark energy and gives me power. I need that feeling again. Baranowski will bring back my vitality when I make him slowly approach the light.

VALUABLE INFORMATION

> "This report, by its very length, defends itself against the risk of being read."
>
> **—Winston Churchill**

PETE'S OFFICE DOOR flew open, and Greg appeared in the threshold with a big smirk on his face.

"It was her, definitely, without a doubt. They call her Lucy, and she was wearing nothing but a bra and panties," Greg said.

Pete rolled his big chair up to the desk and leaned forward.

"Are you shittin' me? I thought this whole thing was some kind of farce, fucking perpetuated by that fake-sounding English ex-spy guy in Michigan, who happened to find some deep pockets to fund his bogus investigation and then have us chase their leads all the way up to that whorehouse, as drama for his gullible clients. What surprises me most is that a girl who looks like Julia would wind up in a place like that," Pete said.

"Boss man, it's definitely her, I'm telling you. I'm one hundred percent sure. She took me to her room, just me and her together. She was about to undress, but then I did like you said.

I told her it was my first time and I'm a good Christian who is waiting until marriage and all that, just like we rehearsed it, and everything happened just as you said it would. I gave her a hundred bucks and got out quick. But I'm telling you, boss, she is one incredible looker." Greg smiled.

"Tell me everything that happened from the time you stepped foot into the apartment."

"First this older woman comes to the door and looks through a peephole. Then I acted like a dork, and she opens the door and lets me in. She's built like an old brick shithouse wearing high heels. Real tough, smart lady though. The madam hugs me like she was frisking me for a gun or something. Then this giant Jewish-gangster-looking guy named Harvey comes out. He likes me and puts his arm around me, like I'm his friend."

"What was he wearing? Do you remember?" Pete asked.

"Like a loose Hawaiian shirt and loose pants. This guy was gigantic. I mean it! He was tall and wide as a barn, real fat too."

"I bet he's packing a pistol under that Hawaiian shirt," Pete said.

"Whatever, so then I go into a room."

"Go ahead, keep talking," Pete said.

"Yeah, so a bunch of girls come out, all different types. But Julia's not there. So I did like you said. I asked if I could have a redhead because that's what I always wanted, and that did it. She yells for Lucy, and out walks our girl into the living room."

"Excellent work, Greg. So that's that, a nice quick job that's successful with a great profit margin. How are the rest of your cases going?"

"Good stuff, boss. That case way out in Suffolk County, you know that guy who said he couldn't get out of bed because his back was broken. Check it out, I got a half hour of video on him pulling out weeds and shoveling rocks in his front-yard garden. Good stuff, huh?”

"Okay, Greg, make sure you get that video copied as soon as you can so I can send it out with a report and an invoice.”

A few minutes later, Pete closed the door to his office as Greg talked with Vicky in the other room. Pete dialed Jonathan Edwards.

"Hello, Jonathan, it's Pete Baranowski here in New York.”

"Yes, Pete, what's the news? Was she there?”

"As a matter of fact, yes, she was definitely there.”

"That's splendid! The parents said that if she's identified they would board a flight to New York in order to get her out of that apartment as soon as possible. Then they plan to take her back home to Michigan,” Jonathan said.

"How are they going to do that? My agent said that there's a gigantic guy guarding the place and no doubt he's got a gun. So how do the parents intend on getting her back to Michigan?”

"Mr. Olsen will be traveling with his wife. They have a private jet, and they are going to have two men with them to assist.”

"Wow, like what kind of men? Like thugs to throw her in a van? You know I can't participate with that part of it,” Pete said.

"I understand, but it appears that we will need your agent to go back up there tomorrow and find out when her shift ends. The parents and their men will be downstairs when she leaves the building.”

"This case is getting a bit shady, Jonathan. I stand to be up against a lot of bad exposure here. If something goes south with my agent up there, I might regret taking this job. To send my man back up there, I'll need the parents to send me a five-thousand-dollar bank check. And they can't do anything until my man gets out of there, far away from that building. I don't want to be an accessory to a kidnapping. My agency will only be involved to the extent that we are identifying their daughter's presence at a location. Maybe instead the parents could just talk it out with their daughter somehow."

"I'm sure they've already considered the strategy expressed in your comments, Peter. I'll contact you when they get settled in their hotel. Then they'll meet your agent sometime tomorrow. The mother is a bit emotional, but the father is a very straightforward businessman. You should have no problem dealing with him," Jonathan said.

"Okay, just as long as we have an understanding that identifying their daughter's whereabouts is the scope of my investigation. It diminishes my liability. You can understand that, right, Jonathan?"

"Jolly good, Peter, brilliant, we'll be in touch, cheerio."

Pete hung up the phone and yelled for Greg to come back into his office.

"Listen, they want you to go back up there and find out her schedule so they can snatch her. I told them they can't do anything until you're out of there. So play it safe. If you see anything bad going down, you quickly get out of there. I've heard of other investigators getting arrested because they were accessories to a kidnapping. At the ION convention, we talked about how two PIs were arrested for felony kidnapping when they walked into a drug-addict's house with the parents and threw an eighteen-year-old girl in a car. They brought her back home and tried to reprogram her back to normality after she was living in a drug cult. As soon as she got to a phone, she called the cops and had the parents and the PIs arrested right there at the parents' house. The parents admitted to forcefully throwing her in the car with the help of two thugs and then holding her as a prisoner in the living room while they tried to deprogram her," Pete said.

"No problem, boss, if I see the parents grab Julia, I'll just get the hell away from them. The case should be an easy time. I told Julia that I was going to be back anyway. She'll be expecting me. The Greg Man will get into the girlie apartment again and get the job done. Besides, I can't wait to see her again. Honestly, she's a very nice person, and smart too."

"I like what I'm hearing. You're doing a good job on this one Greg. Here's a two-thousand cash bonus."

"Nice! Thanks, boss! This makes Big Greg very happy!"

"Listen to me carefully now, don't make any move on this case that I don't know about, especially if you have to deal with the parents personally. Remember, you represent the best interests of Baranowski Investigations when you speak to them. Call me as soon as you finish talking with them, and come back here with the check before you go up to the apartment. A job like this is very sketchy and could involve this girl getting kidnapped by her parents. I need to be insulated from direct liability, especially because there are no contracts, no paperwork, no written instructions, just their word against mine if the kidnap somehow slingshots back to me. Once you get the information they need, leave immediately. Then call them with the information on her schedule. I'll call the parents and arrange for them to meet you tomorrow at a location a few blocks from the subject location to pick up a five-thousand-dollar bank check and five hundred dollars cash. Bring the check back to the office, and keep the five hundred dollars for your operation. I want you to give the cash to Julia, or, uh, Lucy, before you leave when you say you can't have sex again. Make sure you insist on giving her the full five hundred dollars. I need you back here in one piece with no hassles. Do you understand? Don't have any business cards or

Baranowski Investigation ID on you. Leave your phone in your car. You know the usual procedures on an undercover case," Pete said.

"Okay, big boss, the Greg Man has got this."

"So, let's go over the plan. You're going to go up there and tell her that you can't have sex without treating her to dinner. Ask if she can meet you for dinner at a certain time at a restaurant right around the corner or somewhere. Then tell her you will finally be able to get intimate with her after you've had a proper date. If she says no to the dinner, then try to find out her hours. When you leave the apartment, immediately contact the parents and tell them when her shift is over."

Pete knew that he was taking a risk on this one. He would be partially responsible if something bad happened at the Twenty-Ninth Street apartment, but $5,000 just to have Greg go back up there was well worth it. Pete hoped that he had drummed the scenario into Greg's head enough for this operation to be a success. The father could afford the fee. If he could fly in a private jet, then he would be able to pay. Risking the license of Baranowski Investigations demanded hefty compensation. Pete tried to convince himself that this case was just like any other even though it involved more emotion than other cases.

I can't see anything going wrong unless Greg somehow blows his cover while in the apartment. There's also the unknown consequence of Greg meeting the parents. Will he make a bad impression and the parents start complaining to me about him? There is also a possibility that Greg will poach my client. He's such a snake that he'll probably offer to work for the parents directly and try to cut me out of the case. That numbnuts is certainly capable of going behind my back. He's done it before. Eh, considering all those bad things, it's still worth having Greg deal with the parents to keep them out of the office. This will diminish my liability if they kidnap Julia and cause the specter of a felonious charge. And I don't really want the unsavory task of having to talk to the parents about their prostitute daughter. From her picture, she doesn't seem the type, but I guess, you never know.

THE PARENTS

"If the Great Way perishes there will morality and duty. When cleverness and knowledge arise great lies will flourish. When relatives fall out with one another there will be filial duty and love. When states are in confusion there will be faithful servants."

—**Lao Tzu**

EARLY AFTERNOON THE next day, Julia's parents showed up right on time. A large black Cadillac sedan driven by a suit-and-tie chauffeur parked close to the curb, two blocks south from the house of prostitution. A maroon-colored minivan followed behind and pulled up to the Cadillac's rear bumper. In the front seats of the minivan sat two extremely large, buzz-cut blond-haired, thick necked men who looked like serious bodybuilders.

Julia's father got out of the back seat of the Cadillac. He was a big, husky man with a red, bloated face. His rust-colored hairpiece was obtusely placed on top of his head.

The blond Norwegian weight lifters got out of the minivan and stood on the sidewalk next to Julia's father.

The chauffeur opened the mother's car door. It was obvious to Greg by her bloodshot eyes that she had been crying. She dabbed her runny red nose with a white handkerchief as she walked up to Greg.

"Oh my god, my daughter is up in that apartment, isn't she? You saw her up in that apartment building didn't you?" the mother asked, crying more than talking.

"Uh, well, yes . . . uh, madam, yes, I saw her up in the apartment," Greg said.

"Oh my god!" she yelled.

"We want to know when she's getting out. That's all we need to know," the father rumbled.

The two bodyguards stood next to the parents on the sidewalk, looking seriously formidable.

"Yeah, I'll try my best, no problem. So you're supposed to give me five hundred dollars cash and a check for five thousand. But don't you worry now, we'll do a good job. Greg is on the case. You're daughter seems like a very nice person."

The father nodded at a bodyguard, who then handed Greg a brown envelope.

"Oh, please let us know what happens right away. Can you take our phone number and call us as soon as you know? I'm undecided on this. I don't want to snatch my baby off the street," the mom cried.

"Honey, we're doing this. We have to do it. It's the only way. Our daughter is brainwashed. Once we take her home, she'll change. You'll see," the father said.

"I'll be in the car," the mother said, sobbing.

"Okay, Greg, you let us know as soon as you find out anything. Oleg, give Greg our cell phone numbers. Thank you, Greg, we look forward to speaking with you in a couple of hours," barked the father.

After Greg went to the office to drop off the check, he sat in a diner just a few blocks away. As he ate his usual cheeseburger with fries, he thought about seeing Julia again. Although he was on an undercover job and had to stay in character, his real self was attracted to her—not just physically but also to her personality. There was a pureness about her, like the innocent girls he had seen in Catholic church on Sundays when he was younger.

The time had come. The afternoon was cool and bright. The sidewalk bounced warm sun rays into Greg's face as he strode confidently towards Twenty-Ninth Street. He knew that it would be an easy time getting in. All he had to say was that he was finally ready. Getting out wasn't going to be a problem either. Pete's plan to give her the $500 cash would be his ticket to the exit.

Any apprehension or fear regarding this crazy case was not central to Greg's way of thinking. Only the image of Julia was on his mind, and soon he would be with her again.

"Oh, hi, it's Greg. I think I'm ready now."

The apartment door opened and there stood Madam Zeva. She was adorned in a red vaudeville bustier and black spike heels.

"Well come in, my dear. We're so glad to see you. Lucy said she really liked you."

Harvey the giant Jew walked out from around the corner, eating a bagel with cream cheese.

"Ah, my friend, don't be nervous," Harvey said. He put his arm around Greg's shoulders. "Loosen up this time, c'mon, Lucy is one hell of a girl. Go, go, go, have fun." Harvey gave him a little encouraging push.

Greg walked into the living room, and before he had a chance to sit on the couch, out walked Madam Zeva holding Julia's hand.

"Here she is, lover boy. Isn't she beautiful?"

Julia was dressed nicely. She wore a sixties-era tight-fitting one-piece purple miniskirt dress and high white boots up to her knees. Her eyelashes were extra long, and her eyes twinkled like blue stars. Her hair was professionally styled with a part on the left side and large waves of red hair flowed around her perfect face.

Julia reached out and grabbed Greg's hand.

"So nice you came back. C'mon, follow me," she said.

Greg followed her down the darkly lit hallway as she pulled him by the hand. They entered her small room and she closed the door behind them.

"Are you ready for me? Because I'm ready for you," Julia said as she started to slip out of her dress.

"No, wait. Keep your clothes on for now. If it's okay with you, let's talk for a little while first," Greg said.

"Oh, that's fine, I would like that," Julia said, smiling.

"You see, I always imagined, with someone like you, that if I was going to have sex, it would be with a woman I love. Can you understand that?" Greg was a good liar.

"Sure, I definitely respect and admire that. I was actually raised in a family that was very strict and proper. Believe it or not, I was a good girl, but somewhere along the way, I took a side path." Julia frowned.

"Yeah, I thought you looked like a church girl to me. I'm a strict Catholic, so being here kind of goes against what I should believe in. Have you been to church recently?" Greg asked.

"As a matter of fact, I have. There is this church I'm starting to really like. They have a new temple up by Lincoln Center."

"Hey, can we have dinner together some night soon? Maybe even tonight? I didn't want to waste your time, so please, here, take this." Greg handed Julia the $500.

"Oh, that's sweet, but I shouldn't take this."

"What are your hours here? What time do you get off?"

"I get here about two in the afternoon, but they make me stay here until two in the morning every day. So dinner is not really possible," Julia said.

"That's too bad. I would really like to get to know you and see you somewhere besides this place. You're really cool, and I see a good spark in your soul."

"Here, take your money back. I would jump into bed with you for free anyway. You're hot. But I can't see you on the outside. It's against the rules."

"No, please, Lucy, use that money on some nice dinners and think of me. Can you walk me out now? It was a real pleasure meeting you," Greg said.

"Oh, my real name is Julia, but don't tell them that I told you."

As Greg walked uptown on the humid sidewalk, he thought of Julia. Her perfume was still in his nostrils, and he wished that he could stare at her face all day. He felt an emotional attraction to her that went beyond the purely physical. If only she were a normal girl and he could meet her somewhere else, even just to have one dinner, then he could convince her that she should be his and he would be the only one for her. Greg yearned to fall in love with her. However, that probably was not going to happen, and the notion of never seeing her again swept over Greg like a gray, cold cloud, making him shiver at the prospect. He needed to see her again, somehow. Or maybe it was better to forget her? This undercover assignment was now over, and it was time to move on.

Despair haunted his heart, but he resisted the emotional pang.

It was time to call Julia's father and tell him when she was supposed to get off work. The goons would throw her in the van and then drive back to Michigan in twenty hours.

Greg grabbed his cell phone from the glove compartment and talked to Julia's father as he sat in his car.

"Hello, sir, this is Greg. I wasn't able to make a dinner appointment with your daughter, but she told me that she starts work at 2:00 p.m. and gets off work at 2:00 a.m."

"Oh, okay, Greg, thank you. I guess that's all I needed to know," the father said.

"Your daughter is a very nice person. I hope everything turns out okay for you guys," Greg said.

"We'll just have to make her behave, that's all."

Greg was just about to walk into the office building of Baranowski Investigations when his cell phone rang. He recognized the number; it was Julia's father calling.

"Yes, hello, sir, this is Greg. What can I do for you?"

"This is Mrs. Olsen! We're not going through with it!" She screamed into the phone, crying out every word. "I'm not kidnapping my baby, we're not! We need you! We need to meet with you again, over dinner." She burst into a full cry.

"Uh, okay, please don't cry. We'll get a handle on this," Greg said.

"Hello, Greg." The father was suddenly on the phone. "We have a different plan that everyone will be happy with. Can you meet us in the restaurant at the Marriott in an hour?"

"Yeah, sure, see you there in an hour."

This sudden totally unexpected change of events perplexed Greg.

What do her parents have in mind?

He did an about-face away from the office building and

started walking uptown to Times Square. Greg called Pete Baranowski.

"Hey, boss, how's it going in the office today?"

"What happened, don't beat around the bush. Tell me everything," Pete said.

"She wouldn't make a date with me for dinner, but I did get her to tell me when she gets off of work," Greg said.

"What time does she get off work and out of that building?"

"She gets out at 2:00 a.m., but, Pete, check it out. Her parents just called me and want me to meet them at the Marriott Hotel restaurant. I don't know what it's about. I told them I'd be there in an hour."

"Wait a minute, Greg. Remember, I told you that we can't get involved in their mess, especially with what they're thinking of doing," Pete said.

"Her mother was crying hysterically over the phone, saying that she won't kidnap her baby. Then the father says they might have alternatives. So I don't know what they want to talk about."

"All right, Greg, when you find out what they want, call me right away. Then let's take it from there. Don't you agree to do anything without consulting with me first," Pete said.

"You got it, boss. I'll call you from the Marriott."

The cylindrical glass elevators sped up and down over the heads of Mr. and Mrs. Olsen as they sat and waited in the lounge section. When Greg got off the escalator and spotted Julia's parents, he noticed that the two blonde weight lifters sat at a table close by, occasionally glancing at the Olsens.

"Oh, Greg, please sit down. Mrs. Olsen has an alternate plan that she will explain to you," Mr. Olsen said.

Greg sat down on a cushion near the cocktail table.

"Hello, Mr. and Mrs. Olsen, so very nice to see you again.

You can explain to me what you're thinking about, and then I have to call Pete Baranowski and clear it with him," Greg said.

Mrs. Olsen wasn't crying now. She was composed and sitting upright. She sipped tea from a porcelain cup, placed it down gently, and then looked Greg in the eye.

The concerned mother spoke to Greg with composure.

"We would like you to go back up to the apartment one more time, Greg, and talk to our daughter and tell her that we love her and that we're in New York, waiting for her. Here are three pictures to show her so she'll remember our beautiful home in Bloomfield Hills. Here is a picture of our cat in her bedroom, and there's a picture of her best friend from grade school, who lives down the road, and here is a third picture, of our house."

Mr. Olsen leaned forward over the cocktail table, towards Greg. The father's voice sounded deep and authoritative.

"See, Greg, we feel that if you can show her these pictures, she'll remember what a good home she had. Mention her bedroom to her. You know she loved her room. It was decorated just by her, and it was unique. You see, Greg, we want our baby back. We don't know what happened to her. Maybe it was drugs? But we can't accept the thought that she's up in that apartment. So please, do whatever you can do to convince her to get out of there and come back home. Please, tell her we want to have dinner together and discuss her problems and we'll solve them, no matter what the problems are. Please, give her our phone number," Mr. Olsen said. His breathing was heavy and he was on the verge of crying.

Greg was now getting a look at where Julia came from. The house in the picture was a large plantation-type mansion, and her best friend was a cute blonde girl, pictured arm in arm with Julia in grade school. Julia's room was an eclectic mixture of art and figurines, wild modern-type sculptures, and lots of paintings all over the wall. Julia's cute black cat was pictured sitting on her bed.

"Yeah, no problem, I'll show her those pictures and convince her to give you a call. The Greg Man is on the case."

"Oh, thank you, Greg, that's all we want. Just for her to call. If I don't hear her voice soon, I think I'm going to die. Please have her contact us, please," the mother pleaded.

"Yeah, no problem, but listen, I have to call my boss, Pete, to okay all this. So sit tight for a couple of minutes and I'll get right back to you."

Greg stood up and walked away from the parents to make his call.

"Hey, boss, the parents want me to go back up to the apartment to convince Julia to meet them. They gave me three pictures to show her."

"Are they crazy? We can't go back up there a third time. It's too risky," Pete said.

"Nah, listen, no problem, boss, I can do it. It won't be an issue to go up there again. They all like the Greg Man."

"Okay, Greg, if you have no problems with this, then we can do it. Tell the parents to give you another five-thousand-dollar check and five hundred dollars cash. Tell them our risk on this case is huge, and that's why our fee has to be steep. Then come right back to the office, and we'll talk about what you're going to do when you're with her."

"Yeah, sounds good, boss. See you in a little while."

Greg didn't mention to Pete that he would go back up to the apartment for free, just to see Julia again.

LOVE AWAKENS

"Every block of stone has a statue inside it and it is the task of the sculptor to discover it."

—Michelangelo

HE HAD BUTTERFLIES in his stomach, not because he was nervous about what he was about to do but because he wanted Julia to like him after he told her the truth about who he really was and what he was doing there. At the very least, she would be shocked, and at the most, she might scream and he'd get shot by Harvey the giant Jew. Yet his hopes of Julia's affection towards him were pervasive. Greg tried to get her out of his mind, but it was too hard not to think of her in a romantic light. The time had arrived again. He stood on the sidewalk in front of the building, wanting to go inside. This time, he longed to see Julia. The notion of being with Julia again made him yearn to go upstairs to the apartment, more than anything he'd ever wanted to do before. His excitement was churning inside his mind and body. The familiar anxious jitters were happening to him, like the way he used to feel before a big lacrosse game for Marist.

What if she really likes me? This could happen. I want it to happen. I really want her to like me. I want to be with her. Julia is amazing. Why do I feel like this about her?

After she looked through the peephole, Madam Zeva opened the door immediately. She had a big smile on her face and welcoming eyes.

"My boy, the good boy, don't be so good. You can be a bad boy today," Zeva laughed.

Greg explained that he was finally ready and would like Lucy to help him lose his virginity.

Julia lit up the space when she entered the living room. She wore a bright imperial-yellow dress that appeared to be a Japanese tight style, a high hem up to her thigh, exposing her thin legs supported by yellow stiletto heels. Her red hair was in a tight bun on the back of her head. Her eyelids were purple with heavy makeup, and her lips were painted bright red.

Greg trembled a bit when he saw her. She was so beautiful and he felt a yearning to be with her. They walked down the hallway together as she held his hand. Julia closed the door to her room and turned.

"You're not getting out of here this time unless you take your pants off," she joked.

"Hey, it is so nice seeing you again. I didn't think I'd be back here," Greg said.

"Oh wow, I'm really glad you came back too. For some reason, I was thinking about you, and I don't usually think about guys," Julia smirked.

"Same here, I've been thinking about you too. You're a very pure person, angelic, some might say. There's no one like you. Let's sit down here on the bed together. We have to talk about important things."

Greg took both of Julia's hands in his and looked into her eyes. She appeared confused. She smiled at him in a way that seemed innocent, a kind face that showed intelligence and penance. Her eyes sparkled like the time when he first saw her, pinpoint flashing blue diamonds in her pupils that mesmerized anyone staring into them. While Greg held Julia's hands, he guided her to sit on the bed. He faced her; their knees touched.

She leaned over and kissed him lightly on the lips.

"That's just because I like you," she said.

"I really like you too. So much that I've thought a lot about you and I wanted to talk to you about something very important to you and to me. There is a universe where I wouldn't be sitting here with you being the person that I am. But it all happened like this, out of my control, another chapter of fate, of chance, guided by God, and here we are together, and it is real. We are for real. Yet there are forces outside of us. The same forces that happened to bring us together are not as they seem. The happenings of fate that has guided us together are different than you think. The important thing is that we've been brought together. The heavenly forces that have brought us together do not matter when it comes to you and me . . . I have a few important things to show you, and you will recognize them. I am with you, and I am here for you."

Julia shook her head slowly, not quite understanding the heavy gravity of Greg's voice. She listened intently, motionless, hanging her attentions on every word. Greg reached into his shirt pocket, took out three photos, and carefully laid them flat on the bed. Julia stared at the photographs—the photos of her friend, her room with her cat, and her house.

"Please don't freak out. You'll get me killed up here. Your parents sent me to ask you to call them. They love you. They really do. They just want you to call."

Julia's eyes expanded wide and stared into space unfocused. She was silent and shocked. Greg didn't know whether her round eyes were the signs of wonder or of anger. He hoped her view might soften towards her parents, who didn't seem that bad to him. Greg also figured she might get totally pissed at him and kick him out of her life forever.

"Are my parents downstairs?"

"No, they just want to meet you for dinner or something. They really love you and want you to come home to your cat and your room. They told me you have a really cool room that you decorated yourself."

Julia picked up the photo of the cat and started crying.

"Oh, Julia, please don't cry," Greg pleaded.

Her face looked up to Greg with tearful eyes.

"I haven't heard my real name for a long time."

"My real name is Greg Rocco, and I work for a private investigation company that was hired by your mother and father. Everything else I ever told you is true, like I'm a really good Catholic, but, uh, I guess I'm not a virgin." He smiled.

Julia laughed a little and wiped her tears with a tissue.

"Well, the way you look, being all handsome and built, I was having a hard time believing that story, Greg!" she said.

"I have to tell you that I really do want to have dinner with you. There's something about you. I need to give my heart to you. But I'm scared that if you do meet me later, you'll break my heart. It will also be broken if you don't meet me. Do you feel the connection between us, the way we look at each other? There's something I feel when you're next to me that's hard to describe. I love talking with you. We could talk forever, especially about religion and God. We feel the Spirit together, and I feel your intelligence and warmth. When I hold your hand, it's like the whole world disappears except for you."

"Yes, I felt something the moment I saw you too. But now that you've told me the truth, I dig you even more. You're someone I could be with. There must be some kind of magnetic attraction inside us or something. So okay, but tell me, where are my parents now?"

"I think they're staying at the Marriott in Times Square. I met them and they seem okay to me. Your mom was crying over you, and your big dad gets all red faced and cries when he talks about you."

Julia looked down and tears dripped from her eyes onto the bed. Greg squeezed her hand.

"It's okay, Julia, you can meet them, or not. I'll stand behind whatever you want to do, of course, that is, if you'll have me stand with you."

Julia stared into his eyes.

"Greg, I have a million questions to ask you. My first question is, do you really go to church?"

"Yes, I do, every Sunday. I used to go a lot more though, but my job keeps me too busy. I've been working for the private investigation firm for over a year now, and it's a good-paying gig. I get to go to a lot of different places and do some crazy stuff. The best thing about the job is that it brought us together. I was raised in a very Catholic Italian family, so I'll go to church when I'm hanging out with the family. I can see myself going to church a lot more, though, if you'll go with me."

"I've been getting into religion very heavily. Searching and searching for years, I never found the right church. But recently, I've really immersed myself into the Church of Jesus Christ of Latter-day Saints. Have you heard of the LDS Church? You might have known the LDS Church as the Mormon Church. Do you know anything about Mormonism?"

"Is that like the evangelists on Sunday morning TV? After a Saturday night of partying, I get energy watching those guys shout and dance while I'm eating some cold breakfast pizza."

"No, silly, it's a very spiritual faith. The Mormon Church doesn't shout and dance like you were saying. Most just call it the LDS Church. Let me tell you about what I've been learning. I've been meeting with two missionaries, and they're explaining the right way to me. We read the scriptures together, and they tell me all about the Book of Mormon. It's totally spiritual and very fascinating. They are giving me enough knowledge so that I might be baptized soon."

Julia and Greg talked for two hours, all about faith, religion, and belief, and how she believes in the LDS Church. Greg held both her hands as they spoke, the physical connection sending feelings of love through him that he had never felt before. Their discussion was intermixed with tender kissing and hugging. Julia told Greg about Brigham Young and how he forged through the Rocky Mountains to finally settle in Salt Lake City. Julia said she dreamed about going to Utah. Once out there, she'd enroll as a student at Brigham Young University, in Provo, just south of Salt Lake City.

"My dream is to go to college, graduate college, get married, have at least two children, and live in a nice house. I want to be a commercial artist, or at least that's what I would like to do. All that I just said is all that I'd ever want, to always be happy, to have a husband, a family, a house, and a good job, and to follow the right path for Jesus and the Mormon Church."

"I'll be there with you on your journey, if God permits it," Greg said.

"My attraction to you is true. We pray that the Spirit will guide us together for our marriage after one year of being promised to one another. Will you follow God's path to Jesus Christ with me in Utah? Will we be true Mormons on the righteous path to eternity?"

"Yes, I will be your husband. Show me Utah and I swear that I'll be one hundred percent into becoming a Mormon. I'm totally with the program. Big Greg is excited about our adventure to the Far West together, and together we'll find Jesus."

Greg knew that he was laying it on thick, but he didn't care. He also was sure that he loved Julia and believed every word he was saying. If Julia wanted to live in a swamp and raise pigs for pork in Louisiana, he would be her husband there too. Just as long as she wanted him, he would be hers, at any cost.

When they realized how much time they'd spent together, Greg and Julia quickly made plans to meet again. Julia gave Greg her cell phone number and they planned to meet for breakfast on the Upper West Side. She said that she would call her parents tomorrow, to let them know that she was all right and in good health. Although, she'd be making that call begrudgingly because Julia said that she felt very little love for her father and even less for her domineering mother.

Before they left her room, Julia and Greg kissed passionately and hugged tightly for an uninterrupted five minutes. They stared into each other's eyes without blinking.

"I can feel the Spirit in you. Embrace the church with me. Let's take the journey to honor thy Heavenly Father together," Julia said.

"I'm all there, baby. You will have me forever," Greg said.

An hour later, Greg called Pete to tell him that everything went smoothly and Julia was going to call her parents tomorrow. Baranowski was exceptionally happy on the phone and congratulated Greg on a job well done. He also expressed to Greg that he was glad to be over with this case because the prospect of the girl getting kidnapped by her own parents was very unsavory knowledge to have, especially where the authorities were concerned. Of course, what Greg didn't mention was that he was in love with Julia and meeting her for breakfast in a few hours, at two thirty in the morning.

JULIA

"Rebellion against tyrants is obedience to God."
>   **—Benjamin Franklin**

H ER UPBRINGING WAS stricter than most other children—constant berating was the norm of the day. Year after year, she endured her mother and father scolding her to become the perfect student and cheerleader, when all she really just wanted to do was paint pictures, feed her chickens, and play with her friends. Yet nothing was ever good enough. Her grades were low, and her teachers were constantly phoning her mother, saying that Julia needed to work harder. Maybe it was because she was distracted or depressed, or maybe she just didn't like her stupid teachers, who were always a step behind the times? Mrs. Olsen contended that her daughter needed a tutor, so an older woman came over the house twice a week to help Julia with her math and English. This helped somewhat but not enough to make her a stellar student.

It was freezing cold in Michigan. Most of the year brought ice and snow, and Julia hated it; she hated the cold. Her arms were skinny, and her body had very little fat attached to her lithe frame. It seemed that no matter how many overcoats she wore, she was always cold. There was no social life near the ten-room mansion where she and her parents lived. The mall, which was the only place to meet other kids, was miles away. So over the years, Julia withdrew into herself, painting on canvasses whatever came to mind, like the faces of her chickens in the pen out back or freakish self-portraits that pictured distorted expressions topped with a frock of her messed-up cherry-red hair.

For years through her early teens, she imagined what it would be like to run away and just leave everything behind. Her father wouldn't mind. He was a cold, heartless bastard who didn't care about her or anything else unless it had to do with money or his business. At her mother's insistence, he would sometimes yell at Julia to be a better student or tell her that she couldn't watch television unless she did all the dishes in the sink and vacuumed the entire house, even if both maids were working that day.

The cold days seemed to last forever. Darkness came quickly in the late afternoons, which added to her perpetual depression. The all-girl academy where she went to school was her only social outlet; there was no contact with any boys because they just weren't available to her. She became fluent in Spanish and had a knack for speaking different languages. Her dreams of going to Spain never materialized because her parents never let her out of their sight. Not letting Julia go to Spain formed a giant rift in her relationship with her parents. They dismissed Julia's dream of going to Spain as a superfluous request driven by a young girl's folly into her own imagination.

During her younger years, the thoughts of boys didn't enter Julia's mind, but then later, in her early teens, the pervasive ideas of love and sex kept popping into her head, and they weren't going away. Late at night, she'd sneak downstairs to her father's mahogany-paneled office and use his computer to go on the internet to learn about relationships and sex. Wild thoughts of boys became a mental obsession. As the sun rose over the ice-encrusted hills that surrounded their estate, she would tiptoe back upstairs without her parents or the servants knowing what she was doing.

As the years passed, Julia became a stunning young woman, blossoming with a shapely figure. When Julia was an older teen, her parents became even more restrictive. She wasn't allowed to get picked up by her girlfriends who had cars unless they came into the house first and explained in detail where they were going. Then one time, before she walked to the front door, her mother grabbed her by the collar and yelled in her face about not getting into any trouble and forbade her to get into any boys' cars or go anywhere except the local shopping mall.

Every night, before bedtime, Julia's emotions brought on a torrent of tears that ran down her face. She prayed that one day she might be set free to live a normal life like the rest of her friends, without ridicule for being too stupid, too skinny, too silent, or too depressed.

Julia's natural beauty made everyone notice her to the point where she was finally self-conscious about it. It seemed like every man tried to hit on her. She was not able to be herself. People always stared at Julia anytime she went anywhere. Men and boys tried their best to talk with her, even as her mother was standing right next to her.

The rest of the teenage girls her age made their lives all about boyfriends—if you didn't have a boyfriend, then you were an outcast. But in Julia's case, she could have any boyfriend she wanted, but she felt that there was more to life than just getting a boyfriend. Frustration and anger replaced what should have been teenage wonderment and good socialization. She loved dancing. However, out in Michigan, dancing wouldn't get her many places except a stage at the local community center, with a bunch of old people gawking at a well-shaped young person in a spandex-augmented puffy ballerina skirt.

Her mother gave her drugs laced with amphetamines in order to change her depressed mood, which was conveniently misdiagnosed as attention deficit disorder. The actual cause of her perpetual fatigue was severe depression. When her mother stood over her to make sure that she took the drugs, Julia expertly moved the pills under her tongue and pretended that she had swallowed them. Only then would her mother be satisfied that her daughter was sufficiently dosed. Eventually, her mother walked away from her, at which time Julia flushed the pills down the toilet.

The pressure of being a prisoner in her own home was too much. When her eighteenth birthday came around, she was elated at the notion of boarding a bus and making an escape from Michigan. So one day, just after graduation from her senior year at the girls' academy, her mother was at the garden club on a Wednesday afternoon, and Julia asked one of her friends to drive her home to get her bags and then drive her to the bus station. There she bought a one-way ticket to New York City by using cash that she had lifted from her father's wallet.

When Julia got off the bus at New York City's Port Authority bus terminal at Eighth Avenue and Forty-Second Street, she was a bit shocked at the level of noise on the street. She wasn't accustomed to the number of people passing by her and bumping into her, throwing her off balance and making her drop her two heavy suitcases. There was a smell of hot urine everywhere, and it seemed like everyone had a snarl on their face. A skinny black man with shredded clothing stumbled up to her and asked for money. She quickly turned away from the homeless man, right into the face of a grizzled, perspiring man who leered at her. In a slight panic, she ran as fast as she could up the sidewalk, right past a neon light that flashed "Sex Shows 25 Cents." This was not the New York City she had imagined. Where were the art museums, the cool people who would take her under their wing so she could show her great talents on a painted canvass? Julia knew that she had to find a place to stay soon; it was getting dark out, and more unsavory people were walking around the sidewalks. But where would she stay? It was her first time away from home, and she was getting more frightened by the minute. Also, she was tired, almost too tired to walk another block. She had no idea where she was. Julia found a city park, so she sat down on a bench to rest.

Just for a one night's stay every hotel wanted more money than she had. Three hundred dollars doesn't go far in New York City. Julia saw a park bush that she could hide under. She unpacked her heavy coat to use as a blanket. During the night, she heard rats running all around her, which turned her city experience into a loathsome situation. She cried herself to sleep while curled up on top of her coat under a scraggly bush. Julia woke up after just a couple of hours; her soul cried out to the heavens, to be somebody, to love somebody, to be good and not feel bad, to rest between clean sheets again, unlike the animal existence she now found herself in. What should she do? She desperately wanted to feel good about herself, finally, somehow. Her heart and soul were wide open to any sign that showed her which direction to take.

Julia woke up to a gentle nudging on her leg. She opened her eyes and the morning light made her squint. When her sight came into focus, she was looking up at the dark-blue outfit of a New York City policeman who had a serious look on his face. He asked her what she was doing sleeping under a bush. Julia stood up and started crying, telling the cop her whole story about leaving home for New York and wanting to become an artist. The cop said that he would treat her to a cup of coffee, but his generosity was short lived. She got in the back seat of the police car and saw another cop sitting in the front seat. He didn't even turn around to acknowledge her. They drove around the block, where one cop got out of the squad car and bought a cup of coffee from a small deli on Lexington Avenue. He asked her if she would stick around until after his shift as he handed her a cup of coffee in a paper cup. Julia recognized that look in the cop's eyes, the kind of look she was used to seeing from young men who became entranced by her beauty. As soon as he handed her the cup of coffee, she said she had to go. The policeman opened the car door and helped with her bags.

"Wait, I can pull some strings to get you settled or find you some social services," the cop said.

Julia ran as fast as she could, pulling both her bags down some subway steps and then across the platform and up another set of steps. When she emerged back onto the sidewalk, the moving crowd of pedestrians obscured her escape.

A slight drizzle started and her hair became wet. As she stood shivering in the threshold of a McDonald's, a young, clean-cut boy walked up to her. His shirt was extra white under his umbrella, and his colorful tie was perfectly knotted. Another young man stood with him, under his own umbrella. They both appeared similar, wearing ties, white shirts, and short haircuts. Their square black name tags on their shirts read Elder Walton and Elder Elijah from the Church of Jesus Christ of Latter-day Saints.

"You looked cold, and I wanted to know if we could get you something to eat. Please, hold my umbrella while I run in and buy you a cheeseburger."

His features were handsomely soft, symmetrical, and ordinary. His partner was just as pleasant.

Julia felt immediately comfortable standing next to them and moved closer under their umbrellas.

She started to cry.

"Let's go inside and eat. It's warm. Let's sit at one of those tables in the corner. I'll get us some good things, French fries and a vanilla milkshake. My name is Elder Elijah, and this is Elder Walton. We're missionaries for the Church of Jesus Christ of Latter-day Saints."

While the three sat at a table and ate, Julia told the two young missionaries about her life and why she was in New York City, how her parents didn't understand what she was about and how they tried to keep her down. Elijah told Julia that he and his brother missionary, Elder Walton, had been sent by the president of the church to New York, as missionaries representing the Church of Jesus Christ of Latter-day Saints. Their mission was to spread the word of the Church and recruit members into the Church of Jesus Christ of Latter-day Saints.

Julia was intrigued by what he said. She was looking for something pure, an honorable thing to believe in, something to follow spiritually. Elijah was different, as far as guys go; he really wanted to help her and introduce her to God. Elder Walton promised Julia a good life and told her about a community of Mormons who would accept her. This was Julia's answer to her prayers, and these two missionaries would guide her towards God, love, and everlasting life. They told her that she should meet with them tomorrow at the same McDonald's. Both young men reached into their pockets and gave Julia whatever cash they had. With that amount and her own cash, she rented a room at the run-down Martha Washington Hotel on Twenty-Ninth Street. The next day, she met again with Elijah and Walton, who spoke to her for hours about the Book of Mormon and her path to getting baptized. The two missionaries said that they had to go somewhere for a few days but would soon be back. They gave Julia their cell phone number to call and told her to dial the number in exactly one week. They would meet again at the same place, at the same time.

The next day, at the Martha Washington Hotel, Julia met a young woman who claimed she was a prostitute that made a lot of money. Julia was feeling so despondent that she let the woman shoot heroin into her arm. The experience was horrible. Julia vomited and felt sick for ten hours in bed. To ease the pain after taking the heroin, the woman next door gave her opiate pills, which made her feel better. In just a couple of days, Julia was swallowing about five pills a day. The woman told Julia that hooking was easy and great money. The allure of fast money was irresistible, and Julia took the dive into the life of a hooker. She didn't like it at all. Most of the men were fat and smelly, or too old, or too rough. It was a life she hated. In fact, her view of herself as a prostitute was disgust, but the money was great and she was now able to spend on anything she wanted, for the first time ever.

Julia was starting to get herself together and totally went cold turkey on the opiates. If there was one thing she knew about herself, it was that her mental toughness could be absolute. She decided to kick the habit, and she did, just like that. However, her next step was unknown. She had a place to live, but it was being supported by a disreputable profession she did not like.

During the next few weeks, she met with Elijah and Walton once in a while. LDS Church rules mandated that the two missionaries must stay together at all times. Elijah kept trying to indoctrinate Julia into his fold of Mormons, but she resisted. Julia had found a way to support herself and, for the first time, became enthralled by the large amounts of money. The right path towards religion took second seat. She had real freedom and it felt good. She had her own place and lots of money. What more could a city girl want? For a while, she felt shallow but didn't care. She could wear new clothes or eat at an expensive restaurant. New York City was a place to have fun and shop, if the money was there.

Julia's time flourished at the "working" apartment just a few blocks away from the Martha Washington Hotel. The work was steady and the salary fantastic. She made enough money to live not only comfortably but lavishly in a city that offers everything to those who can afford anything. Even though her newfound wealth permitted her to feel liberated, Julia knew deep down that it was not going to last long. She would put a stop to her work just as she had put a stop to taking the pain pills.

The days of prostitution turned into weeks. Julia was speaking to Elijah twice-a-week. She'd delight in calling Elijah on her cell phone. Sometimes they might talk for an hour. Elijah, Walton, and Julia would meet in city parks if the weather was nice or maybe at a museum if it was raining. They started to speak of baptism, and it was soon time for Julia to embrace Jesus and the Church.

Julia wanted, more than anything, to believe in something good. She looked at the Mormon culture as pure goodness. The Church of Jesus Christ of Latter-day Saints filled her heart with serenity; the Church made her feel like she wasn't a bad person at all. She could embrace God and be forgiven for everything that she had done in the past. She'd be a righteous person once again. It was something to believe in, and she really wanted to embrace proper morals, which made her feel excellent about herself.

She despised her life. In fact, she was going to draw a line. The time had come to accept the Heavenly Father and the teachings of Jesus Christ. Julia finally decided she was leaving her life of shame and stepping into a new world of true belief in the Church of Jesus Christ of Latter-day Saints. She looked forward to being baptized by Elijah and Walton.

For a few seconds, she reflected back on her actions during the past couple of months.

What was I thinking? How could I do this? Was I greedy? I'm a painter, not a whore! And I'm a good girl, not bad! I believe in God. I believe in purity and love! There is going to be another way, the way of the Church. They will help me, and I will believe in them and Jesus Christ and the Heavenly Father. Then I will believe in myself with their help.

The money that she made at Madam Zeva's gave her the opportunity to paint again. The room at the Martha Washington Hotel was big enough to set up an easel for large canvasses and grand paintings. Her talented hand had uniqueness and was recognized by many. When she walked downtown to show one of her paintings at an art gallery in lower Manhattan's SoHo section, they liked the sample so much that they scheduled a showing of three of her paintings. Things were looking better for Julia. Her art might sell, which would be her dream come true—to support herself by selling her art. Julia often daydreamed in a constant loop of hopes, about going to college, getting married, having at least two children, living out West, and practicing total spirituality by following the teachings of Jesus Christ.

With the help of the missionaries, Elder Elijah and Elder Walker, through the divine teachings of the Church of Jesus Christ of Latter-day Saints, she would find God and Jesus Christ, and she would find herself.

Oh, Heavenly Father, our Lord Jesus Christ, please guide my spirit to the Saints in Salt Lake, for I long to be at Thy doorstep as Your child with my other brothers and sisters. My devotion will be total to Thee. My spirit awaits Your acceptance to guide me into Your lands. May You forgive my past transgressions and accept me as I was before, a pure and truthful servant of Thee. May my path be towards baptism, may the Spirit show me the correct path, and may I choose the right.

GAZING AT DEVOTION

"Life is what happens while you are busy making other plans."

—John Lennon

G REG WAS ALREADY seated at a booth in the diner when Julia walked in. Her hair was bunched up in a knit hat, and her black wool sweater was buttoned up to her neck. When she slipped into the booth, her wry smile had Greg's undivided attention. He was enamored with her presence; she smelled like powerful lemons and fresh soap. It didn't matter if she was a prostitute, because he liked her too much.

Besides, people can change. She could leave the hooker life behind and go straight and just be with me. If that happens, she'd make a great girlfriend. Better still, since she wants to follow the church, that's good, 'cause religion might steer her away from prostitution. She's so hot, and she's a nice girl too, man, a true keeper for sure. I'm hers and she's mine.

Julia reached across the table with both hands for his. Greg put his hands in hers and looked into her eyes. He felt himself melting right before her.

She is definitely the one.

"Tonight was my last night in that apartment with Zeva and Harvey. I'm turning over a new leaf. I can be a good girl again," Julia said.

"That is really excellent news. Maybe we're on the same wavelength. Are you thinking about me as much as I'm thinking about you?" Greg asked, softly.

Julia smiled and slowly nodded yes.

"I want to make a home with you, in a place I really want to call home. I want to live in Utah," Julia said.

"That sounds like something I'd like to do too. When do you want to go?"

"Let's accept Jesus together and bring the Spirit into our lives. Together we'll become Mormons, forever with the Church of Jesus Christ of Latter-day Saints, at the same time, and move to Utah and live there. What do you say?" Julia's eyes were bright.

Greg thought about the possibilities of getting out of New York—taking a jet from JFK airport with this hot chick and flying out West, where everything is brown with mountain vistas, golden sunsets, and silhouetted cowboy hats.

Maybe I could do private investigation work out there? I'll do all the religious stuff with her, that won't be any problem. Going with her to Utah would be an awesome adventure for Big Greg!

"Uh, Julia, are Mormons like those Amish people in Pennsylvania, driving those little horse and buggies, and the women churn butter all day? What got you into all that? I never met any Mormons except when those Jehovah's Witness people came around with their magazines. I always tell them no, thanks." Greg smiled.

"First of all, that's funny you think that Mormons are Amish—they're not. Second, we should talk deeply about the right way. I need to tell you how I became such a fuck-up. I came to New York on a bus just to get away from my controlling parents and started snorting heroin with some people I met at the hotel. Then to support my habit, I became my character Lucy, doing tricks for Harvey and Zeva. I was drinking myself to death too. I found true Jesus when I needed Him most, by God's will, with the help of two missionaries from the Church of Jesus Christ of Latter-day Saints. I got on my knees and crossed my arms and said 'dear Heavenly Father.' At that moment, the Heavenly Father hugged me from the inside, and I knew that Christ was real."

"Yeah, I think you're following the right path," Greg said.

"Do you want to follow the right path with me?" Julia asked.

"Uh, yeah, sure, definitely, I'm totally with you on this. I bought something for you at a jewelry shop. It's a ring. Check it out . . . here."

Greg held out a silver ring that had the gold-inscribed initials *CTR* inside a small green shield. The look on Julia's face lit up like a bright bulb.

"I don't believe that you got me that ring! How did you know about it? Do you know what CTR means?"

Greg took Julia's hand and placed the ring on her finger.

"It means 'choose the right.' I asked the guy who sold it to me."

"Yes! That's correct, my love!"

"And you are my love too." Greg's eyes focused on her.

"My ring is special. Thank you so much."

"How does it fit? It looks a little loose. I didn't realize your fingers were so thin."

"That's okay. I'll make sure this special ring always stays on my finger."

Julia took Greg's hands across the table and began singing. Greg thought that Julia sounded like a beautiful bird; her voice was astoundingly good.

Choose the right when a choice is placed before you.
In the right the Holy Spirit guides;
And its light is forever shining o'er you,
When in the right your heart confides.
Choose the right! Choose the right!
Let wisdom mark the way before.
In its light, choose the right!
And God will bless you evermore.

The transfixed diner patrons listened intently to Julia's heavenly singing voice. When they realized that she had finished her song, everyone, including the waiters, broke into enthusiastic applause and standing ovations.

Greg was impressed.

"Wow, excellent voice, Julia! You should make a recording," Greg said.

"Maybe someday, but you and I have our priorities first. If you're joining the Church of Jesus Christ of Latter-day Saints with me, then we have to get baptized."

"No issues there, Julia babes, I'll get Mormon baptized no problemo. I want to feel the Spirit of Jesus with you," Greg said.

"Oh, that's so good! We can get baptized together! Before I call my parents, I'm seeing the missionaries about going to a holy place for consecration in a Sacred Grove, where we will learn to build the Kingdom of God on the earth and for the establishment of true Zion."

After breakfast, Greg suggested that they take a walk in Central Park at sunrise. Julia loved Greg's idea, and as the sun peeked above the horizon and lighted the park, the lovers walked and talked for hours, hand in hand, sometimes giggling, sometimes squeezing each other's hand, and sometimes kissing. They walked, holding hands the whole time, around the pond and over an arched stone bridge. The couple kissed again by the shore. The morning sun's rays rippled off of the reflective pond water, highlighting the lovers in a sparkling array of moving light.

In a few hours' time, they got to know each other well, and their passion grew with every sentence, every touch, and every intense eye contact. The connections of love helped to transmit each other's spark to one another, and their souls connected. It was the most special time of their young lives.

They got into a taxi for a fifteen-minute ride back to the Martha Washington Hotel. After just thirty seconds into the taxi ride, Julia put her hand on Greg's hand and looked into his eyes, pursing her lips into a timid request for a kiss. Greg froze. All of a sudden, out of nowhere, he felt shame. He awakened to the reality of this new day and suddenly worried. The experience was too complex for his simplistic, straightforward way of thinking. In this short moment, a strong pang of guilt shot into his gut: he loved the girl he had spied on, and now, in a few hours, should he reveal to his boss and her parents that he was romantically involved with Julia? That he loved her? Maybe he should, because he could never walk away from Julia, ever.

Pete is going to go ballistic. Also, Julia's parents, if they find out, they'll also be super pissed and tell those hard-core Norwegian blockheads to kick my ass.

Julia reached behind his neck and pulled him onto her lips. A feeling of weightlessness flowed over Greg, and he got lost in the moment. The rest of the taxi ride downtown became a physical connection between the two young lovers in the back seat of the yellow sedan, kissing, hugging, passionate, the whole way downtown.

Greg threw a fifty-dollar bill on the front seat of the taxi as he was pulled out of the car by Julia's hand. They rushed upstairs, she unlocked her door, and they fell into each other's arms. Neither Greg nor Julia could contain their passion. There was no conscious thought to what they were doing. It had to be; there was nothing that could stop their coming together.

Their pillow talk was in soft voices just a few inches from each other's face. They held each other, arms swirled around arms and naked bodies; small kisses were sudden and without warning as they whispered vows to each other. They also talked about how their love was going to be spiritual and they would both follow the road to complete love by walking down God's path.

"I have so much to tell you," Julia said. "My faith is absolute, and I've found where I need to go."

"The place that you need to go, will you take me? For I will be by your side, through either the gates of hell or the entrance to heaven," Greg said.

"We will be together, a couple who love to walk in the name of Jesus and of the Heavenly Father. Our love is pure, our touch is real, and our devotion is absolute. I totally need you to follow me to the church I've selected. I don't even want to think about the past. Let's move forward and not look back. Our love is the most spiritual thing that we can do, for when we have our own family, with at least two children, our destiny will be complete," Julia said.

The sun rose above the late-morning cityscape, and Greg had already dressed. He walked over to the bed and kissed Julia.

"I'll see you later, after you call your parents."

She remained in bed, under the white sheets, her smiling face and bare shoulders exposed. They agreed to meet at a restaurant after she called her parents and then, later, to have dinner with the parents all together. They kissed one more time.

She asked him to stay, to call in sick. She begged Greg to remain in bed. Tears came to her eyes and a tear rolled down his cheek, feelings of loving passion filled their hearts, even though they had practically just met. They knew that they were meant for each other. Greg's emotions overwhelmed him, and he took off his shirt and jumped into the bed. Greg leaned forward and Julia's arms encircled his neck tightly.

Later came more whispers between them on the pillow when they spoke of the faith that they were destined to follow. They agreed that the Church would be their new life together. The mutual move was going to be a big change for both of them. To follow God and Jesus, to study the scriptures, to "choose the right" was their ordained purpose. The trip out West was to be a physical commitment to their faith. Living in the heart of Mormonism was Julia's goal, and Greg was there to share this life with her. Together they would find true faith and an honest life among people who believed in the same purity of the Spirit. Julia and Greg were joined by a shared mind, which added to their newfound love for each other.

As Greg walked back to his parked car uptown, he thought about Julia and how she wanted to make him a Mormon and take him to Salt Lake City. It was a drastic change, but he didn't care. He was in love, and she was the girl he wanted to marry.

Life felt simple to Greg, quite basic, actually. He wanted what he wanted when he wanted it, which was usually right away. Greg's life up until now was one movie scene after another, and the main plot was always selfish gratification.

I want to believe in her so much. I would do anything for her. Jesus says to forgive people, and I can forgive her for anything that she's done. Yes, I want to believe . . . I want to believe . . . I'll be a Mormon too. And I'll believe it . . . I'll believe in it. I want to find love . . . I can't stand not having anything or anyone. If I'm looking out for numero uno, then Pete Baranowski will just have to wait until I get things straightened out for myself. My job is just a stepping stone. I need to find love and find myself, and do what is good for me, myself, and I, just for the Greg Man and no one else.

REQUIEM FOR INNOCENCE

"Do not trust all men, but trust men of worth; the former course is silly, the latter a mark of prudence."

—Democritus

"JULIA! YOU'RE HERE! What a special morning this is going to be!" Elijah elated.

Elijah wore an all-white suit—even his tie was white. "Yes, hi, guys. I'm here. How is everyone today?"

"The day is special and will be such an exciting time. Are you ready for baptism?" Elijah asked.

"I didn't know you were doing the baptism today? My boyfriend and I decided that we want to be baptized together. I thought we were meeting today just to go over the scriptures," Julia said.

"Certainly the scriptures are within our realm for today's prayers, but today we have the Sacred Grove all ready for your baptism, and it won't take very long at all. Please join us for baptism and introduce thyself to God and Jesus. We can baptize your boyfriend when he is ready at a later date. We feel now is the time for your holy baptism," Elijah said.

"Okay, yes, I'm ready for baptism," Julia said.

She made a decision and there was no going back on it. Her new path would be that of righteousness with Greg. This was the first step, and from here on, she could move forward and fulfill her dream of getting married, going to college, having children, and living like a pure family should. Elder Elijah and Elder Walton told her that baptism was the first step towards entering into a covenant with God and obtaining Church sisterhood status.

A white van was parked on the curb. Walton smiled at Julia from the front passenger seat.

"We'll drive there," Elijah said as he slid open the van's side door. "You can sit in the back. Then we'll soon be in the Sacred Grove."

"That's in Central Park, right?" Julia asked.

Elijah just smiled like he didn't hear the question. He slid the van door shut.

When Julia sat on the back seat, it was covered with a plastic sheet. She noticed someone behind her in the third-row seat.

"Hi, Julia, I'm Brother Jessop. I'll be a witness to your baptism."

He was a big man, with long hair and a big bushy beard. Julia thought he seemed nice enough, but he looked rough, kind of like someone who might have been in jail.

They asked for her cell phone because it was their rule that nothing should interfere with the discussion of the scriptures and she wouldn't want to get it wet during the baptism.

As they drove off, Walton spoke loudly from the front seat, proselytizing scripture.

"Now I say unto you, if this be the desire of your hearts, what have you against being baptized in the name of the Lord, as a witness before Him that ye have entered into a covenant with

Him, that ye will serve Him and keep His commandments, that He may pour out His Spirit more abundantly upon you."

After she noticed that an inordinate amount of time had passed, Julia thought the car ride was lasting too long. They had been on the road for twenty minutes, and she realized they weren't on the streets of Manhattan anymore. They were driving on a three-lane highway. She knew that Central Park was supposed to be in the middle of Manhattan. Why did she see what looked like the Hudson River?

"I thought that the Sacred Grove was in Central Park. Why are we going this way?"

"The Sacred Grove is in a town called Palmyra that is a few hours' drive."

"Wait, I have to meet my boyfriend. So I can't be baptized right now. Please let me off at the next exit and I'll take a subway back, unless you can drive me back to where you picked me up," Julia said.

"We told you that the Sacred Grove was in Palmyra. Maybe you just didn't hear us when we spoke of it. It is the most sacred place in the world, the site of the First Vision, where Joseph Smith saw the Heavenly Father and His Son, Jesus Christ, when he was just fourteen years old. This is the most important event that humanity has ever experienced. The First Vision is the resurrection of the Lord in these latter days of the Bible—Jesus has returned. Now please sit back and remain quiet in prayer until we reach the Sacred Grove."

"Don't tell me to remain quiet! Let me out of this van right now. I can't be here. Let me out or I'll scream!"

The presence of Jessop, an extremely large older man with a gray-streaked black beard and long hair past his shoulders, brought on an intimidating air. He leaned forward and whispered into Julia's ear: "Quiet."

"I'm not going to be quiet. I want to get out of this van right now! Why do I have to sit on this uncomfortable plastic sheet? Please let me off at the next exit. I want to take a bus back to New York City," Julia said.

Jessop leaned his big face over the back seat. He looked at her for a few seconds, just inches from her face. Julia was frightened by his strange expression. Suddenly Julia was gazing at the largest knife she'd ever seen, just inches from her face. It had a wide blade and was a foot long. Jessop held the knife in his right hand and turned it slowly back and forth. Its curved blade scared Julia so much that she started hyperventilating, her chest heaved, and she looked shocked.

"Oh, sister, we are progressing on a holy transport to the baptism in the Sacred Grove. Therefore, we cannot stop. The plastic you sit on will prevent your blood from staining the seats. If you decide on the path of an apostate, the blood atonement mandates that I slit your throat to let the evil blood flow out. The devil will be in your soul no more. Of course, this is spiritual talk and may not be the course of our actions here. If we simply pray, the knife will not be present and the blood atonement will not be required. Oh, Satan, stay out of our sister and may she complete her journey to the Sacred Grove and our Holy Land," Jessop said.

Julia remained silent. Jessop was a large man, as wide as a refrigerator. When he introduced himself as Elder Jessop and shook her hand, it seemed like maybe he was faking sincerity, somehow. Julia noticed motorcycles riding on the road in front of and behind the van. She realized that these people must have been some kind of gang that had nothing to do with the Church of Jesus Christ of Latter-day Saints.

The ride continued for hours. She had been fooled, which was something that seemed to happen to her often. She had chosen the wrong course for a while, but this time, she was deceived by people she thought were good.

Jessop explained to her that they were a fundamentalist sect of the Church of Jesus Christ of Latter-day Saints and theirs was the only true religion paying homage to God the Father and His Son, Jesus Christ. The Promised Land awaited their arrival to the west, and their location was called Zion, an enclave of true believers of the real Mormon Church. Jessop said that the Fundamentalist Latter-day Saints were the only true Mormons and that Julia had been selected to be a true sister in the beautiful community of the FLDS.

Five hours more of highway driving and the van finally got off at an exit.

"I have to go to the bathroom."

Julia thought that if they pulled over to a gas station, she could feign cooperation and then leap away while she screamed for help. Her hopes of escape were soon dashed.

"If you got to go, there's a little seat behind me with a garbage bag under it. You'll have privacy back there," Jessop said.

After a few minutes of driving on country roads, they arrived at a small grass patch, where Elijah pulled up under some trees. The sun was setting over the forest, and deep shadows extended in thick lines through the woods. Walton opened the side door of the van, and Julia was tempted to make a break for freedom. They all stepped out, and that's when she impulsively decided to run, but Jessop quickly grabbed her arm and took out his knife. The sight of the large blade sent a wave of fear through Julia that stunned her into silence. From that moment on, she cooperated.

"We have arrived at the Sacred Grove. It is time. There are white clothes for baptism in that travel bag. You step back into the van, and we will let you change in private. You will have three minutes to change," Jessop said.

When the darkness of night slowly fell upon them, Jessop grabbed Julia's arm.

"It is time now that we enter the Sacred Grove," Jessop said.

Elijah and Walton led the way down a path to a remote part of the forest. The land was flat and the forest very green with low grass and leafy trees. They walked off of the path for a few hundred feet and stopped. Walton turned on an electric lantern and placed it on the ground. A small, blue plastic pool was on site and filled with water.

"Your faith will build. This is our first step, and you will repent and you will accept God and feel peace," Jessop said.

"Let the baptism commence," Elijah said.

Elijah gently grabbed Julia's wrists and led her into the small pool. The water was just past their knees. Elijah raised his right hand up and square angled his elbow at ninety degrees.

"Julia Anne Olsen, having been commissioned of Jesus Christ, I baptize you in the name of the Father, and of the Son, and of the Holy Ghost. Amen."

"Amen," Walton and Jessop said at the same time.

Elijah tilted Julia backwards and dunked her in the pool. She was totally immersed for a second and then brought back up to a standing position. The water flowed off her. Walton handed her a towel. The look in her eyes showed fierce anger and total remorse. All she could think about was Greg waiting for her; he must have been wondering why she wasn't there with him. Her self-esteem had hit rock bottom, and it was her own fault.

They walked back to the parking spot under the trees, and Jessop had her change back into her clothes in the privacy inside the van. Walton said there were plenty of towels in the van to dry off. Julia looked quickly around the van for her phone, but they must have had it in one of their pockets. Suddenly the van door opened, Elijah got in the driver's seat with a towel around his shoulders, and Jessop sat in the back seat with Julia. They drove a short distance to the backyard of a house.

Jessop grabbed Julia's arm, led her inside, and directed her to sit at a kitchen table. Elijah asked Julia if she was hungry and if she'd like a salad or a steak. Jessop said that he had to go to the bathroom. Julia told Elijah that she wanted a steak and a salad. Walton said that he was going to change his clothes upstairs. When Elijah turned his back to the fridge, she saw her chance. Julia tiptoed over to a phone she saw attached to a wall near the kitchen. The dial tone was a welcome sound, and she called the one number that she had put to memory: Greg's phone.

"Greg! It's me, Julia! I'm—"

Jessop ripped the phone off the wall. White plaster chips broke and scattered on the floor.

"Calls are not allowed while we are in a time of thoughts and prayers. Now go sit down and eat your meal, young lady. We are in a solemn period of solitude and reflection of our souls. May our thoughts be pure without the intrusion of outside interference with those of us who seek to follow the path of Jesus," Jessop said.

Julia sat down at the table, frightened that Jessop would rip her head off the same way he'd done to the wall phone. She ate some of her salad and steak, the whole time feeling disheartened. A depraved human soul is the only force that would enslave Julia. The men who surrounded her were all monsters. Jessop was the obvious ogre, a callous blood-thirsty giant who would have no compunction about slitting her throat. Those two so-called missionaries were the really bad people; they pretended to be good, but they were just bad to the bone. Elijah and Walton were heartless young go-getters who wanted to advance in the ranks of their FLDS radical sect. They were not concerned in the least about what happened to Julia as long as they could deliver her to Zion.

Greg, the person I really love, is probably thinking that he's been abandoned and discarded by a floozy. How could he possibly think that I love him now? Help me, Greg, help me. Let my prayers reach you, and you will somehow find me and save me. I love you, Greg. Please, Jesus, help Greg find me and free me.

After a few more bites of steak and salad, she was no longer hungry. Walton took her hand and led her down to the basement, where she saw two girls asleep on mattresses on the floor and another girl reading a book while sitting in a chair. Jessop told Julia to sit in one of the chairs and either pray or read the Book of Mormon. There were other men in the room. Some were sitting on pillows, reading, and a few were lifting weights. They all seemed like large men, and most had full beards and long hair down to their waist.

Depression had taken hold. Julia finally realized the gravity of her dire situation. There did not seem to be a good way to escape this basement, especially with all these other guys down there who looked like football players.

Julia thought back on when she had so much promise in her life. Her art, she could be a commercial artist, and there was so much she wanted from life, especially faith, the belief in the Heavenly Father and His Son, Jesus Christ.

These guys in this basement are not of the true LDS Church. They are self-described fundamentalists, some offshoot that is a cult. Looks like I'm kidnapped. These other girls must be scared and depressed too. I wonder if they want to be with these guys. I need to get out of here. Let's see what happens if I talk tough with them.

"What do you think you're doing? I want to go back to New York City right now. You are holding me prisoner," Julia said.

Jessop looked down at her from his great standing height.

"But, sister, we are traveling to Zion to meet the prophet and anoint you with the blessings of our church. This is just days away."

"Don't make me scream! I want to leave here right now!"

Jessop unsheathed his knife and held it in front of Julia's face.

"This Bowie knife will perform the blood atonement if you choose to become an apostate. The blood atonement mandates that I slit your throat. Yet that is only in the scripture and in an extreme circumstance. I'm sure our trip to Zion will be peaceful and quiet. Don't you agree? We will be there in a day plus time, my sister. We ask of thee that you behave and follow the precepts of our prophets and the promise to the seed masters."

Julia was stunned and didn't answer. She sat down and stared straight ahead. The other girl reading a book didn't even look up. The other two girls remained asleep on their mattresses.

All Julia wanted was to become a Mormon and follow the righteous path to God the Father and Jesus Christ. She started to cry.

"Let's not resort to crying, Julia. Jessop was just stating verses from long ago that are not necessarily relevant in today's day and age. Once we are in Zion, you will see that you belong and we'll open our arms to you. It will be a righteous mating within our holy land," Walker said.

How did she get herself into this mess? Things were going so well. What happened? She became despondent with severe depression. Julia felt sleepy and wanted to lie down. The other girls in the basement did not want to talk. They looked more frightened than Julia. A mental picture of Greg's face was the only thought that kept Julia sane. Somehow she knew that Greg would rescue her, no matter what. He would get her out of this basement and they'd be together forever in Utah.

I can't believe these guys fooled me into this place. There's no escape from that big guy. He's watching me like a hawk. That knife of his really scares me, and I want to scream, but he might cut my throat like he said. Oh, God, save me, please don't let them take me away. Please, Jesus Christ, I pray to You to save me and help me get out of this place. Only You can help me, Lord. I beg Your forgiveness of my sins and promise that I will be a good, loving person from now on. My only love will be Greg. He and I will get married and have a family in Utah. Please, my Lord, save me and permit me to continue to do Your pure work. Release me from this place so I may continue to strive for Your true goodness, and may the Spirit move me to do great things for the Church. Oh, Father of Jesus Christ, please answer my prayers and release me from the confines of this prison. Thy men here are not from heaven but are instruments of hell. They will hurt me and do me wrong. Please, oh God, please, in Thy infinite wisdom, answer my prayers. Please release me from this bondage and make gone these soldiers of Satan. Oh please, Thy Heavenly Father and Jesus Christ my Savior, I've never prayed to You like I'm praying to You now. Please save me from this place.

A TURN OF EVENTS

"There is frequently more to be learned from the unexpected questions of a child than the discourses of men."

—John Locke

J ULIA NEVER SHOWED up. How could this possibly be? Greg was beside himself. She was supposed to meet him at the diner on the Upper West Side at 2:30 p.m. He waited three hours, but she never walked through the door. It was now 6:00 p.m. He called repeatedly, but Julia didn't answer her phone. He couldn't stand it any longer. Before he sprinted from the diner, Greg asked the waiter if he would give a message to a red-haired girl, if she walked in alone and looked like she was waiting for him, that he would be back in an hour.

Greg jumped into his car and screeched his tires pulling out from the parking spot. When he got to the Martha Washington Hotel, he learned that she wasn't in her room. He even put his ear to her door for ten minutes to see if he could hear anything inside. She still didn't answer her phone, so Greg thought about the only other place he figured she could be. If he found her there, it would be a total betrayal, and he wasn't emotionally ready for that. The shock over her going back to hooking after what they shared was too much for Greg to bear. He thought about just walking away from everything, thinking that maybe she didn't want him anymore and it was all a play. But he had to know, so he went to the Twenty-Ninth Street apartment to find out, one way or the other.

An eye poked through the peephole, and Madam Zeva opened the door with a big welcoming smile. Greg tried to calm down and not seem too intense. He didn't want to raise any suspicions from Zeva or Harvey. So Greg smiled a big, toothy, nervous grin and said that he would love to see Lucy again. Madam Zeva said Lucy didn't show up for work today but there were many other beautiful girls inside. Greg said that he only wanted Lucy and he'd be back tomorrow—maybe she'd show up then.

Greg was beside himself. Julia had suddenly disappeared, and he couldn't wrap his head around the idea that she would abandon him on purpose. The streets were abuzz with people. Greg wanted to find her so badly that he relied on chance, hoping against all odds that he would see her on the sidewalk and grab her and never let her go. So he frantically started walking fast through every street he could traverse in a one-mile radius. He became angry, very angry, wanting to lash out at all of society, anyone, scream at his boss, Pete, give the finger to Julia's parents. Rage filled his heart, boiling out into the world. People on the sidewalk were mildly noticing his frenetic neck movements, a desperately searching man with darting eyes.

After a while, a reality filled Greg's void: she was not in his realm anymore. As quickly as Julia had entered his heart, she now disappeared. Her vanishing was just as surprising as when she appeared. He thought of her face, her smile, the upturned corner of her eyes when she laughed. The touch of her soft hand on his hand was transformational for Greg. There was a pure understanding with Julia. Could there ever be a more beautiful face to wake up to in the morning? There was some kind of elemental connection he shared with her. The true faith in God and Jesus that she expressed was the real thing that captured Greg's heart. For him, she would have been his guide to authentic spirituality while experiencing the love of a woman at the same time.

He went back to the diner and sat in a booth. It was the only thing that he could do, just sit and wait for her. The minutes ticked by, every second like an irksome nudge making him more pensive with every time fold into an uncertain future. He never wanted to speak to someone as much in his life as he wanted to speak with Julia at those moments that kept passing by.

When his cell phone rang, he quickly answered it, hoping that it was Julia, but it was Julia's parents, who said that their daughter never called them. Greg acted ignorant by saying that he thought the case was over and that he didn't know what to do. The parents said that they were going to call Pete Baranowski's office in the morning. The parent's dissatisfaction because Julia didn't call added to Greg's distress. Everything was supposed to be good by now; Julia and he were supposed to have dinner with the parents and reveal that they were going to be a couple. Depression settled in, a novel feeling for Greg. He hadn't been this sad since he wrecked his motorcycle, but this agonizing now was much worse.

A few more hours of sitting in the diner, eating two chicken dinners and drinking seven cups of coffee, and not knowing what was going on gave Greg a sick feeling in his stomach. The anxiety of falling into an emotional abyss felt like torture.

Where is she? Is this it? Am I broken? I meet thousands of people and none of them have affected me like Julia. How can one woman change my life forever?

Greg looked out the diner window and noticed the light from apartment windows and colorful traffic signals in the night, reflecting off the wet street asphalt. The sidewalk filled with evening people looking for a good place to eat or simply walking their dogs. Greg didn't know what else to do, so he just sat there, doing what he did best: waiting for something to happen. Passing time during surveillance was easy for Greg, but this kind of anticipation was something he couldn't do anymore. It was too painful, and he thought about just going back to his apartment in Queens and falling asleep due to his depression-filled mood.

Is my life really worth a dime without her? The Greg Man never feels like this about a girl. What is it about her? How could I fall in love so quickly? I'm hurting! Man, this sucks! Am I all alone, a useless person, with no real soul for her to love?

Suddenly the dull sound of a ringing phone emanated from his jacket pocket. He fumbled trying to answer it.

"Hello? Hello?"

"Greg! It's me, Julia! I'm—" The call suddenly disconnected.

Greg frantically tried calling the number Julia had called from, but she didn't answer. He kept calling the telephone number, but it just rang. He also continued to call her cell phone, but it had been turned off.

The parents called Greg a few times after Julia's call, but he didn't answer his cell phone. What was he going to tell them?

The situation is now totally worse. Julia calls and hangs up, and the parents are crying for their daughter's return. This all leaves the Greg Man in a state of big despair. Where are you, Julia? Why don't you answer your phone? Are you okay? Julia!

Greg felt frustrated and exhausted. He drove back to Queens and slipped into bed but couldn't sleep. He tossed and turned, felt hot and cold, and then his eyes closed at about 7:30 a.m. A half hour later, Greg sprang out of bed and walked into the kitchenette, where he opened the fridge for a stale slice of cold pizza and ate it while sitting on the couch in his underwear. Sleep was not in the cards anytime soon. He had too much anguish over Julia and thought about how his role in her life had definitely gone to another level. Greg also thought about the possibility that she double backed on her whole commitment to him and to God and just flew the coop, just to get away from it all.

Then he had a morning epiphany: he could reverse trace the phone number Julia had called from. He opened his company laptop and went on a website that traced the phone number to an address in Palmyra, New York. Greg thought that maybe he should just go there right now to see if Julia was there. Yes, that's what he was going to do.

Just a little rest on the couch first, and then I'll drive to Palmyra.

Big Greg knew that he had stepped over the line with her. He had made love to her and confessed his love for her, but now it was time to fess up to both the parents and Pete Baranowski. Perhaps he might call them later when he was on his way to Palmyra, wherever that was.

When his phone rang at nine in the morning, he was dozing on the couch and the TV droned with commercials. He awoke excitedly, rolling off the sofa, and answered his cell phone, but it wasn't Julia; it was his boss, Pete Baranowski.

Oh man, shit, first thing on a bummed-out morning. Pete is going to be really angry at me. How do I handle this one? Should I just hang up this cell phone and move out of this fucking city? Maybe my cousin in Jersey might let me live with him for a while?

I'm heading to Palmyra today, and nothing is going to stop me. My love Julia waits for me up there. I don't care what happens. I'm going to follow my heart on this one.

"Greg, where are you? The parents called me and said that their daughter never called yesterday. Got any ideas why she didn't call? The parents seemed pissed, but I'm not giving any of their money back if they're going to start bitching about their daughter not calling them. It's not our fault she didn't call. We were there just to locate her, that's it," Pete said.

"Uh, boss, I have some things to tell you that you're not going to like. Also, I might need your help on something. I better come up to the office. Um, uh, see you in a little while."

"But today's not your office day. What's up? What did you do? Did you get us involved in something that we shouldn't be involved in that's going to get us in trouble? Can't you just tell me over the phone what you're thinking about? I mean, why drive into Manhattan when you don't have to? Just tell me over the phone now what's on your mind."

"Uh, well, Pete, it's kind of an involved story. Let's just say that things have gotten more intense and I think that we need to talk about our options," Greg said.

"Oh man, this doesn't sound good. What the fuck. Okay, Greg, see you as soon as you can get up here."

It was time to expose his love for Julia and their relationship with each other. But it was also imperative that Greg tell Pete straight out that he was going to Palmyra to find Julia. Greg figured that he'd be out of Baranowski's office in just over an hour, and then he'd hit the road up to Palmyra. Even if Julia went on a binger or something like that, Greg wanted to see and hear it for himself. Whatever the case, Julia tried speaking with him and then she was cut off. It didn't matter why. The only thing that mattered was getting to that address in Palmyra.

I'll be seeing you again very soon, Julia. Your face, your lips, your deep soul, my love for you reflected in your eyes. I love you, no matter what. Please stay where you called from, because I'll be on my way to you. Come hell or high water, I will see you again, to tell you that I love you.

SHOCKED AND DECEIVED

"Sailed this day nineteen leagues, and determined to count less than the true number, that the crew might not be dismayed if the voyage should prove long."
—**Christopher Columbus**

WHEN PETE HUNG up the phone, he knew that Greg had betrayed him again. There was an incident just a few months ago, where Greg worked an insurance company case for Pete and then gave that case to the lawyer of a personal injury firm, who was also Pete's client. If it weren't for Greg writing his name as the referring person on the claimant's fact sheet in order to get a percentage of the case for himself, Pete's client wouldn't have caught Greg's malfeasance. The personal injury firm's CEO called Pete and said that the referring name on the claimant intake form was Greg Rocco, whose investigator name he recognized on previous work received from Baranowski Investigations. If Pete's big-time insurance company client found out that his agency was referring insurance cases to a personal injury client, his firm could be shut down with criminal charges pending. Pete was going to fire him, but Greg begged for his job and professed his deepest regret over the transgression. Greg pleaded for Pete's trust again and said that he would do all his cases one hundred percent for a minimal cost. At times, Pete wondered if he should have fired Greg right then and there. But Baranowski Investigations needed Greg's robot-like surveillance stamina to obtain videotape on cases that went on for long hours, where he'd have to stay in the stiflingly hot van to get the video they needed. Greg also possessed neat handwriting skills and would be able to secure signed statements that were college literate and written with nice penmanship. Greg's work produced large profit margins for Pete; consequently, the distrust was tolerated and Greg kept working. Greg's phone call brought on feelings inside Pete that were reminiscent of the double cross from a few months ago.

The secretary buzzed Pete on the intercom; Greg was in the front office.

"Send him in please," Pete said.

Pete's frosted-glass door opened and Greg had the expression of a kid who had behaved badly. His mouth went to the right side and he looked up at the ceiling. Pete knew for sure that Greg was about to deliver bad news.

"Boss, I got a little too close to the case. She and I kind of had a thing going, but then she just disappeared," Greg said, contritely.

"I fucking knew that you were going to say that shit. Just answer one quick question for me and then we'll talk more. Did you have sex with her?" Pete asked.

Greg sheepishly nodded, looked at Pete in the eye for a second, and then looked down.

"Yes," Greg said, with his head bowed.

"Holy shit! Even after we discussed that you weren't sup-posed to do that."

"But, boss, you don't understand. It's more than just sex between me and her. We really love each other. I'm serious. We love each other. She was supposed to meet me, and she disappeared but called and then hung up quickly," Greg said.

"What do you mean she hung up quickly?"

"She called from this number I didn't recognize and said 'It's Julia!' and then she hung up," Greg said, perplexed.

"What's the number she called from?" Pete asked.

Greg opened his flip phone and read off the number to Pete.

"I reversed it on my computer, to a town named Palmyra," Greg said.

Pete pressed the button on his desk intercom.

"Vicky, could you please come in here and take this number from me?"

"Yes, what do you have there, Pete?" Vicky asked.

"Please reverse this telephone number and get me all the information on whoever it goes to. Also, please call the number and see what happens. If anyone gets on the phone, transfer the call to me," Pete said.

When Vicky walked out and closed the door behind her, it was Pete's opportunity to get the whole story from Greg.

"You have jeopardized my operation once again, Greg. What happened? Tell me the story in a nutshell from the third time you went up to the apartment."

"Well, what can I say, Pete? We connected on many levels. She met me at a diner, and then we walked through Central Park. When I took the taxi back to her hotel, she jumped all over me and pulled me into her room. So that's the story," Greg said.

Pete couldn't help but think that Greg was a complete lummox. All those qualities that made him a great surveillance agent now played against Pete. Greg was a mindless automaton guided by the external programs of nature. He exhibited total disregard towards the company's welfare.

"When were you supposed to meet her?" Pete asked.

"She was supposed to show up at two thirty in the afternoon yesterday at the diner on the Upper West Side. When she didn't show up by six, I checked the whorehouse and her hotel, and she wasn't at either place. Madam Zeva said she didn't show for work, and the hotel lobby guys said that they hadn't seen her. So I go back to the diner and wait for her, and she finally calls, but from that strange number, and then hangs up."

"This is probably going to lead to hot water for me with the parents. They are pissed, big time. Is there anything you're not telling me? Did you forget any important details to your sorry-assed story?" Pete was angry.

"Well, she said that she was going to team up with some missionaries before meeting me at the diner. We were going to have dinner with the parents later in the day. And well, I was going to go move to Utah with her."

"Holy shit, this gets better with every fucking sentence from your mouth. Looks like I need to do some major damage control on things that are still happening, and I have no fucking idea of what's going to happen. You have to clean this mess up! Do you understand?" Pete glared at Greg.

"Yeah, sorry, boss, I apologize. I lost control for a while, but she is so cool!"

The buzzer on Pete's desk intercom sounded. The secretary's voice boomed over the speaker: "Peter, about that number you gave me, it goes to a private house address in Palmyra, New York. I called the number. It's out of service."

"Where did you say?" Pete asked.

Vicky's voice crackled through the intercom again: "Palmyra, it's a small town near Rochester."

"Thank you, Vicky." Pete let go of the intercom button. "So, Greg, she called from a town called Palmyra, like you said. Does that strike a bell with you at all?" Pete sounded frustrated.

"No, not at all, I'd never heard of that town, and she never mentioned it. She did say something about going to a sacred forest or park or something like that. Pete, I have to go up there. I have to check that address. What happens if she's kidnapped or something?" Greg asked.

"Don't go overboard with your crazy theories now. Let's remember that Julia lives on the wild side, and her phone call from Palmyra might be from a sugar daddy's estate and she called you because now she's tired of him. Who knows? I'll engineer it so the family will want me to go up to Palmyra. This way, you and I can get paid for going up there and we can even get the Palmyra cops rolling on this case, if need be. Once I'm in Palmyra and I lay the groundwork with the local cops, I'll call you. When you get up there, check in to a motel near the town and then you'll go to the address. We'll set up a strategy depending on what you find when you're there. Let's try to keep playing this case the smart way."

"Okay, boss man, let's do your plan. I was going to rush up there, but if you can work it now so the parents come up with more bucks and get the cops to help me out, well then I can go along with that. But don't make it too long now, because Big Greg needs to find his love mighty quick and there's no wasting time when Julia is in Big Greg's picture."

Thirty minutes passed, and the long stretch of time doing nothing made Pete feel worse every second that he procrastinated calling the parents. What should he say? There was no way that he could tell them the truth regarding his agent Greg having sex with their daughter. Yet his scruples compelled him to at least tell them about her call from Palmyra. Pete knew that the scenario was going to be that the parents would tell him to drive up to Palmyra to find their daughter for a handsome sum.

Pete finally picked up the phone to call the parents.

"Hello, Mr. Olsen, it's Peter Baranowski. I have some updated information regarding your daughter's whereabouts."

"Well it's about time you called back, Baranowski. What do you have for us?" The father's tone was gruff.

"My agent Greg, who you've met, just got a call from your daughter, but then she hung up immediately. However, we were able to reverse trace the number she called from, and it originated from a location in Palmyra, New York. It's a small town in the western tier of New York State, about forty minutes from Rochester," Pete said.

"Do you think that she's totally irrational? Why would she be in Palmyra?" the father asked.

"I'm sorry, sir, I can't answer that. I know that you love her very much. We could go to the Palmyra address and coax her to call you or even go home," Pete said.

"Yes, you do that, Baranowski. Can you go up there right away? I don't care what it costs. I want to find my daughter and have my wife and myself stand face to face in front of her and ask her to come home."

"Sure, I could handle that for you. I'll plan on spending a couple of days up there and form a team. We'll try our best to find her and have her call you or give you her new address. It's going to take me about six hours to get up there. So I'll leave this afternoon and give you my report tomorrow once I'm up there. My agent Greg will also assist me in the investigation. Can you have one of your men stop by with a $10,000 retainer? How does that sound?"

"Okay, Baranowski, you get cracking. I want my daughter back in Michigan as soon as possible. Her mother is physically sick from this ordeal, and I'll do anything at this point to get her back. So please find her for me. We'll drive to Palmyra when you tell us you've found her."

Mr. Olsen did not sound happy.

Pete hung up the phone and unconsciously let out a gust of pent-up air.

I'm going to need some help on this one. Herbie Schwartz is the man to set me up on this case. I might need to speak to the cops up there about this missing girl or even have them gain access to the premises she called from.

As Pete left the building, he called Herbie Schwartz on his cell phone and filled him in on the missing girl and the phone number going to Palmyra. Pete asked Herbie if he could pave the way for a sit-down talk with the police up there and, if necessary, help him check out the address that Julia had called from.

More recently, Pete had purchased a Detonics .45 Combat Master automatic pistol from Herbie, which was a vast improvement over having to carry his great-grandpa's enormous Colt revolver that was manufactured in the early 1900s. The new Detonics .45 was small; it fit in the palm of Pete's hand. Yet the powerful Combat Master's .45 ACP round packed tremendous energy. The pistol's magazine held only six rounds. It certainly wasn't a lot of bullets compared with Herb's NYPD Glock that held seventeen nine-millimeter bullets; however, the .230-grain hollow-point .45 was wide and heavy, and full of enough energy in one shot to stop a murderous three-hundred-pound maniac swinging an axe on a small stairwell. For many years now, Pete had only carried his great-grandfather's pistol, which sported fancy-looking white deer-antler grips. The old revolver was frequently displayed to his clients when the private opportunity presented itself. Pete's pistol was an advantageous marketing tool while pitching his investigation services to lawyers. The repeat clients would invariably ask Pete to show off his revolver. However, Pete rarely carried this long-barreled gun. It was so large that he had to wear it in an uncomfortable leather shoulder holster under an extra-large-fitting sport jacket. The only time he'd carry the revolver was during marketing visits to clients. The pistol made a noticeable bulge under Pete's suit jacket, prompting his clients to notice it and then ask wide-eyed questions.

While not as impressive looking as his great-grandfather's Colt revolver, the new Detonics Combat Master was manufactured to be the quintessential compact-carry firearm. Pete bought the Detonics auto from Herbie and kept it in the file-cabinet safe in his office. He never carried it, because guns made Pete feel uneasy. He couldn't relax while knowing that he was strapped with a device of death at his side. Self-defense experts talk about a state of "condition yellow" when one wears a firearm; a person who wears a gun must always be on guard. What would happen if it fell out and landed on the floor of a busy nightclub while the person was dancing? How about an altercation in a bar? Someone could grab the gun. Carrying a gun is not a relaxing endeavor, and for Pete, it was a constant source of anxiety and paranoia.

An hour later, Herbie Schwartz sat in front of Pete in Katz's Deli on Houston Street. The table was loaded with a bucket of pickles surrounded by tins of mustard, ketchup, and other condiments. Herbie was a unique sort of person, a gun-loving Jew who formerly worked as a detective for the NYPD in the burglary division. He also sold guns to cops and security personnel through his Federal Firearms License. Corpulent Herbie was Pete's police contact when hard-to-get information was necessary to complete a case. So far, Herb's performance was stellar; he always produced accident reports and detectives' notes every time the case called for official documentation. As they shared pastrami sandwiches and spooned chopped liver onto rye bread, Pete engaged Herbie on the case.

"I'm starting out soon and driving six or so hours to Palmyra. What's the name of this detective I'm supposed to meet up there?" Pete asked.

"He's a slow-talking rancher-sounding cowboy, originally from Salt Lake City, but he seems like he's a real nice guy. I talked to him for a good fifteen minutes. His name is Orrin Culver. You're driving all the way to Palmyra? Shit, it's fucking way-out remote, like the fucking boondocks up there in western New York. What are you getting yourself into this time?" Herbie asked, kiddingly.

"This is a big-money but touchy case, Herbie. The parents are having a shit fit, and I'm in the middle of a shit storm. Listen to this, first the daughter runs away. Then we find her in a whorehouse. Then my agent Greg has sex with her against my specific instructions not to . . . but the parents don't know that my agent had sex with their daughter, and I'm sure as shit not going to tell them. Then she skips out of New York City and calls Greg from Palmyra and then hangs up after a few seconds. The number she called from is disconnected, and she's not answering her cell phone," Pete said.

"Holy shit! Is that the same numbnuts Greg I worked with on that Albany marital surveillance a couple of months ago when he got pulled over by the troopers after the husband spotted him and called nine-one-one? Good thing I was there. He would have definitely been hauled into the station. That jerk Greg was up in the troopers' faces, saying shit like, 'You're not so tough.'"

Herbie took a giant wide-mouthed bite of his softball-sized pastrami on rye.

"Yeah, he was the agent on that Albany case with you. I remember that case. Needless to say, Greg is a fucking strange bird," Pete said.

"So what you're telling me is that after Greg had sex with your client's daughter, she runs away up to Palmyra? And now the parents want to find her again after Greg defiled their precious little girl?" Herbie laughed.

"Not funny, Herbie, I'm on the hot seat here. It's a sad situation, I know, but I can't tell her parents what really happened, and I'm probably going to need backstabbing Greg sometime in the future on this case," Pete said.

"Ah, ha-ha-ha! I don't envy you and your crazy shit. If the parents ever found out, they'd probably kill Greg and then you!"

Herbie noisily slurped the last of his Dr. Brown's Cel-Ray soda and smirked at Pete's misery.

Pete hit the table with his clenched hand.

"Now you can see what a fucked-up situation this is. At least I'm getting paid a shitload of money to patch up my own fuck-ups." Pete chuckled.

"But why would the daughter go all the way to western New York? What the fuck is so important up there? There's nothing there except cows and farms," Herbie said.

"I have no fucking idea why she called from there or why she didn't just call from her cell phone. This is the bullshit on my plate, and now I have to eat it. I fucking hate western New York too. I was out there a few years ago, and it is one boring place. I mean, there was absolutely nothing to do out there and everything closes down by 10:00 p.m. No restaurants, no attractions, nothing, it's fucking boring," Pete said.

"Well, good luck in Palmyra. You've got a long drive ahead of you. Hey, what's interesting is that Orrin Culver is a Mason, and you are also, right? He's going to like you just because of that," Herbie said.

"I went through the rituals at the Masonic Temple on Twenty-Third Street just to get more business for my private-eye office. This is a taboo thing to do, as Masons firmly believe that one should join solely for being in the club and not to gain profit by association. Learning all that crap was a pain in the ass, but at least I got to meet some good people, and I got a bit of business from the guys there."

"Sorry you have to go all the way up to Palmyra just to find a runaway teenager. Hey, what happens if your agent Greg gets her pregnant? Will Baranowski Investigations be ordered to pay child support? Ah, ha-ha-ha!"

Herb's high-pitched cackling laugh annoyed Pete.

"Oh, Herb, why must you rub salt in my wounds. Isn't it enough that I have to go to bumfuck western New York and try to salvage a fucked-up case?"

"Ha! You're so fucked, it makes me laugh!" Herbie changed his tone from mocking to reassuring. "Eh, you'll be okay, just find the girl and tell the parents where she is. Then you're in the clear, right? If they find out about Greg, who cares? Your job's been totally completed satisfactorily, and they couldn't sue you for anything, am I right?"

Pete shook his head and let out a long breath.

"I'm either going to just squeak by the trouble on this case or I'm going to be totally fucked."

WELCOME TO PALMYRA

"Let my skin and sinews and bones dry up, together with all the flesh and blood of my body! I welcome it! But I will not move from this spot until I have attained the supreme and final wisdom."

—Buddha

P ETE DROVE PAST the city of Albany while traveling west on Route 90. The tall gleaming towers of white marble denoted the government buildings of Rockefeller State Plaza. The State towers appeared like sparkling spires in the distance, like in the movie *The Wizard of Oz*.

The Detonics Combat Master .45 pistol was tucked inside Pete's waistband. His heightened sense of his surroundings was always prevalent when he wore a pistol. Yet traveling into the unknown, on a possible criminal kidnap case, did raise questions as to being a fool for not carrying. So even though he agonized for a few minutes about taking it to western New York, he still felt that it would be better to have the pistol. Forever being paranoid about a possible misfire, Pete carried the .45 without a bullet in the chamber, making it impossible for the gun to misfire. He'd have to cycle the slide using two hands in order to make the pistol operable. Pete didn't bring any extra magazines for the Detonics. He simply slid it into its leather holster and drove out of the city.

After he passed Albany, the rest of the drive to Palmyra was going to be another three hours. It was a long drive, more than two hundred miles into New York State's western frontier, north of the Finger Lakes region. The view from his front windshield was mundanely consistent and scenically boring, an endless scrubby flat ground that brought on feelings of dullness—nothing to look at but a few dilapidated homes plopped down on endless bushy plains. The early summer day was cloudy. An overcast sky hovered over Pete's car the entire way. Finally, after what seemed like a longer ride than it should have been, the exit sign for Palmyra appeared.

It was already dark, a lot of houses looked down in the dumps, and Pete knew he had a lot on his plate before he could get to a motel for a nap. He drove by the Palmyra Inn and his problem was solved for the night's stay. After he drove north on Route 21 for a few miles, a sign on the side of the road said Welcome to Palmyra. He passed a few clusters of private houses as he drove towards the center of town. The notable intersection in Palmyra, at Route 21 and Main Street, had a religious Christian church on each street corner. The different denominations were evident from the contrasting architectural style of each church. The unique four corners made Pete conclude that Palmyra must be an especially religious town.

The right turn onto Main Street brought him past an old two-story 1800s red brick building with a sign that said Town Hall. Pete knew that the Palmyra police department was inside the building, but Detective Orrin Culver was explicit about not meeting with him there.

Pete noted how all the two-level buildings in town appeared as interconnecting brick and timber structures with antique wood-framed windows, built around the same time, more than a hundred years ago. A two-story tiny stone building with just two windows in front had a date carved in stone on top that read 1922. Pete noticed a nice early-American building with a sign over the door; Book of Mormon.

To Pete's right was the Lock 29 burger bar where Detective Orrin Culver wanted to meet. It was a small place, kind of a dive, with neon beer signs in the windows, a street-level burger joint below a three-story brick building that was probably built in the early 1900s. As Pete drove by, he looked into the front window of the Lock 29 and noticed a girl cooking on a grill, with a few customers bent over the counter, their beers in hand.

Now that he was finally here in Palmyra, Pete decided to waste no time and check out the address that Julia called from. He turned left and headed to a remote section of town. There were thornbush-lined sidewalks and broken-up concrete streets. The map denoted that the house was just a couple blocks away from the old Erie Canal, which was a manufactured waterway used in the early 1800s to transport goods on barges.

The house was painted white with green trim, a small two-story colonial style, positioned in the middle of the block. The paint-chipped house looked in total disrepair, with rotted wood siding sticking out of some places and the roof's shingles were somewhat askew with green moss growing from the cracks. The house was partially surrounded by a bent chain-link fence broken in places where jagged spokes stuck into the air.

The street struck him as somewhat serene; there was nothing really happening in this quiet neighborhood. Sidewalks were on both sides of the narrow road, yet no one was out of their house, walking around. The neighborhood looked deserted.

Pete stopped his car about a hundred feet past the house and watched it from his rearview mirror. Not five minutes went by when a squat man with long hair and a beard stepped outside and looked down the block towards Pete's charcoal-dark Buick.

Holy shit, I'm burned in less than five minutes!

Pete drove away, acting as if he did not realize that the bodybuilder was scrutinizing him.

Fucking A, that's going to be an impossible location to pull off a good surveillance. I've got to call Greg and tell him to come up here. I'll send him right into that crocodile nest. At least we'll find out if she's there or not.

The front of the Lock 29 burger joint had glaring electric neon signs in the window. Inside the place were two pinball machines, a small wooden bar with rickety black stools, and two booths on the left that were empty. A pool table in the back area had a large light over it.

Pete took a seat at the second booth. He noticed that the locals were staring at him—not threateningly but in a curious fashion, like someone had entered their cage and they wanted to know why.

"Can I get somethin' for ya, honey?" the nicely featured twenty-something girl bartender asked.

"Sure, I'll take two cheeseburgers, some fries, and a large Coke," Pete said.

Without saying a word, she turned to the cooking counter behind the bar and threw on two thick pads of chop meat that immediately sizzled from the hot grill. The big burgers and thick-cut potato fries were a welcome late dinner after such a long drive.

When Pete looked up from his plate, it was easy to recognize Orrin Culver from his tan cowboy hat on top of his narrow head of short silver hair. He was about Pete's height, perhaps a bit shorter, maybe five foot eight. His black, pointed cowboy boots had two-inch heels. His appearance might be described as looking like a thin rail, someone with a very slender body. However, even though his body looked skinny, he had an air of wiry strength. Orrin Culver wore a navy-blue sport jacket and blue tie with a white shirt. Pete thought that Orrin looked like a well-preserved man in his mid- to late fifties who had an athletic appearance. Orrin's square jaw and cleft chin featured a strong facial appearance and lent to his serious countenance. As he stood turning his head back and forth, some patrons turned away, others gave him a half-hearted nod of recognition. It was obvious to Pete that Orrin Culver was a well-known man in town.

"Hey, you must be Pete. I'm Detective Orrin Culver, pleasure to make your acquaintance. How you been doing today? You made a long trip up here driving all the way from New York City."

His voice was deep, a baritone usually reserved for somber men. Pete felt the excessively strong grip from his right hand. Orrin's accent sounded Southern but with a seldom-heard out West twang.

"Yeah, you said it. Long trip as hell, I wouldn't be out here if it wasn't for the money. Thanks for meeting here and talking with me. My friend Herbie tells me that you're a fellow Mason," Pete said.

"That means we share a lot of good common values. Sorry to meet you in this place. Ya know, I didn't want to talk in my office because it's probably bugged," Orrin said.

"Yeah, shit, I always think that my office is bugged too, but then after a while, I just don't care anymore," Pete said.

"No one has the right to listen to my every word, no matter who they are."

"You could always deploy electronic countermeasures. I specialize in that on occasion," Pete said.

"Those electronic doodads might give a false sense of security, so I don't bother with technical things. I just like to discuss matters in places I know are not bugged. I gathered from talking with your friend on the phone that you're a private investigator looking for a missing girl, is that correct? At least that's what your New York City detective Herbie told me. He also said to let you know if I might need to buy any guns from him," Orrin said.

"All true. Herbie will give you the best prices. So we found this girl for her parents in New York City a couple of days ago, but now she's flown the coop again and her parents want to speak with her no matter what. The girl's name is Julia Olsen. She called my investigator, but the call got cut off. We traced the number she called from to a house on Canal Street here in Palmyra, specifically, 419 Canal Street," Pete said.

"Ya know, that's interesting because I've seen some young girls walking around Main Street who don't look like they're from around here. That makes me curious because I'm good at recognizing faces, but these young girls were walking around town and then I suddenly didn't see them anymore. Little things like that bother me when they just don't fit into life as they should. There're some things going on in this town that aren't apparent on the surface. There's a lot I can tell you. In fact, there is a lot I need to tell you. Because maybe you can help me as much as I can help you," Orrin said.

"Oh, how so? I'd be happy to do what I could," Pete said.

"That house you're talking about. I know there are some shady things going on there, but I can't get a warrant because there's no probable cause. It's a hard block to get a surveillance going too. It's too easy to get spotted by the guys who come out of there," Orrin said.

"Yeah, I was just over there for a minute before a muscle guy with a beard and long hair stepped out of there. Tonight I'm thinking of calling my young agent, who I'll send up to the door and see what happens. I'll get him up here tomorrow," Pete said.

"Well, Pete, I have to get back to the office now before some eyebrows get raised. But how about you give me your cell phone number and we meet up tomorrow night for some homemade beef stew over at my place?" Orrin asked, looking around like someone might be watching him.

"Sure, Orrin, that sounds great. In the meantime, can you help me find out more about that house on Canal Street and what's going on in there? The girl called from there, but I don't want to go up to the place myself and spook her or whatever."

"In due time, Pete. Let's talk tomorrow night, and we'll see what we can do about finding that little runaway girl. Your hamburgers here are on me, welcome to Palmyra."

Pete noticed Orrin wearing a ring that had the initials *CTR*.

"Nice ring, what does CTR mean?"

"Choose the right."

"Oh yeah, I agree with that, but sometimes choosing the right can be a hard decision when the only thing left to do seems wrong but, in the end, is the right thing. Kind of like doing bad so you can be good," Pete said.

"If you always choose the right, then you never have to worry about anything," Orrin said.

"So then choosing the right might seem wrong at the time, but in the end, it was the right decision. Is that what you're saying?" Pete asked.

"Choose you this day whom ye will serve. But as for me and my house, we will serve the Lord."

Orrin stood up and threw a twenty-dollar bill on the table. He nodded to the young female bartender on the way out. Other local patrons glanced up at Orrin's exit but then quickly turned away, to not get caught looking. The young girl bartender glared at Pete for a couple of seconds.

Pete made a hasty retreat from the bar after feeling like he was in a fishbowl being studied by curious children,

On the way to the Palmyra Inn motel, Pete wondered about Orrin Culver and the strange interaction he had with him at the burger place.

Why is Orrin so paranoid about everything? He constantly looks around like something bad is about to happen. He seems to virtually dissect everyone with his steely stare. And what's the real reason that he wants me to come over to his house tomorrow night for dinner?

HARD KNOCKS SURVEILLANCE

"Although nature commences with reason and ends in experience it is necessary for us to do the opposite, that is to commence with experience and from this to proceed to investigate the reason."

—Leonardo da Vinci

EARLY THE NEXT morning, Pete woke from a pleasant sleep at the Palmyra Inn. It wasn't every day that he got the opportunity to sleep alone in a king-sized bed. The big beef burgers he ate last night were the perfect comfort food to nod out on. Palmyra was a quiet place, very little traffic and no large industry of any kind. Main Street consisted of Mormon bookstores and little drinking bars. The original printing press for the Book of Mormon was the only attraction on Main Street, but even that innocuous façade was subdued to the point of looking like nothing more than an old restored three-story 1800s brick building.

Thoughts of Orrin Culver persisted into Pete's morning. He wondered why Orrin was so nervous and paranoid, especially in light of the fact that Orrin was a cop.

Shouldn't Orrin be confident and fearless in his own town?

Maybe he thinks there's an upper echelon of corruption in his police department and they think he's a Goody Two-shoes who will rat on their illegal activities? Or maybe he's some kind of religious zealot who has gone off the deep end and is ready to snap at any time? He seemed friendly enough, and there's a certain goodness and confidence that I'll go along with. He could be very instrumental in getting into that house to determine the whereabouts of Julia Olsen. If she's there, that would be great news for me. I'll cash in on the parents' retainer and my job is done. Hopefully I can spot her out in front of the house, playfully interacting with her new long-haired boyfriend. Then it would be case closed.

Downstairs, in the lobby of the Palmyra Inn, a few tables were set up for a quick breakfast before Pete embarked on a tight surveillance on the Canal Street house. Pete figured that he would do just a couple of hours in a box to see what was going on there. If he happened to see Julia walking freely in and out of the house, then she was there by her own volition and was a faker to Greg by leading him on. To perform surveillance, even a short one, often brought up more questions than answers. But it was worth a shot for a few hours' surveillance until he had to call Greg to come up to Palmyra to knock on that door. Moreover, Pete was a corpulent five-foot-nine, 230-pound lug with a black mustache. His overweight appearance was often misinterpreted, and people thought that he was a donut-eating cop. Pete's experience told him that he'd better use Greg on that Canal Street door; otherwise, the occupants might never open it up for fear of staring into a police badge.

Through his many turbulent years of private investigation, Pete had learned the hard way how to perform surveillance in a tight neighborhood. He invented his own technique for close-up surveillance without getting noticed. The first time that he used the box routine was in the late 1980s, for surveillance in the Bronx. The only way not to get spotted by the "target" was to find a large-appliance cardboard box and sit inside it on the back-seat floor of a car. This was a tried and proven technique. Nobody ever knew that he was inside the box, sitting, watching every movement on the street through a peephole. The box technique got him a big insurance client one time when he sat in front of the house of an elderly woman who claimed that she was disabled due to an accident. Pete took pictures of her digging a garden in front of her house. He then arranged a vegetable delivery, made by Herbie, the gun-dealing police detective, who loved the extra money he pocketed by working on Pete's PI cases. The old woman told Herbie that she didn't order anything but to bring the crate of vegetables inside. Herbie told her that union rules didn't allow him to go inside the house. The lady then bent down and easily picked up the thirty pounds of vegetables while Pete videotaped every motion. As long as the box didn't get too hot inside, as he peered out from a cutout peephole the size of a quarter, it was a fantastic surveillance technique. The only drawback to this method was that during summertime, it was over a hundred degrees inside the box. Herbie was supposed to come back to the car after walking away from the lady's house and then drive from the parking spot that was in front of her house. On that hot summer day, Herbie didn't get back to the sweltering car for thirty minutes. Herbie had gotten lost walking around the unfamiliar Bronx block and had forgotten where he parked the car with Pete roasting in the back-seat box. Bronx drug dealers leaned against the car, doing business, and Pete dared not move a muscle. In a less-active neighborhood, it was a simple matter to pop out of the box when no one was around and then drive away undetected. In a neighborhood with residents standing on the sidewalk, it was best to have a driver park and then walk away from the car, leaving the surveillance agent secreted in the back-seat box.

When working alone, the real trick was to get into the box when no one was watching and then remain still until ready to leave the vicinity. This could be a very tricky thing to do if someone decided to sit on their porch for a couple of hours and stare at the car or a dog walker let their pooch meander and sniff near the car for what seemed like an eternity when the surveillance agent was having a bathroom emergency.

On Canal Street in Palmyra, Pete parked the car about two hundred feet away and then slipped into the cardboard dishwasher box in the back seat. Pete focused his attention on the front of the house by using the telephoto feature on his video camera. The two-inch hole was cut in such a way that Pete could sit on the back seat and look through the cutout through the front windshield. Pete also cut a second two-inch hole in the box so he could look out the back window if he had to. He covered the second hole with a piece of black tape so no revealing light entered his box. The small video camera in his hand zoomed up to ten power, enabling Pete to see every detail of the house. The condition of the place was slightly ramshackle and paint chipped, and there was a driveway on the side that led into a backyard that Pete was not able to see from his vantage point. He settled down into surveillance mode and focused his attention through the two-inch hole, looking out from the box.

When he was a child, Pete always wondered what was going on inside all those apartments in New York City. The many thousands of apartments, they each had their own story. At night, the light from each apartment had its special tale that Pete thought about. His young mind would ask, who lives in that apartment? What are they doing in there right now? Those memories came back to him as he stared at the Canal Street house. There's just no way to know what's going on inside a house. Anything could be happening, and those on the outside are left to postulate.

After just fifteen minutes, Pete saw a white van with a Utah license plate drive up to the front of the house. Two Caucasian young men got out of the front seats of the van, wearing white short-sleeved shirts and bright ties. Pete focused his camera on the young men and the van's license plate. They walked inside the house like they lived there. He recorded every action on telephoto video. Then a minute later, both young men exited the front door of the house, got back in the van, and drove it into the side driveway, out of sight, to the back of the house.

Those guys in the nerd outfits are probably the missionaries Julia was supposed to meet in the city. So it looks like she's flown the coop from Greg's embrace and fallen right into the grasp of these evangelists. Greg's going to be heartbroken when he finds out, but that's the way the love cookie crumbles when you fall in love with a wild chick. This box is getting too hot. I'm going to have to get out of here soon.

A grueling hour passed. Pete had reached the limit of his endurance and was more than ready to pop out of the box, but just then two motorcycles rode out of the driveway. The riders were large men in long, dark duster coats. The two motorcyclists looked similar: big beards, long hair, and sunglasses. There were no license plates visible on the front of the bikes. They rode right by Pete's car. The large motorcycle engines vibrated his seat as they passed. Pete quickly twisted his torso and ripped the black piece of tape off the box's second hole in back. He strained trying to get the camera's lens up to the hole. The motorcycles were almost at the end of the block as Pete struggled to align the front lens of the camera with the peephole. With two seconds left, he pushed the record button and was able to acquire a telephoto view of the back license plates of the motorcycles. They were also from Utah.

Ten minutes later, Pete popped out of his box and drove back to the Palmyra Inn for a much-needed shower after a very sweaty surveillance. He thought about how the house on Canal Street was an odd mix. It was strange, how two young nerds were living with two older bruisers on motorcycles. Moreover, the van had Utah license plates and so did the motorcycles. Pete called his office and had Vicky use their Department of Motor Vehicles connections to run the Utah plates. All the plates came back to a remote address in the southern Utah desert. The motorcycle's license plates reversed to the same address as the registration of the license plate on the white van, to a town called Hildale, Utah.

Pete started to wonder if they had the right house, or maybe Greg's phone number was totally off-kilter and these people from Utah had nothing to do with Julia—unless there was something going on in that house that was criminal in nature.

Is Julia in there, a prisoner, held by nerds and a motorcycle gang?

This idea did not strike Pete as a likely fact. Another more-plausible thought was that she was on a party binger, snorting crystal meth cooked up by the bikers, and the nerds were the unobtrusive drug distribution team selling meth to the yokels up here. This seemed a more likely theory, but now it was time to really find out what the mystery was inside that house. There were too many questions and not enough answers for Pete to feel comfortable taking on that house by himself.

I'm not going to blow the chance of finding this girl by prematurely investigating the house by myself. I look too intimidating. If anything is going on in there or if Julia is hiding for some reason, whoever is in there, they'd probably clam up on me. I've got no other choice but to call Greg up here for a look into that house. Then maybe we'll find this girl. The story all seems to fit now: she tells Greg that she's meeting some missionaries, and then she doesn't show up to meet Greg. And guess what, I just saw those two tie-wearing evangelist missionaries just now. Greg is going to be devastated when he finds out that Julia has left him for the two nerds. However, who really knows? I'll get him up here and find out what the real story is. The father is footing a handsome retainer, so I'll give him his money's worth by using Greg as a backup on this case.

New York City was far away from Palmyra, and Pete wished that he was back home, playing with his kids and watching TV with Cathy. The money was good on this case, so Pete gritted his teeth and was determined to do the right thing by the client. Getting a look at Julia and reporting where she was holed up was the only thing Pete was concerned with. He thought that Julia was probably some kind of wild child. Whatever the case, if Pete didn't work Greg into this case, then Greg might get pissed off and do something stupid. In the end, he wanted Greg to get a look inside that house. If Julia was there, great, case closed. If Julia wasn't in the house, then this matter would become an unsolved missing-person case.

I really hope that Julia is in that house. Then everyone is a winner. Greg gets his girl, or not, and the parents get their daughter. Moreover, I get a nice fee for all of it. If Julia's father starts getting in my face about Greg, I'll tell him that I found his daughter and that's all I was supposed to do. If Greg and Julia are in love, that's got nothing to do with Baranowski Investigations.

CALLED INTO ACTION

"It is even better to act quickly and err than to hesitate until the time of action is past."

—Carl von Clausewitz

ALTHOUGH HE WAS torn up emotionally inside, Greg concentrated on his regular case load, making believe as if nothing significant had occurred. Julia was gone and there was little he could do about it for the moment. He would honor his word to Pete and not go up to Palmyra right now; he'd wait for Pete's call, but only for a few hours. Greg was intent on going to Palmyra even if Pete didn't call. He had to find Julia and look her in the eye. If her love was true, then maybe she'd been kidnapped. But if she was just a super player, then she ran off with some rich dude who had a country estate in Palmyra.

Other girls had been short-time paramours until he got bored of them. He never experienced girlfriend love before. All the one-nighters and short-term girlfriends were insignificant. The only meaningful relationship he ever wanted was the prospect of being with Julia. Her presence lingered inside his heart. Greg couldn't believe that she would just take off on him as if nothing had happened between them. However, he had been down this road a few times before, where he was easily deceived by supposed love. Even he was guilty of changing his mind about a girl he thought he loved. Yet no girl was ever like Julia. She was the best, the one he felt real love for, even after just a few days. He could drive up to Palmyra right now, but Pete would definitely fire him and then he'd be stuck with a bartending job. Greg tried to play it cool, but his emotions for Julia were too overwhelming.

Maybe I should just say fuck it to Pete and drive up there and see if I can find Julia. I should go get her. So maybe I should. In fact, I'm definitely going up there, no matter what. To hell with Pete and the parents, I'm going up there to find her. I'm not going to wait for Pete to call me for his okay to go up there. It's something I should have done right after I reversed the phone number to the address in Palmyra. I'm such a fuck-up!

Greg had just finished an early-morning workman's compensation fraud surveillance in Long Island and was speeding back home to Queens to pack an overnight bag when Pete's call came in.

"How soon can you get up here to Palmyra?" Pete asked.

"As soon as I can, boss. I'll go back to my apartment, get a few things, and then I'm off. So maybe seven hours, I guess?" Greg said excitedly.

"It's Exit 43 off of Interstate 90, just north of the Finger Lakes region in western New York. It's closer to Rochester, about forty miles east. Take the 87 Thruway north to 90 West, and yeah, you should get here in about six or seven hours," Pete said.

"Definitely, Big Greg is on the way! Hey, boss, thanks for the chance to find Julia. I really appreciate that. I was wondering when you were going to call me. The Greg Man needs to find his love today for sure. Guess I'll be seeing you in Palmyra there, boss man. Did you find out any new information up there today?"

"As a matter of fact, I did find out some interesting stuff to tell you about. Let's wait until you get up here, and call me on your phone."

"Greg Man will soon be on the case, and everything will be solved. Good thing you got me, right, boss?"

"Yeah, well this is your fucking mess and now you have to help me clean it up. On the upswing, you'll still get paid, the parents coughed up more money, and for now, they don't know that you got yourself intimately involved with their daughter. But listen up, Greg. You're going to help me turn things around on this case. I can't believe you twisted everything and made this case a lot more complicated. You're a fucking jerk-off! You fucking did this to me again, and it's important that you fix this by helping me find this girl," Pete said.

"Sorry, boss. Mi mucho sorry, but you know this time, it's 'cause of true love. I really love this girl. It's for real," Greg said.

"Please, spare me. Get on the road as soon as you can. Check in to a small motel off of Exit 43. Go to this burger joint on Main Street in Palmyra. Then call me from your car when you're in front of the bar. It's called the Lock 29. Have a burger, but call my cell from your car before you get in there," Pete said.

The stimulating call to action gave Greg jubilant hope. Traveling up to find his true love on the boss's dime was the best of all worlds. He could fulfill his emotional promise of going to Palmyra to find Julia and get paid for it at the same time! Greg would pack a small bag and leave without thinking about anything else. Getting on the road to Palmyra was his only consuming thought. He stepped on the gas and sped back to his Queens apartment. The Long Island Expressway runs down the center of the island for seventy-one miles, and Greg was maintaining a steady eighty miles per hour the whole way by weaving in and out of traffic. He was determined to keep up this high-speed pace until he reached Palmyra.

Introspection was one of Greg's specialties, yet his deepest thoughts often lacked common sense. His roller coaster of profound emotions was caused by thoughts of Julia. He hyper focused his mind, and he reflected on some of his faults. He frequently deduced false assumptions about people. Also, he was often clueless as to what his role was supposed to be within the context of an investigation unless specifically instructed as to what scenario to perform. Without Pete guiding his every action, he would turn into a fumbling idiot with a false pretense about his own intellectual virility. Adding further to his intractable stoicisms was his robotic, uncaring attitude that he had perpetuated throughout his young life, so far, until now—because he would change, for love.

He wanted to be a good man to Julia. Her past didn't matter. Greg just desired to be with her and grow with her. He loved all of her. The overly opinionated Greg Man was now open to more understanding and forgiveness. People move on and become different people. He could change and so could Julia, together. Sometimes people will love each other for each other's future and what they will become together.

Julia was on his mind like a constant picture, her face framed in a mental image. When Julia spoke about her faith in God, her words made Greg warm inside. He felt a connection with Julia through her chosen faith, the Mormon religion. He wanted to learn more about Mormonism and the Book of Mormon after Julia had so vigorously espoused the religious merits of the Church of Jesus Christ of Latter-day Saints. Did she take off with those missionaries she was supposed to meet? Greg thought about Julia running away with Mormon missionaries but figured that idea was very unlikely and didn't give it much serious thought.

When someone just disappears, it changes the reality of the person who misses them most. I'm suffering differently somehow, maybe because I miss her so much and I feel she might be in danger. I'm going to get a look inside that Palmyra house one way or another.

As he drove too fast, speeding past other cars on the highway, he thought of Julia.

Her voice sounded desperate until the phone cut out. So maybe she's kidnapped? That's the best explanation. Julia must be kidnapped! That's got to be it. They took her against her will. Now I know it! Julia, if you can hear me, please hold steady and try to wait for me in Palmyra. Our love for each other was too true. God, I've got to find her! Heavenly Father, please forgive me for not rescuing her sooner. Oh, Julia, please forgive me, I'm so fucking stupid! Hold on, babe, I'll be there soon! My God and Jesus Christ, please help me find her!

After quickly packing and telling his aunt that he'd be gone for the night, Greg screeched his small black car out of his building's back parking lot. There was thankfully no traffic on the Whitestone Bridge as he drove north. The highway was monotonous and endless. He wished he could get there faster. Adrenaline shot into his body like a hit of amphetamine. He was elated about finally getting on the highway north, which offered a pipeline to reunite with his love, Julia.

The hours on the road dragged his energy down and he got bleary-eyed. Exit 43 on Route 90 couldn't come soon enough. Flat, endless brush and then a few low hills, not much else on the way, the car was low on gas, but he knew he'd make it to Palmyra without stopping.

Greg drove directly into town and, contrary to Pete's instructions, did not check in to a motel right off the highway. He parked in front of the Lock 29 burger joint on Main Street in Palmyra. Greg thought what a little dinky town this was. Julia would not have come here unless she had been kidnapped.

He sat in his car and called Pete on his cell phone.

"Okay, boss, I'm parked right outside, here at the burger joint like you wanted. I don't see you inside. You're not meeting me here, are you?" Greg asked.

"No, Greg, of course not, you're supposed to be undercover, remember?" Pete asked.

"Yeah, I figured, but I was just asking."

"Listen, Greg, I want you to see if you can get a look inside that house. Okay, so the address is 419 Canal Street, or at least that's the address the telephone number you gave me reversed to. I staked it out in front this morning, doing a short surveillance with the box routine. I saw two motorcycles come out of the driveway and a white van with two well-dressed young guys. They looked like those missionaries you said Julia mentioned, the kind of guys who hand out magazines and knock on people's doors. Funny thing, all the vehicles had Utah license plates. See if you can get some information on that house by getting a look inside. Go up to the door and tell them you got a good job in a nearby company and you're thinking of buying a house on the block and ask them how they like the neighborhood. Put on the personality of a young Wall Street guy, be authoritative and self-assured, like you have a lot of money. Then sap them for any info about people living at their residence. Try to talk your way into the house by saying how great their house architecture is and you want to buy a house on the block just like that one. Ask them if you can take two measurements of their rooms or something like that. Who knows, maybe Julia will answer the door? Remember to leave your IDs and cell phone in the car, and park far away. Let me know how you do. Call my cell right after you finish. If we happen to see each other in town, don't acknowledge me, okay?"

"I got it, big boss. Okay, I'm eager to get a look inside that house. Maybe she's there and these missionaries have brainwashed her into thinking something crazy," Greg said.

"Make sure you call me right after you finish at the house, no matter what you find. Maybe she'll jump into your arms, or maybe you'll come face to face with her new biker boyfriend. Just make sure you call me right after you find out what the story is."

"Roger that, boss, the Greg Man is on the case. Julia will soon be in my arms again, and everything is going to be all right. You'll see."

SEARCHING FOR HER

G REG WENT ABOUT life with a cavalier attitude, which frequently got him successful investigative results, but sometimes there were outrageous repercussions, like the time he left his "garbage grab" investigation garbage in a dumpster at Pete's office building. The janitors called the target company and told them not to throw away their Queens garbage in Manhattan. The next thing that happened that day was a contingent of angry businessmen from Queens trying to find out how their garbage ended up at a Thirty-Fifth Street office building in Manhattan. If there was an investigation that required a bold agent, Greg would go in headfirst without a second thought. That's why it was always important for Pete to give him an exact scenario of the way events should progress within a time frame and what kind of character he needed to play. In the absence of specific instructions from the office, Greg blindly charged into every case, always thinking that everything was going to be all right and people would talk to him no matter what. Interestingly, Greg's confidence did get him results, people actually did talk to him on the street, and his neighborhood information was spot on.

Parking the car a ways down the block on Canal Street was an easy first step because there were plenty of spaces on the curb far from the house. The sun was slowly setting through the trees, which lent long shadows over the street, a dark block of quiet—maybe abandoned—houses, with many lightless gaps in between. When Greg walked up to the Canal Street address from the sidewalk, he noticed a small red barn in back. Boldness is an attribute of the brave and the stupid. It was hard to say what Greg was thinking when he simply walked down the dirt driveway of the house, to the barn in back, in order to take a look inside.

When he opened the unlocked door, he saw the space was jammed full with motorcycles, about eight bikes, the cruising type, not the motorcycle gang, typical chopped Harleys. These bikes had big windscreens with dashboard electronics and hard-case saddlebags, the type of motorcycles meant for long-distance cruising. He used his small flashlight to scan around the inside; Utah license plates were on all of the motorcycles. When Greg put his hand near one of the motorcycles in the front row, he felt warmth, which meant that it had been ridden recently. Greg quickly walked out of the barn and tried to remain quiet as he closed the wooden door. Parked up on the back lawn, behind the house, was a white van with Utah license plates. Greg figured there could be many people in the house, with all these motorcycles parked in back and a big white van by the back door, so he quickly stepped off the property and hurriedly walked down the sidewalk to his car.

Time to call Pete.

"Hey, boss, listen to this, they got a lot of motorcycles with Utah plates parked behind the house in a barn, and there's a white van also with Utah plates parked in back."

"Slow down, Greg, are you talking about the house on Canal Street? Were you just there? Where are you now?" Pete asked, nervously.

"Yeah, I got the plate number off the van, and I got one plate off a bike, but I couldn't get the plates off of the other motorcycles because I snuck back there into the barn and didn't want to stay too long."

"Any indication of what's going on inside that house?"

"Nah, boss, I wanted to call you first. The house looks like there's no one there. Only one light is on upstairs and one light downstairs. I'll knock on the door now and see what's up."

"Okay, but please be discreet. Don't get us into any trouble. If anyone opens the door, do like we planned, act like you want to buy a house in the neighborhood and you want to know what they think of the street. You got that? Then if you get them to trust you, ask to see their house because it's just like the type of house you want to buy. Got all that?"

"I got it, boss, loud and clear. I'll beat around the bush with your story and then try to walk inside to see if Julia is there. Don't you worry, big boss, I'll take care of this case for you. I really need to find Julia though, case or no case. I hope she doesn't break my heart. I need to see her and ask her how she is and tell her that I love her."

"Why don't I feel confident that this operation will go smoothly?" Pete asked.

"No worries, boss, the Greg Man has everything under control."

"And listen, Greg, if she happens to be there with other guys, don't have a conniption, that's just life. I know you're not one to cause a scene, because you won't care by that point anyway, right?"

"Yeah, Pete, if I see her there with another guy, I'll just be disappointed and walk away, no hassles."

There were many possibilities going on in Greg's mind about what was happening in that house. It was hard to believe that Julia would hook up with a motorcycle gang. Then again, maybe she would. The uncertainty of what was about to be discovered at that house catapulted Greg to new heights of awareness. He was on the precipice of depression and excitement at the same time; he'd be sad if she voluntarily left him, but he'd still be elated just to see her. The inside of that house had the answers, and it was time to find out what was going on. Greg, for the first time that he could remember, was anxious, maybe even scared.

What if she's hooked up with some guy and I'm totally on the outs? Will she choose a big motorcycle biker dude who will show her the fast life, better than what I could do for her? She was so sincere with her beliefs in God and Jesus. I don't believe that she hooked up with a motorcycle gang. Damn! It's time to see what's happening inside that house and find Julia!

Greg put his cell phone in the glove compartment and walked back down the sidewalk towards the house.

Guess it's time for Big Greg to give the door a knock and see what the deal is.

Greg knocked three times on the door and waited about a minute without hearing anything. The door suddenly opened, and in the threshold, filling the space, stood a muscular, stocky, buzz-cut blond-haired man in his thirties, wearing a Wrangler western shirt with metal snaps on his breast pockets. Greg noticed that the man was clean shaven and figured him to be an athlete of sorts. He looked at Greg suspiciously with a furrowed brow.

"Can I help you?"

"Hi, how you doing today? My name is Greg. I was thinking of buying a house on this street, and I was wondering what you thought about the neighborhood?"

The square-jawed muscle-pumped man was steely at first, without expression. Then, suddenly, he seemed to spring to life.

"Oh great, so glad you are thinking of joining the neighborhood. Hey, where's your car? Who are you with today?"

The man had a Southern Bible Belt-type accent. Greg thought that maybe he was a fellow athlete who was from some other part of the country, maybe the Midwest.

Is this the guy Julia chose to hook up with?

"I'm parked way over on Main Street, figured I'd walk through the neighborhood and ask a few residents if they liked living here. Seems like a great town. Easy to get over here too, so it might be just a couple of weeks until I close on a house around here. Hey, it looks like we might be neighbors soon."

"Well, come on in, let's get you some iced tea and I can tell you all about this great place."

The man affectionately grabbed Greg's shoulder and gently pulled him into the house. He smiled at Greg and acted extra friendly.

"This is an old house, isn't it?" Greg asked. "So what year was this house built?"

"Oh, this house is very old. I'm not exactly sure what year it was built. The houses in this neighborhood have been here a long time. As you can probably see, a lot of houses on this block are in some need of repair. Are you a handyman?"

"Sure, I can fix a lot of things back up. It looks like most of the houses on this block are of similar size. My cousins and friends are going to put up the financial backing on the house we buy, and we'll fix it up. We all come from a plumbing background. So who else lives here? How many people live in this nice house? I just wanted to figure out how many bedrooms there are in the houses around here because maybe we'll use some of the bedrooms for offices. This looks about the same size as a house I looked at down the block."

The man just smiled. It was a creepy smile, like when some-one knows that you're a fool but they're not telling you to your face. Greg felt suddenly exposed. Deep down in a primal sense, he felt danger. Greg realized he was all alone in a house that was occupied by a motorcycle gang that must be hiding upstairs, maybe scoping him out.

From behind, he felt a presence. Greg turned, and there stood the hulking frame of a very large man. He was about six foot four. Greg's fears were quickly materializing. He was getting cornered by a crew of hardball dudes who rode motorcycles.

Of course, all those guys were in this house but keeping the lights low and keeping their bikes hidden in back. I think these guys might have kidnapped Julia. Look at these fucking guys. No doubt, they're fucking psychos from Utah. I'm going to have to rip this place apart to find Julia if they don't give her up!

"Oh, that's my roomie. He likes it here in the neighborhood too," the blond man said.

Greg noticed, out of the corner of his eye, another man, a bit older than the others, with long black hair down to his waist and a full beard that extended to his chest. He was just as big as the other guy but heavier overall. The odds were really against Greg now, three giant dudes against just him. Greg's svelte 175 pounds was not going to be a match against the 800 pounds of combined weight facing him. The guy blocking the door would be the first guy to get punched in the face. Then he'd grab the doorknob and get out quick if he had to.

Maybe it would be better if I leave now and get Pete to come over here with me?

"So it's just you guys living here? Where you guys from? You have kind of a Southern accent."

"Why yes, we're a big family from out of state, enjoying the summer here. Where are you from?" the large man with long hair asked.

"Up from New York City, I'm thinking of getting away from all the noise. So it's just you guys here in this house, no girls?"

Greg started to stroll around the room, poking his head around a corner to look down a hallway.

"Some of our sisters might come over sometimes. Is there anything else we can do for you?"

"Yeah, sure, this is a cool house. How about if someone shows me the rest of it? If I could measure all these rooms, it will really help me out," Greg said.

"We're so glad you can visit. Now how about someone gets you that iced tea?"

When he focused his attention on the face of the blond man asking the question, Greg suddenly felt a sharp pain on the side of his neck and a snapping electric sound under his ear. Then all went black, like the time before he was born.

THE RETURN OF TOMMY KARATE

"If you prick us, do we not bleed? If you tickle us, do we
not laugh? If you poison us, do we not die? And if you
wrong us, shall we not revenge?"

—William Shakespeare

IN 1998, HE was agile and athletic. A steep mountainside
would not have been a problem to run while wearing a full
sixty-pound pack. Yet now, in 2002, his left arm was gone
and replaced with an ebony steel limb, and his impaired vision
necessitated thick glasses with heavy black frames. Sometimes
his right eye involuntarily blinked at the same time that his
entire head suddenly twitched to the right. His facial quirks
were caused by a man who was able to shoot him in the head.
This same man shattered his forearm with a bullet. The attacker
was Peter Baranowski, a gumshoe now marked for a certain
painful death.

Dominic had been beaten. There were times that he squeaked
out a win, even if it meant a retreat, but he never imagined
such a complete defeat at the hands of Pete Baranowski. It
felt demoralizing; Tommy Karate had never been bested by
any man until Peter Baranowski shot him up in the woods on

that fateful October day. This was his emotional anchor, the embarrassment over getting beaten by a stooge. His old crew now viewed him as a laughingstock, snickering behind his back. He knew the crew was derogatorily referring to him by saying he was now weak and retarded. Somehow, in just a few moments' time, Baranowski had taken away almost all that he ever had. He felt feeble, diminutive, humiliated, and self-loathing. His rage had festered over the years, simmering for too long and now ready to explode. The bottled anger had taken away years of his life. His hair had turned silver-gray, and his face was skeleton gaunt.

Alone in a dark room, his thoughts wandered to revenge. The overwhelming anger would often make him cry; the salt of flowing tears stung his sensitive eyes, which angered him even more, creating a loop of depressed emotions. The feeling of deep melancholy gave him a corrosive power to maim and kill without hesitation or regret. The rage, the madness, the frustration, the whole miserable life experience must have an end. His wrath must have an outlet! Hate, murderous hate, cold and senseless in a self-consuming way, the mental pain must vent on the face pictured in his mind: Peter Baranowski! A quick assassination with a silent bullet to the head was just too easy for Baranowski. The suffering that he should go through should be the same as what Dominic had gone through but a hundred times more. A fantasy popped into Dominic's head, of Baranowski being electrocuted on a cross. The thought of this torture was the only thing that gave Dominic enjoyable contemplation. In his sick mind, Dominic felt good when he tortured people. It had been that way for decades. Now that he was back in New York, it was time to experience that pleasure again.

Revenge upon Baranowski would soon be Dominic's gleeful endeavor. The glorious moments of killing him would make a substantive world of difference for Dom. Killing Baranowski would propel him to feel good again, like when he was his former self. He would become the Tommy Karate that everyone feared once again, to finally and slowly sink his ten-inch tanto blade into Peter Baranowski's chest with gleeful enthusiasm.

This time around, Dominic needed help, but there was no help to be had. The days of doing things alone were here once again; it's the way he started off years ago.

Anyway, doing things alone is so much easier than having to rely on someone. Some guys always worked alone because once someone sees you kill someone, they could be a snitch and have power over you.

At least he convinced himself of that axiom for the moment. He had no other choice; the deed had to get done soon, one way or another. The tension was just too much because Baranowski was still breathing.

When Dominic barely escaped with his life from the Catskill woods, he was thankful. After his recuperation in Japan, when he finally got back to Brooklyn, the family treated him coldly and he could never count on his crew to be faithful again. Life wasn't so good anymore. Killing Baranowski would be the start to a long road of recovery. Prestige and power would be his again. Soon the time would come when respect and fear for Tommy Karate would be prevalent inside every Gravesend diner.

Waiting in front of Baranowski's Upper West Side apartment building wasn't fruitful. Dom noticed that Baranowski would leave at different, unpredictable times, making the operational window too difficult to effectuate a snatch off the street or plug him with a silenced pistol. Moreover, Dom couldn't afford witnesses calling the police. There were surveillance cameras all over this neighborhood now. In New York City, Dom's van might get stuck in traffic, where the police would have an easy time boxing him in. Besides, he wasn't his old self. Kidnapping was easy with a crew, but now, working alone, there would be too much of a risk of failure. The moment would arrive. He just had to wait, like a cat waiting for a mouse to come out of its hole.

The latest surveillance electronics were fitted into compartmentalized foam inserts arranged symmetrically in Dom's briefcase. His prized unit was called the Interceptor. With just the touch of a button, Dom could key in on any cell phone call and even descramble its signal if the phone was digitally coded for security. The Interceptor was a small handheld unit that looked more or less like a walkie-talkie, but the abilities it had were far beyond anything that was commercially available in America. The Japanese connections that Dom had cultivated over the years enabled him to acquire the latest in technical surveillance gadgetry. Dom's plan was to listen to Baranowski while he talked on his cell phone, and when the moment was right, if the opportunity to shoot Baranowski presented itself, he'd welcome the chance.

The ubiquitous white van parked on the Midtown Manhattan street displayed the logo of a handy-dandy dry cleaner on the windowless panel sides. The van actually served as a darkly lighted electronic listening post that glowed on the inside with multiple computer monitors. The light from the computer screens reflected images of green- and orange-colored graphs fluctuating in shape and brightness off of the thick glass of Dom's black-framed bifocals. The high-backed leather office chair let Dom sit back for endless hours in total comfort while he intensely listened for a voice that sounded like Peter Baranowski. The computer signature of any voice intercepted on a cell phone call would display on a colored graph. The computer then analyzed Baranowski's cell phone frequency with the caller's voice and matched it up to the recording previously acquired by Dom when he scam called the private investigator's office and was able to get Baranowski talking on his cell phone.

Dom knew that Baranowski was sitting up in his new office, enjoying the benefits of having a successful business, while Dom sat in his van in front of the midtown office building, in pain and not enjoying himself. Japanese electronics and German headphones cupping Dom's ears cackled with different cell phone conversations from all over the area within five hundred feet. The laptop computer that was wired into the Interceptor flashed different frequencies of the cell phones on the screen as the conversations simultaneously popped into Dom's headphones.

After three days of listening, the computer screen flashed red in a sign of recognition, and Dom recognized Baranowski's voice immediately. That annoying voice, it needed to be silenced.

He sounds like he thinks he's mister know-it-all. He's got a big surprise coming soon, a big surprise.

Dom heard that Baranowski was traveling up to Palmyra on some missing-person case . . . to find a young runaway girl . . . in Palmyra.

Perhaps torturing and killing Baranowski in Palmyra is a good plan? Yes! Why not? It should be easy to pick up his signal in a small town. Finally, I will reap my vengeance upon Baranowski!

Dominic drove to Palmyra in his Cadillac.

Listening to Baranowski's conversations enabled Dom to know just about every movement and every plan that Baranowski made. He discovered that Pete was staying at the Palmyra Inn and planted a remote booster device outside the motel, permitting him to listen to everything Pete said.

I love this electronic stuff! Using this Japanese technology gives me so much power. The Interceptor is the best. Out in the ether of the spectrum's signals, the stream of Baranowski's conversations will be recorded and listened to, by me, with great, great interest. Maybe I should let Baranowski find this runaway girl and then snatch her away! Just to spite him first before I kill him! When someone's soul has been taken from them, their power is gone because of a culprit. Then revenge against the culprit is a right of the victim. Of course, if I was a thinker without emotion, a purely logical thought dictates that I should move forward, with only profit as my life's goal, without the hindrance of costly retribution, making me step backwards. But revenge can be an itch that never goes away until it's scratched. The vendetta is a curious pact with oneself that revenge must be upon a certain person who has done me wrong. Perhaps it is the best therapy and this is what I must do, to eliminate the source of my troubles. For me, revenge is in my DNA.

ENTER THE SERPENT

"Having gone as usual at the end of another year to the place where they were deposited, the same heavenly messenger delivered them up to me with this charge: that I should be responsible for them."

—Joseph Smith

ORRIN CULVER'S RESIDENCE was a modest, single-level manufactured home that looked more like a long rectangular trailer than a conventional house. It was sided with painted white wood and had a brown shingle roof, located out in the middle of a sparsely populated, country grass field that had one house every quarter mile. The area was very quiet; only the sound of bugs and the breeze could be heard. Even though the residence was apparently in a remote farm landscape, the house was only a couple of miles from the center of town. A large field with mowed grass was in the back. Orrin's house had a small front yard that bordered an asphalt country road. To the left of the house was a large storage shed. A single wooden utility pole stood in front of the house.

Pete parked his Buick in the dirt driveway and walked up a small concrete path to the front door.

When Orrin stood in the threshold, Pete was reminded of just how thin he was. Orrin's five-foot-eight frame was even shorter than Pete's normal five nine. Orrin extended his strong hand, and his grip enveloped Pete's when they shook. As Pete stepped inside, he noticed that Orrin's place looked like a tiny museum of contemporary early-American furniture. Everything was arranged perfectly in its place, and there wasn't a speck of dust anywhere, not even near the legs of the colonial wood rocking chair in the corner.

"Have any trouble finding the place?" Orrin asked.

"Not really, this town is too small to get lost," Pete said.

"I cooked up some barbecued beef stew with vegetables, homemade sourdough bread too. Have a seat."

Orrin walked over to a small, white gas range in the kitchen, where a large stainless-steel pot steamed from the top. Orrin lifted the pot off the stove using oven mitts and placed it on the table.

The food was delicious and Pete asked for more. As Orrin dished out more stew with a ladle, Pete voiced some concerns.

"So, Orrin, this all is very nice and I appreciate the hospitality, but I know there was something on your mind that you wanted to talk to me about in private. Otherwise, we could have just chatted over some burgers in town."

"Well, Pete, it's interesting, I now have to trust a stranger with the most important thing in the world. Since you're not from around here, you're the only one I can trust. People are meant to cross, double-cross, and collide. Whether it's in a car accident or by meeting someone in a market, our lives get woven together, maybe forever. I think that's why you showed up in town all of a sudden. You were sent to help me."

Pete felt both perplexed and apprehensive.

"Sounds like there's some drama going on in this town, Orrin. Whatever you're talking about goes beyond what I'm up here for. All I wanted to do was locate this runaway and get back to the city. What else are you trying to put on my simple menu?"

"Well, you see, Pete, it still has to do with this missing girl you're looking for. I'm going to directly help you with finding her. She might tie into something else that's going on in this town that you're not privy to," Orrin said.

"I don't understand what you mean. Please go ahead, tell me more," Pete said.

"Pete, are you a very religious man?"

"Nah, not really, I'm not religious. I was born Jewish but stopped going to synagogue a long time ago. But I respect people who are religious. If people want to believe in something, that's a good thing."

"Pete, do you know anything about our Mormon faith or the history of the Church of Jesus Christ of Latter-day Saints?"

"Not really, I know this town seems very religious with the four churches on the four corners."

"So then you've never heard of Joseph Smith?"

"Nah, who's that supposed to be?"

Pete was starting to wonder where all of this was going.

"On September 22, in the year 1827, Joseph Smith received the golden plates from the angel Moroni. The golden plates detailed the culture of the ancient Nephite people who lived here in America. Jesus came to visit the Nephites in about 400 AD. They had the perfect society. Jesus approved of them, but there was an evil group nearby, the Lamanites, and they killed off the entire civilization of Nephites, who were descendants of the thirteenth tribe of Israel. Before all the Nephites were killed, however, their leader, Mormon, wrote about the Nephite culture on the golden plates. The golden plates are like a stack of metallic pages held together by three large rings. Mormon's son, Moroni, ran with the golden plates and buried them, in

Hill Cumorah. Then, on the date that has changed the world, on September 22, 1827, a plowboy prophet took a horse and wagon and, in the dark of night, rode to Hill Cumorah, where he received an ancient record from the angel Moroni. In a remarkably short time, this untutored young man translated a record detailing one thousand years of history and then prepared the Book of Mormon for public distribution. Are you following me so far, Pete?"

"There's a lot to keep track of, Orrin. I'm certainly doing my best to understand everything that you're talking about. Are you saying that the Nephites, who lived here in North America in 400 AD, were Jews from Israel?"

"You got it, Pete. You're a good listener, aren't you now?"

"Well, Orrin, I wouldn't be a great private eye if I wasn't a good listener, right?"

"We of the Church of Jesus Christ of Latter-day Saints believe that this life is just a test. You are a child of God. Before you were born, you lived in His presence. God knows you and has a plan for your progress and growth. His plan involved you leaving His presence so that you could learn and improve by experiencing the joys and challenges of mortality. The Book of Mormon explains that this life is the time for men and women to prepare to meet God."

"Orrin, you know, some science says that we're nothing but two dollars and sixty-seven cents' worth of chemicals. The rest is water. But I know you'd disagree with that. I respect that you're into your church."

Pete was doing his best to be polite while visiting someone else's house.

"The vicinity around Palmyra is the holiest land to the Mormons in the entire world. A mile from here is the Sacred Grove, where Joseph Smith had the First Vision of God the Father and Jesus Christ in the year 1820. Then, seven years later,

Joseph Smith was presented the golden plates by Mormon's son, the angel Moroni. There were twelve witnesses in total who signed affidavits that they saw and hefted the golden plates. Joseph Smith translated the scriptures from the golden plates and wrote them into the Book of Mormon. A rich farmer believed in the Book of Mormon and put up the money for five thousand copies, which were first printed right here in Palmyra circa 1830. Joseph the prophet said that the angel Moroni took the plates back . . . but I had a vision, a dream, but more real than reality, many years ago. My beautiful wife had passed, leaving this world all to me, alone. I felt an emptiness that made me sleep for days. I did not wake but a few times. Joseph Smith, the first prophet, himself, came to me in the dream and spoke to me. Joseph told me that the golden plates were buried in Hill Cumorah, and it is upon me to recover the golden plates and protect them for our temple in Palmyra."

"Well, uh, yeah, that sounds like a worthwhile project. It's kind of like an archeological dig that stems from where you think the gold is. Curiously enough, I've traveled down this road before. How's the search going?"

"I've found the golden plates," Orrin said.

Pete was now apprehensive about this whole night and wondered if he had made a mistake coming to Orrin's house. This guy was supposed to be a police detective, but instead, so far, Pete thought that Orrin was turning out to be a zealous loon.

"The golden plates you speak of, what do they look like? And where are they now that you've found them?"

"They're just as the prophet described them, bronze-like pages that have a golden sheen, with reformed Egyptian hieroglyphics written on them. They are bound by three elliptical rings."

"Okay, that's great, Orrin. I bet they're worth a bundle. So why are you acting all paranoid, and what's up with all the secrecy? Shouldn't you tell the world of your find? They'd make you a hero, right?"

"It's a lot more complicated than that, Pete, a lot more complicated," Orrin sighed. "There's a group called the Fundamentalist Latter-day Saints, or FLDS as they're known. Very bad people, the kind of people who will have no problem hurting you to get what they want. Those heathens marry off underage twelve- and fourteen-year-old girls, which is something that must be stopped, no matter what. They've infiltrated the government here in Palmyra up to the highest levels. They want the golden plates too. It was my mistake talking about the golden plates with someone I thought was my Mormon brother, Police Lieutenant Clayborn Taggert."

"Oh, that sucks, are you talking about a cult that you didn't know existed in your own police force, and they were right under your nose?"

Pete was surprised at this information. Out here, in the plains of western New York, in this quiet town, was a crazy fundamentalist Mormon offshoot cult?

"I also think they've been convincing young girls to join their heathen cult by sending in missionaries who look like regular LDS missionaries and forcing wayward girls into their fold of becoming a sister wife, but what these girls probably aren't told is that they'll have to report to FLDS seed masters for impregnation. Seed masters are men who are specially chosen by the top tier of the FLDS to defile underage girls and young women and then make them part of the clan's sister wives."

His account might fit into my case, because Greg told me that Julia told him about meeting some missionaries.

"Uh, Orrin, to be straight with you, one of my agents, this guy Greg, said he started up a relationship with my subject runaway, without me knowing what was going on. He said that she was meeting some missionaries and then she just disappeared. She made a short phone call to Greg with a Palmyra phone number that reversed to that house on Canal Street. You don't suppose those motorcycle guys you're talking about are missionaries, do you? Today, I did a bit of surveillance and saw two young, white-shirt missionary-type guys who hand out the magazines at your door, and get this, they had Utah plates that go back to a town called Hildale, Utah."

"The FLDS is now using upstanding-looking young men who dress nice and proselytize the scriptures. So they're using guile to get what they want . . . but they're far away from home. You know, the present circumstances are, I can't trust anyone, not even the cops up here. That's why we need to talk this out. I told my lieutenant in the police department that I had found the golden plates and needed his assistance in getting them out, but then I learned that he was an FLDS agent and associated with those guys at that house on Canal Street," Orrin said.

"Now this is entertaining. Fill me in, Orrin. There's certainly a lot of excitement up here. You're saying Lieutenant Clayborn Taggert, a fellow Mormon, is some kind of radical who now has a gang up here from Utah to steal your gold?"

"Let me tell you more details about the Church of Jesus Christ of Latter-day Saints, or Mormons, you might say. Did you say you were Jewish?"

"I was born Jewish, but I'm not religious at all. Never was."

"What do you know about Mormonism?"

"I know that Mormons don't look like the guy on the Quaker Oats box."

"That's funny, Pete. No, we look like everyday normal people. A Latter-day Saint is quite an ordinary individual. We are taught to be in the world but not of the world. Therefore, we live ordinary lives in ordinary families mixed in with the general population. We are taught not to lie or steal or cheat. We do not use profanity. However, let me tell you, this Fundamentalist Latter-day Saint sect, or FLDS as they're known, is a radical, dangerous cult that has nothing to do with real Mormonism. These cutthroats are here in town, and I think they're grabbing future sister wives, and now they're waiting for the perfect moment to steal the golden plates from me," Orrin said.

"But why would they come here to Palmyra. Is it just because they want to steal your gold? Couldn't they get girls to be their wives anywhere in the country?"

"It's because Palmyra is the mecca of the Mormon world, but I guess you didn't know that. Right here, under your nose, in your own state, our holiest land is where you and I are sitting right now, in western New York. I couldn't say for sure, but I think they're holding consecration ceremonies in the Sacred Grove at night, which is only a mile from here."

"So that's why my client's daughter is here? She is searching for her religious identity and has been tricked into becoming a fundamentalist?" Pete asked.

"Yes, I think you hit the nail on the head. This radical fundamentalist group owns a whole town on the Arizona-Utah border. I suppose you never heard of Short Creek? It's also known by its two town names, as Colorado City, Arizona, and Hildale, Utah. It's the most remote town in the country, away from any major city. The FLDS like to refer to their home as Zion. If they possess the golden plates, then they'll claim that they're the legitimate followers of God the Father and His Son, Jesus Christ," Orrin said.

"Okay, I'm starting to get the picture. There are no new girls where they are, so they need to go to faraway places to get their underage sister wives. Those big guys I saw on the motorcycles fit into your idea about them also being here to steal the golden plates."

"Exactly, Pete, those fundamentalists are here in town now,

and they're looking to cause me big trouble. First of all, they've been taking young girls, last seen in Palmyra, and then driving 'em back to Short Creek. Second, they make those young girls part of their stable of sister wives. They practice polygamy with underage girls on a major scale. Genetic defects are starting to show up in their society from having children with each other in the same family. They need a fresh genetic pool, and these teenagers are the perfect candidates for them. A local FLDS group existed here when I told Clayborn Taggert about finding the golden plates and asked for his help getting them out," Orrin said.

"But now that they know you found the golden plates, how come they're not trying to take them from you as we speak? Where did you say those golden plates are?" Pete asked.

"The FLDS know I found the actual golden plates left by the angel Moroni because I told my former brother Mormon, Lieutenant Clayborn Taggert. But I did not tell him exactly where they were or any other details. I imagine he might suspect they're in Hill Cumorah if he's been tailing me. The golden plates are beyond any price to the LDS in Salt Lake City, and I intend on securing them for our Church. The significance of the golden plates to the Church of Jesus Christ of Latter-day Saints cannot be overstated. The difficult part is yet to come, and I need your help tonight," Orrin exclaimed.

A wash of nervousness came over Pete and hollowed out his stomach. He suddenly felt queasy.

"I don't know how much I can help you against a gang of radical fundamentalists led by a crazy police lieutenant. Seems like the odds are heavily against you? If you don't mind too much, maybe I should just get back to New York City."

"No, Pete, I don't need you to fight the FLDS. I'm asking you to help me excavate the golden plates. They're just the size of a real big, thick book. Like a big dictionary. The golden plates of Mormon are in a place where I can finally see them. I almost excavated the golden plates a few days ago from Hill Cumorah. They're still at the base of a rock the size of a tractor trailer, ensconced in a fitted panel located on the bottom side of the rock. Joseph Smith saw the angel Moroni, who told Joseph where the golden plates were buried in Hill Cumorah. Joseph then buried them again after he translated the Book of Mormon. But no one has ever found the golden plates . . . until now."

"That's a big find, isn't it? But how come, for 175 years, no one has ever found these golden plates when everyone knew where they were?"

"No one but me had the vision that the golden plates were ensconced in a compartment under this massive rock. The rock is made up of iron ore, so no other metal signatures were ever discernable, even by the best metal detectors. And you know, Pete, my find is the biggest there is. Before the golden plates, the most historical thing found was the Jupiter Talisman that the prophet Joseph Smith carried in his pocket when he and his brother Hyrum were martyred by a murderous mob in 1844."

"That still doesn't explain why those fundamentalists from out West are suddenly here in Palmyra. They got on their bikes and rode all the way here from out West? Who called them, Clayborn Taggert?" Pete asked.

"Yes, they want the golden plates for themselves, but I believe they're also on a mission here in Palmyra to indoctrinate young sister wives by using the aura of this holiest land. They probably go from region to region as to not raise too much suspicion when a whole lot of young girls disappear from a town, and they're bringing them into Palmyra as some kind of ritual before sending them to Short Creek. They've sent special men from their FLDS Danite army who are called the Destroying Angels.

It goes way back to the 1800s, when Saints like Porter Rockwell forcefully defended the Latter-day Saints. Porter Rockwell had long hair because the prophet Joseph Smith said no harm would ever come to him as long as he kept his hair long. After Joseph Smith was martyred, Porter Rockwell became the bodyguard to Brigham Young, who called Rockwell his "Destroying Angel." The FLDS guys lift weights all day and practice with guns and knives. Some have long hair to honor Porter Rockwell. They're bad spirits sent by Satan, who've trained at hurting people and enforcing their illegal ways. They keep chopped-down .44 magnums in their coat pockets and Bowie knives on their belts. They ride heavy Harley Davidson motorcycles with windscreens and every bell and whistle you can imagine, big saddlebags too, not those stripped-down choppers like those outlaw bikers have. These guys can ride cross-country without stopping except for gas."

"Yeah, well, there you go, Orrin, I saw the kind of guys you're talking about ride out from the Canal Street house this morning, and they had Utah plates that reversed back to that town you mentioned, Hildale, Utah. Those bikes seem to come out of nowhere too," Pete said.

"So they're here then. So be it. These people have to be stopped. They are pure evil. It used to be our way to take many wives, but no longer. The prophet spoke to God and decreed that plural marriage is wrong and if any member partakes in the practice, then they must be excommunicated. The Church of Jesus Christ of Latter-day Saints sanctifies the marriage with one wife, period. Those people from Short Creek are purveyors of forced child labor too, making young children farm all day and gather almonds. Yeah, that's my problem with them. I have lots of problems with them, and it's not worth trying to figure those people out. Those fundamentalists are like a cancer. They're spreading everywhere, even here in Palmyra. I know they're here and they're up to no good at that Canal Street house. Sometimes the FLDS looks regular and that was how I got hoodwinked by the guy in my department. Palmyra is about a good forty percent Mormon, and most of 'em are great people. It's just this FLDS sect that has all of a sudden ridden in like a swarm of locusts, in all shapes and forms."

"Yeah, I follow you, Orrin, you're in a world of shit up here . . . but I just wanted to locate that girl. If you can help me with that, I would be most appreciative."

Pete was a bit nervous at this point. Things were tipping into the realm of the surreal.

Why is Orrin telling me all this? I just want to find this girl and call her parents. That's all I want to do. I can't get involved in this guy's supernatural drama up here. And I sure don't want to go digging holes anywhere for him.

"There's something I'd like to show you. Follow me." Orrin smiled.

Orrin stood up from the dinner table, turned, and motioned for Pete to follow him. They walked down a small hallway to a brown door. Pete watched Orrin move a thermostat from the wall, which revealed a lighted keypad. Orrin touched in a code and opened the door.

Pete went through a steel doorframe into a small ten-foot by twelve-foot room with brown shag carpet. In the middle of the room, lit up on a shoulder-high pedestal and under a rectangular showcase of glass, was a revolver, a combination of Old Western style and futuristic-looking silver rail-gun. It was a stainless-steel Colt Python revolver. The six-inch barrel of the gun had a narrow aiming rib on top that was ventilated with three low rectangular slats. The sides of the barrel had an engraved *.357 Magnum* along with the inscription *Python.*

"This is the Serpent of Justice."

Orrin carefully reached to the top of the glass showcase, lifted a hinged lid, and took out the Colt Python. He held the barrel straight up.

"I am a real Danite, a member of the historic army that our Prophet Smith formed in 1830. I have carried on the Danite traditions. With this gun, I enforce God's will and the righteousness of mankind! The Spirit through the Serpent of Justice always guides my hand correctly to do what's right and proper. When Brigham Young led the Saints through the hostile western frontier, he made sure there was a fighting army of men to take up arms against those who attempt to murder us. Weapons for defense have always been a Mormon tradition. We Danites, the direct descendants of Brigham Young's army, following the precepts of the Hebrew tribe of Dan, the unspoken army of Mormons have progressed into the CIA, the FBI, the Defense Department, and every important fabric of our great society you can think of. Yet there are evil Danites, the FLDS who come from Short Creek. The FLDS has subverted the real intent of the LDS Church into a horrific and immoral cabal of perverted criminals. They have their thugs, the Destroying Angels, to undertake a kidnap program of young girls because they're starting to have genetic mutations down there from all the inbreeding. Basically, they need new girls to sustain their culture. An FLDS group called the Selected Order get favors in the Short Creek community and then graduate to be seed masters. Those selected men get to mate with the underage girls. My holy mission is to acquire the golden plates before they get stolen by the hands of the FLDS Destroying Angels. The FLDS will claim theirs is the true religion if they acquire the golden plates of Mormon."

Orrin quickly holstered the gun.

Pete noticed the wood-grained checkered grips on the revolver's stainless-steel frame sticking out of the basketweave tooled black-leather belt holster. There were also two black-leather pouches that contained speed loaders on Orrin's belt.

"That's a mighty nice gun you have there, Orrin. I used to carry my great-grandfather's .45 revolver, and I think it was even bigger than your, uh, Serpent of Justice. I carry this little .45 here." Pete lifted his shirt and showed Orrin the holstered Detonics.

Orrin drew out the Python revolver so quickly that it looked as if there was a frame of film missing between when Pete saw him reach for the gun and when he became aware of the gun hovering overhead in Orrin's hand.

"All those fancy automatics with their high capacities and firepower and whatnot, that's all fine, of course, for those guys who prefer modern pistols, but when the Serpent of Justice comes out, it takes on a life of its own, to pursue the righteous way of law and God's way."

Orrin got down on his knees while he held the stainless-steel revolver in his right hand; he folded his arms across his midriff, eyes tightly closed. The Colt Python remained in his hand and stuck out from the side of his folded arms. A tear rolled down Orrin's cheek and he spoke softly.

"Oh, Heavenly Father, please protect me on my mission for You, and protect all those around me. May my Serpent of Justice reign supreme amongst the evil that pervades our lands and vanquish those who are immoral. Oh, Heavenly Father, thank You for the Spirit that guides my hand and my power to make things right, to smite the armies of the devil before me, who do us wrong. Our love transcends our souls. I am affected by the Spirit and from goodness that I may unleash the Serpent of Justice."

Orrin stood up and slid the .357 Colt Python back into his belt holster.

"That was a very nice prayer. I like what you've done with this room, very private," Pete said.

"There's that one small favor y'all got to do for me before we find us that girl of yours."

Uh-oh, here it comes, too bad I just had to wait through a whole dinner and endure this guy's supernatural ravings. The moment of truth has arrived, and the reason for coming all the way out here for this meeting.

"Yeah, sure, Orrin, what do you need?"

"When I was in Vietnam, I volunteered to be a 'tunnel rat' for the US military. I'm proud of my service even though it was an irksome mission. The lessons I learned from my time in Vietnam, inside the Cu Chi Tunnels, combined with my BYU geology major, gave me a deeper understanding of what's possible when it comes to hiding things underground. My vision of the golden plates has sealed my fate. Could you please, my brother, hold a rope and drag me out of a deep hole in the ground, later tonight? There is no way to back out of this hole, especially while I'm holding the heavy golden plates. I can see them ensconced in the rock underground, but then once I chisel them out, you've got to pull. There is no one else available to me but you, in the coming hour. The FLDS might find my trapdoor tonight. The golden plates are under this thirty-ton rock that I dug under, at an angle. My body will be tilted almost upside down, and I won't have the leverage to get out of this narrow-sized hole. I almost died down there last time, but the Heavenly Father saved me, and I somehow got out. So that's my request of you, to pull me out of this hole using a rope tied around my ankles. Then, I promise, we'll find that runaway girl you're looking for."

At this point, Pete wasn't about to say no, although he wished none of this was happening. There wasn't anything in it for Pete, except Orrin would later help him find the girl, which was a good thing, considering the potential hot water Pete was in.

"Yeah, okay, it all sounds a little crazy, but I'll help you out. Let me ask you, Orrin, are you absolutely sure that you saw these so-called golden plates?"

"As sure as I'm looking at you right now, that's how certain I am. The golden plates of Mormon are down there, and I need your help getting them out."

"What if someone got a hold of these plates from under your nose? How much would the LDS Church pay for those plates?"

"I don't even want to think about that. My vision was to find and protect the golden plates. To the Church of Jesus Christ of Latter-day Saints, they are beyond earthly wealth. The golden plates are our spiritual affirmation."

"Okay, Orrin, I'm with you on this. I know how to do a rope belay. I was an Eagle Scout in the Boy Scouts, so I'll get you out of that hole. What time tonight?"

"I'll be in the parking lot at the Palmyra Inn tonight at twelve midnight, waiting for you." Orrin bowed his head and grasped Pete's hand. "May this night complete our sacred work that will be accomplished here as a token of Thy love for Thy children of all generations and of the provision Thou has made for their eternal progress and happiness. The Temple speaks of the everlasting covenant between Thee and Thy children. All that will take place herein will be concerned with the things of eternity. The golden plates stand as a gift from God to all the world of the certain immortality of the human soul." Orrin lifted his head; his eyes stared into Pete's. "What's your room number, in case you're sleeping and I need to wake you up?"

"It's room 218, but don't worry, I'll be up."

"Okay, see you in a couple of hours then," Orrin said.

The drive back to the Palmyra Inn gave Pete the opportunity to call Vicky before it was too late. The whole conversation with Orrin about Mormons and fundamentalist Mormons intrigued Pete. However, while Pete had no problem with very religious people, he did not like the talk about a motorcycle gang of Destroying Angels. That information disturbed Pete.

"Hi, Vicky, sorry to call you so late, but I need to know about a few details on this case up here in Palmyra," Pete said.

"Sure, Pete, no problem. I happen to be here on my screens. Is this overtime right now?" Vicky asked.

"Yeah, of course, you know you always get overtime when I have to call you at crazy hours. I just spoke with this detective named Orrin Culver, who told me some far-out stuff about radical religious fruitcakes who might be involved with our missing-person case. There are a few specific things I'd like you to get information on. Take this down. Find out about the Mormon golden plates and what the story is. Most importantly, find out if they're real or just some notion by a soothsayer in a book. Also, please see what you can dig up on a Mormon army called the Danites. See if they have a special group called the Destroying Angels—not the spiritual type though, they're supposed to be some kind of extreme Mormon motorcycle gang. Lastly, there's a radical Mormon group called the FLDS, which is the acronym for Fundamentalist Latter-day Saints. Please see what you can find out on them."

"That's it?" Vicky asked.

"Yeah, that's all. I just want to know about what I'm really dealing with up here. I'll call you back in a half hour or so."

"Give me forty-five minutes to be safe," Vicky said.

"Okay, excellent, thanks, speak to you again soon."

ORRIN CULVER

"One of the grand fundamental principles of Mormonism is to receive truth, let it come from whence it may."
—**Joseph Smith**

S ALT LAKE CITY, the most beautiful place on earth, is an important home to the Mormon religion. Sixty percent of the people who reside in Salt Lake are Mormon. Most Salt Lake people are true believers in the Church of Jesus Christ of Latter-day Saints. The Saints have lived in their sacred city since 1848. Brigham Young declared, "It is enough. This is the right place. Drive on." Brigham Young, the second president of the LDS Church, led the Saints into the Promised Land of the Great Salt Basin. He ultimately fathered fifty-seven children by more than two dozen wives. The original Mormons were polygamists; they believed that three wives were the minimum, but there were some of the faith who had many more wives than just three.

Utah is an amazing state both socially and geographically. It has a homogenous culture and vast designated park landmarks—the Mormons are in control of all of it. By most conservative standards, it's more than acceptable that a society that's faithful to God is in charge of the operations of the State of Utah. A Mormon does not drink alcohol or ingest any mood-altering drugs, including caffeine in coffee. The LDS Church member never utters a curse and is in control of his emotions. Many would say these personal attributes are a good thing for a politician, whose sole purpose should be to serve the people he represents without the specter of political corruption.

In June of 1946, Orrin Thaddeus Culver was born in Salt Lake City, Utah. In the 1950s and early 1960s, the era was an innocent time for kids growing up there. Going to good schools, playing in neighborhood backyards and following the Mormon faith were cornerstones.

Fortunate residents of Salt Lake can gaze upon the open vistas that are seen for miles all around. The whole city is surrounded by mountains on one end and the Great Salt Lake on the other. Even as a child, Orrin felt that Salt Lake City was a magical place to live in. The Mormon faith, otherwise known as the Church of Jesus Christ of Latter-day Saints, is a religion that is as binding as the warmth of a tightly woven blanket. Communities take care of each other, and people help each other out. There is a dependable cohesiveness within the city and amongst the residents. One person's family is another person's family; the sharing of food, resources, and affection is a common practice within the Mormon culture.

The Great Salt Lake presents expansive views of clear-blue skies and offers sights of serenity for those who look to the heavens for inspiration. It is the Jerusalem of the Western United States, a holy land to all those of the LDS Church. The mountains, the big blue sky, the crisp air, and the Great Salt Lake give the location a unique panorama like nowhere else on earth. There were some nights when Orrin looked up to the night sky and wondered if he could speak to God one day or if Jesus could hear him. Will Jesus Christ answer his prayers?

Much like his father and brothers, he was lean of body and sinewy, but even more muscular than his siblings. He had three brothers and two sisters, with a doting mother and a "stand-up kind of guy" father, who was an auto mechanic with a repair shop that did quite well. All of Orrin's family members were followers of the Church of Jesus Christ of Latter-day Saints. The Culver family was tight-knit and loved being part of the holy land. Orrin's childhood was more or less ideal; to grow up in a loving, God-fearing family was more the norm in Salt Lake City than the exception. Other Mormon families participated in group functions with the Culvers, leading to an atmosphere of family and community. The Salt Lake maturation for Orrin was perfect due to the sensible environment for a young boy.

The LDS Church was Orrin's rock, his solid belief, his entire life structure. He cherished the church, with every heartbeat; his soul was for the Church of Jesus Christ of Latter-day Saints. Orrin treasured those great times as a teenager, going to high school and wrestling for his team. Then he went on to enroll at Brigham Young University, which is nestled on a flat plain below the majestic rocky cliffs of Y Mountain and Squaw Mountain in Provo, Utah. BYU has been considered by the LDS Church to be "The Lord's University." Ninety-eight percent of Brigham Young's student body is of the Mormon faith.

A young adult is expected to spread the word of the Mormon faith by becoming a missionary for a couple of years. Mormon missionaries are sent to different countries all over the world to indoctrinate local inhabitants and convince them to join the LDS Church. Halfway through his college years, Orrin completed his missionary work in Argentina, where he spread the holy gospel with his partner, referred to as an "elder." It was a totally different society at the bottom of the southern hemisphere. His mind opened up to other cultures and foreign beliefs. Orrin proselytized the scriptures the best he could but was only able to convert two Argentineans the whole time he was there.

After graduating from Brigham Young University with a Bachelor of Science degree in geology, he went on to become a police officer with the Salt Lake City police department, gaining a reputation as one of their fairest and most likable officers, and he received many commendations during his short career there.

His loving wife Beatrice was his whole being during his young twenties; she and Orrin were inseparable. They had met in high school, gone to BYU together, and then gotten married soon after graduation. It was their dream to have a family together, and they were just about to start trying for a child when she tragically and suddenly died of heart failure due to a genetic disorder. Orrin's love of his life died in her sleep the same night she and Orrin talked about having a family. Orrin became socially despondent and slept for long periods of time, too depressed to get out of bed. He only had the strength to get out of bed when he felt the Spirit in him to pray. His prayers for his wife were filled with emotion.

"Oh, my Father in heaven, help me, I pray Thee, to so live that I shall be worthy to meet Beatrice in eternal glory, to be united again with her, never again to be separated, throughout the countless ages of eternity. Help me to be humble, to trust in Thee. Give me wisdom and knowledge of heavenly things that I may have power to resist all evil and remain steadfast to Thy *truth*. Oh, Lord, help me, grant unto me eternal life in Thy Kingdom. Guide my footsteps in righteousness. Give unto me Thy Whole Spirit. Help me to protect the Saints with only righteous law, and when I have finished my course, take me unto Thy Celestial Kingdom, I pray Thee. In the name of our Redeemer, let it be, Amen."

Orrin's depression was obvious to all those around him. The Salt Lake chief of police told him to take a few months off in order to get over the death of his wife. The public admission that he was depressed beyond function embarrassed Orrin. To get away from it all, Orrin joined the Army. The Vietnam War was forefront in the news. The images on television drew him in to the idea that he must help his country win the war. He joined the Army because of his belief in and love for the United States. It is believed by the LDS Church that serving in America's military is only second to serving the Church. The LDS Church believes that the United States is "God's Country."

As a young man, Orrin had watched the numerous World War II television shows about dramatic violent conflict, which influenced him towards inclinations of guns and honor. Shows like *Combat!* starring Vic Morrow were ingrained on Orrin's mind, which made him want to be like those tough-acting characters. He thought about it a long time and thoroughly decided that putting his life on the line for America was the only honorable thing to do.

During his in-country tour, Orrin asked for the most dangerous assignments; he was a troop leader by example. He became a tunnel rat, stationed in the communist stronghold of Binh Duong province, north of Saigon near the Cambodian border. The region was known as the Iron Triangle. A network of underground enemy tunnels extending for hundreds of miles. The mission was simple: rout out the enemy from their extensive underground tunnel network, where they often sustained living quarters and even hospitals. During the hot and physically difficult two years "in country," Orrin became an expert tunnel rat, a term used for those soldiers on a search-and-destroy mission into the depths of the Cu Chi Tunnels, holding nothing but a flashlight in one hand and a .45 automatic pistol in the other. His thin rail-like body slithered like a snake down into the Viet Cong tunnels, pistol in hand and ready for anything. It turned out that the Army-issue .45 pistol was too loud and its blast too powerful for such an enclosed space in those claustrophobic narrow tunnels. Luckily, his uncle in Utah shipped Orrin a Colt Commando .38 four-inch barreled revolver, which he used to greater effectiveness against the Vietnamese down in those hellholes. Hunting the enemy in the claustrophobic tunnels was described by the tunnel rats as experiencing the "black echo." The trick was to stop and listen in the darkness within the tunnel, or pick up the auditory "black echoes," the only effective way to get a notion that an enemy soldier was close by, around a tunnel bend, crouching with an automatic AK-47. A rope was sometimes wrapped around the waist of the tunnel rat but only if that particular soldier wanted the tether. Use of the rope often hindered the underground crawling process, where men had to lie on their stomachs and squirm forward like a worm for hundreds of feet. The rope tether wasn't important for some soldiers, but others wanted to be pulled out if they were wounded or dead. Orrin often chose not to wrap the rope around his waist and crawled into the tunnels with the blind loyalty and a sincere belief that he was helping America win the war against communism. Also, his strong faith in God prompted him to crawl into the most awful situations a human could put themselves in: covered by giant centipedes and rats, poison snakes lunging with fangs, razor-sharp stakes at the bottom of pits, and Viet Cong to the sides of the tunnels with spears to jab an unsuspecting heart. On a patrol one time, he saw a dead Viet Cong soldier with ants crawling all over the body. Afterwards, Orrin reflected on this scene over and over in his head. For many years, then decades, it was unforgettable and this image of horror pushed him further towards his faith in the LDS Church. He prayed for that dead soldier's soul and undertook blessed ceremonies around his unnamed memory.

After his discharge, Orrin went right back to Salt Lake City, but he continued to feel depressed. Instead of facing his depression and treating it with a therapist, he wallowed in endless self-pity. Now that he was back from Vietnam, his heart and mind were empty. Deep depression and hours of sleep took over. Orrin found it impossible to get out of bed unless he had to go to the bathroom or take a shower. His reoccurring terrifying dreams due to the war persisted for years.

One morning, during a long sleep, Orrin had an incredibly realistic dream that was more like a profound vision. The thoughts in his head were as pronounced as printed words that he could see through his mind's eye. He saw the first prophet, Joseph Smith. Orrin could repeat word for word what Joseph Smith said in the dream:

Convenient to the village of Manchester, Ontario County, New York, stands a hill of considerable size, and the most elevated of any in the neighborhood. On the west side of this hill, not far from the top, under a stone of considerable size, lay the plates, deposited in a stone box.

Although he had never been to New York State, Orrin found himself standing on the edge of Hill Cumorah in Palmyra, New York. It was a surreal experience for him. The vision . . . the moon was shining bright above him, like a spotlight on a stage. Was it a mental picture or an actual occurrence? He couldn't say for sure if what he experienced was real or imaginary. The prophet himself, Joseph Smith, was standing in front of him. The prophet's face was very close, only inches away. His eyes stared into Orrin's eyes. Joseph Smith's voice was loud and directed at Orrin. He placed his right hand on Orrin's left shoulder and spoke:

Only you, Elder Orrin, only you, must protect the golden plates. Go to Palmyra, and uphold the law. Spend your lifetime there, and revere the temple that will soon be. The golden plates are directly under the largest stone on Hill Cumorah. Secure the golden plates forever in the inner sanctum sanctorum of the new Palmyra Temple.

Orrin then dreamed that he saw the golden plates under a massive rock the size of a truck. His dream then flashed to an unfamiliar man standing at a podium, talking about a new Palmyra Temple. Orrin listened and memorized every word.

Then suddenly, Joseph Smith was close again. The moment was too real. He was there; it felt so poignant, standing next to the prophet. Orrin was overcome with emotion and started to cry. The prophet then bestowed a declaration.

On the twenty-second day of September, 1827, having gone as usual at the end of another year to the place where they were deposited, the same heavenly messenger delivered them up to me with this charge: that I should be responsible for them; that if I should let them go carelessly, or through any neglect of mine, I should be cut off; but that if I would use all my endeavors to preserve them, until he, the messenger, should call for them, they should be protected.

"You are my prophet," Orrin said.

Don't cry, my elder, I am here. I will always be with you.

Joseph Smith leaned forward and wrapped his arms around Orrin's shoulders.

Orrin cried again.

When he suddenly awoke, Orrin continued to feel the arms of Joseph Smith around him. It was the strangest feeling, to be fully awake yet continue to be squeezed by two arms. He hoped that the feeling of being hugged by Joseph Smith would continue as he lay there. Unrelenting tears continued to flow from his eyes.

After about two minutes, the pressure of Joseph's arms subsided. Orrin did not want to move. He wanted to feel the embrace of Joseph's arms again. He lay in bed, totally still, for another twenty minutes, looking at the ceiling and trying to grasp what had just transpired.

I had a holy vision!

Ordinary people can have visions too. He was a chosen one, a special soul among his Saints. His holy vision was for real. He would follow the precepts of the task laid out before him. Orrin's quest for the golden plates of Mormon had been inspired by this poignant vision. It was incumbent upon Orrin to fulfill the request from the prophet Joseph Smith.

Salt Lake had always been his home, yet now he was destined for a cold remote place in western New York known for two things: the birthplace of the Church of Jesus Christ of Latter-day Saints and the historic Erie Canal. Palmyra is a small town, pretty much unknown and innocuous to the general public. It is a small western New York enclave that is the place where the founder of the Church of Jesus Christ of Latter-day Saints, Joseph Smith, was given the golden plates by the angel Moroni. Orrin also firmly believed that he would unearth the golden plates.

It was no small effort to abandon Salt Lake City, Utah, for Palmyra, New York. Orrin had been used to a dry climate with wide-open spaces and rocky-cliff mountains jutting out into the sky. In Palmyra, the weather was raw, gray, and wet. There were some sunny days but none like the crisp Utah days that he loved so much. The long-forsaken Erie Canal went right through Palmyra. Orrin thought often about the remoteness of his chosen new town. Palmyra used to be a bustling municipality back in the 1800s, and the Erie Canal was attributed to the growth of the Industrial Revolution. The canal is just a tourist attraction now, but in the old days, barges pulled by donkeys traveled for hundreds of miles. The canal used to be the best way of transporting goods from the Great Lakes to Albany and then by way of the Hudson River to New York City. Present-day trucks on superhighways, jets, and mile-long cargo trains now overshadow the circa-early-1800s canal's usefulness.

People in Palmyra seemed a little sad to Orrin. With the exception of a few good drinking bars for non-Mormons, there wasn't much to do except mix with neighbors in local places where everyone knew everyone else. New people in town were a rare happening. If someone was passing through from New York City on their way to Niagara Falls or Rochester, the locals might swarm the fresh newcomers with detailed questions about what they were doing in town.

The Hill Cumorah had its usual July pageant celebrating the entire story of the Book of Mormon. Other than the Hill Cumorah festival event in July, the town was a hushed community with a working-class population.

Orrin was able to parlay his police experience from Salt Lake into a job on the Palmyra police force as a patrol cop. It was a step in the right direction towards his vision of recovering the golden plates.

On April 6, 2000, the dedication of the Palmyra New York Temple took place 170 years after the birth of the Church of Jesus Christ of Latter-day Saints. Orrin was elated to be at the dedication. His feeling of spiritual fullness peaked during the ceremony. With the completion of the Palmyra Temple, Orrin's vision from over twenty years prior was finally coming to fruition. Upon the dedication, LDS President Gordon B. Hinckley said words that were in Orrin's dream. Orrin had put the entire speech to memory and often reflected on it, word for word:

In this same vicinity, Joseph received the plates from the hands of Moroni, and there ensued their translation into the Book of Mormon Another Testament of Jesus Christ, which was published here in Palmyra . . . Dear Father, we acknowledge that it all began here. We marvel, and we gather today in these precincts which were sanctified by Thy presence and the presence of Thy Son, to dedicate unto Thee and unto Him this the Palmyra New York Temple of the Church of Jesus Christ of Latter-day Saints . . . Now dear Father, as we speak from this place of great beginnings, from this sacred and holy house which we have dedicated unto Thee, may the solemnities of eternity rest down upon us and may our understanding of Thy great work broaden and deepen from faith into certain knowledge. Thy work, begun here so humbly and with so few, has now blossomed into a vast family. Thy people are spread over the earth. They speak many languages. Great has been the growth, and greater yet it will become as it moves forward in the nations of the earth.

Orrin knew he was alone in his quest to secure the golden plates. It was an obsession for over two decades, and now, finally, he was just one night away from retrieving the most holy of all precious artifacts for his Church. His vision and geological skill, coupled with his years of perseverance, resulted in finding the golden plates.

Oh, Heavenly Father, I am so thankful for Peter Baranowski. For with him, I may retrieve the golden plates and bring them to the sanctum sanctorum in the Palmyra Temple. This will complete my mission for You, Our Father in Heaven. Please bless my endeavor, and may I be successful in my quest to obtain the golden plates. I humbly beseech these blessings, oh Father, in the name of Thy only begotten Son, Jesus Christ, Amen.

He now realized that his years of friendship with his fellow Mormon Clayborn Taggert had been a big mistake. He should have never told Clayborn about the golden plates. Getting past Clayborn, and his FLDS Destroying Angels from Short Creek, was going to be a challenge tonight. There was no one else available he could trust, given such short notice. Peter Baranowski was his only option: Peter was sent by the Heavenly Father to help in the quest for the golden plates.

If I can get the golden plates to the temple then that's all that matters. The golden plates will be secure in the inner sanctum sanctorum and only then will I finally rest. Heavenly Father, I am thankful for all You have done for me. I will complete Your charge and will let no man or circumstance prevent me from fulfilling Your Word.

Suddenly Orrin's intense thoughts were broken by the sound of a car engine passing his house on the road outside. The road was usually empty during the night, but Orrin kept hearing cars and motorcycles pass by. Orrin thought that he had every right to be paranoid; tonight had to be the night he recovered the golden plates.

They're probably watching me right now.

REVEALING DISCOVERIES

> "In marriage do thou be wise: prefer the person before money, virtue before beauty, the mind before the body; then thou hast a wife, a friend, a companion, a second self."
>
> **—William Penn**

IT WAS AN interesting night, one that Pete felt a bit apprehensive about. He was not a religious person and doubted the sanity of Orrin. His exaltations made Pete feel uneasy about going on a secret midnight archeological expedition to find some sheets of brass.

These religious whack jobs scare me. They actually believe in all this mumbo jumbo, which doesn't make any sense to me.

Pete looked at his watch. It was 11:00 p.m. and he was worried about Orrin picking him up at midnight.

What am I about to get into here? Maybe Orrin is using me as a sacrificial pawn, playing me for some totally different motive other than these so-called golden plates? His vision is something right out of a folk-tale book with angels and ancient armies. Damn! I should have had him meet me later at someplace else, other than my damn motel room. I could've had the option of not showing up. Since he's coming here, I've got to tell him face to face that I'm not going anywhere tonight.

Pete parked his car in the front lot of the Palmyra Inn and looked up at the large window of his room on the second floor, to the left of the motel's front entrance. He noticed that the sliding-glass window had been left open and figured that it was a cleaning person airing out his room and they forgot to close the window.

A car is a great place to talk on the phone. An enclosed metal and heavy glass vehicle is like a capsule of privacy when it comes to talking loudly and freely with gusto. It was Pete's usual practice to leave his office and go downstairs to his parked car in the Manhattan garage to boisterously talk with friends or make a confidential deal on a case that he didn't want his secretary, Vicky, to know about. Since Pete was distrustful of all hotel rooms, he always made his private calls from his car when on the road. Even though the Palmyra Inn looked safe, it could have thin walls that would enable an opportunistic snoop to press an ear to the wall.

Pete called his wife, who was at home with their two children at their West Side New York City apartment. Normally, Pete would make a standard call when away at an investigator's convention or on the occasional case that demanded travel, but tonight he really wanted to talk with her at length, to tell her everything and let her know how crazy things were up here and how he felt. When she answered, his relief was immediate; most of his anxiety ebbed out of his body and right into the phone. Cathy told him the boys were asleep and everything was well.

After Pete and Cathy discussed the kids' school and some other interests, Pete went on to tell her about the cast of characters up in Palmyra who contributed to an unexpected twist on a simple missing teenage-runaway case.

"I'm telling you, honey, this guy Orrin said that the golden plates have to be protected from a radical Mormon cult called the FLDS," Pete said.

"So your story is that a cult is going to steal the church's gold? What's really going on up there? How did you get involved in all this? At first, all you were doing was looking for a missing girl!"

"Honey, I thought the same thing myself. Here I am, three hundred miles away from the city, working a normal missing-person case, and then all of a sudden, I'm wrapped up in some kind of archeological church drama. I didn't ask for this either."

"Since these plates are worth so much, I guess they're paying you a lot for this case. That's right, isn't it? You're making good money on this case, right? I could see how your friend up there would be nervous about someone stealing them if they're worth so much. If you're helping him, you should get paid," Cathy said.

"Yeah, well, he's going to help me find the girl, but I'm not sure if that's going to be enough compensation for what he's asking me to do. According to Orrin, there are some nefarious individuals from a radical Mormon sect who want to get their hands on those golden plates. The golden plates supposedly have the writings of the Book of Mormon pressed onto the metal. I don't know, honey, he's a Vietnam vet and he had that faraway look that they tell you about. Maybe he's just a scary religious zealot? The only thing is, he seems like a really nice guy who's telling the truth."

"Why do you keep calling them the golden plates? Are they dinner plates or cocktail-sized plates? What do they look like? How much gold are we talking about here?"

"They're like sheets, or metal pages, like license plates on a car, but they were made a long time ago. I'm not sure, honey, but they've been described as metal plates banded with three rings, like the size of a big encyclopedia book."

"So how can it be worth so much if it's just the size of a book? If all the pages are gold, then it's worth a lot but not a super-giant amount."

"I think the golden plates are worth more as a museum-type piece significant to the Mormon Church. In spiritual terms, they are worth more than the actual gold. The Mormons put all their faith into the reformed Egyptian writings on the golden plates, and that information was translated into the Book of Mormon, so it's more of a religious worth than an actual worth. Any way you look at it, the belief of millions of Mormons will be affirmed, if we can secure these plates in secret. Keep all this confidential in case Orrin Culver is telling the truth. If someone ever stole the golden plates and wanted to ransom them back to the Church, I think the Latter-day Saints would pay a billion dollars to get them back," Pete said.

"Worth is a relative thing, honey. If the Mormons think the golden plates are worth a lot to them, then that's what makes them valuable. How historic are these golden plates? Who made them?"

"Uh, yeah, well, Orrin said that an angel named Moroni gave the golden plates to their prophet Joseph Smith in 1827 and that Joseph Smith translated what was written on the plates into the Book of Mormon. But c'mon now, honey, this guy Joseph Smith could have just melted down a lot of brass buttons and made these golden plates himself. What do you think about that?"

"Well, I don't think so. You may have your doubts, but those with faith believe that the golden plates were given to Joseph Smith by God's angel. It's just like Moses in the Old Testament, the time he saw the burning bush of God. Remember? He came down from the mountain with the Ten Commandments written on two tablets of stone, by the hand of God Himself! So it's good to believe. The golden plates could be the most valuable treasure on earth. Not everyone in the world is an atheist like you," Cathy said.

"I'm not a total atheist. Sometimes I believe in God, like when I've prayed to Him and He saved my ass. People believe in their faith, or whatever, just to believe in something, anything. Even an atheist believes in something . . . he believes in nonbelief. But I think I'm what you call an agnostic. One time I made a deal with God and I'm not going to renege on it. If I didn't have to hold up my end of the bargain with God, then I would have to say that I'm a Darwinist. I believe in Darwin because he said we all came from monkeys, and that's what I believe," Pete joked.

"You know, Pete, you're a monkey. But really, honey, sometimes it's good to believe in something. I believe in God. I think there is a heaven too," Cathy said.

"Yeah, it's good to believe in something. I'll have to admit that there is a God, or something that we interpret as God, that is beyond our mortal understanding."

"What's the problem with that runaway-girl case you're supposed to be doing?"

"It's a long story. The thing that irks me is that I don't want to go traipsing around the forest in western New York. I came up here to look for a missing teenage runaway, and now I've been lassoed into helping excavate a museum piece!"

"Pete, are you saying that you're doing this as a favor? You should get paid. We have a lot of bills, you know, with the kids and all."

"Yeah, I agree, honey, except this Palmyra police detective said that he was going to help me if I can help him. That's the deal. I'm not sure if he's totally off his rocker or if he really means and believes what he says. I guess I'll find out soon enough. On top of everything else, I've got some volatile clients on this teenage-runaway job, and I've got to score for them and cover up some big mistakes that Greg made. I'll have to explain it all to you later when I get home. I'm not sure how all this is going to turn out."

"Uh-oh, Pete, that doesn't sound good. What did Greg do this time? What's happening up there in Palmyra?"

"Let's just say that he screwed me over again, and now I have to clean up his mistakes or the client is going to be on my ass big time, with his lawyers and his thugs. It's a mess. Sorry, Cathy, I can't talk about all that right now. It's too much. I'll tell you the whole story when I get home."

"When are you coming home?"

"I'm not sure yet, honey. Hopefully I can get home the day after tomorrow. Oh and, honey, check this out, Orrin Culver has this big silver revolver he calls his Serpent of Justice, and he keeps it in a glass case with spotlights on it."

"What is it about this fascination with guns? Why do these people give their guns names and put them on display? There are too many guns and too many people who want to handle them. I mean, what's going on? That seems a little psycho, no?"

"Yeah, well a couple of hundred years ago, everyone had to have a gun. Then you also have the Second Amendment in the American Constitution, which guaranteed the right for everyone to own guns, big guns, small guns, and even pink guns, all to be had for the purpose of killing something or someone. Although, shooting for target practice, I have to admit, is a lot of fun. So there you go, it is what it is."

"Please be safe up there, honey. All this talk of guns makes me nervous," Cathy said.

"No worries, everything is good. How are the boys doing?"

"They're great. Both are sleeping now. I love you. Stay safe, honey," Cathy whispered.

"Call you soon, love you."

Pete hit the speed dial button for Vicky's number, his second and last call for the night. Pete knew that he was fortunate to have such a good secretary-researcher.

"Hi, Vicky, what were you able to dig up regarding the golden plates and Orrin's ranting about the Danite army and their special forces, the Destroying Angels?"

"The golden plates seem to actually exist. After receiving the golden plates at Hill Cumorah, Joseph Smith had to fight his way back to his farm while holding the golden plates. Men were jumping out of the bushes and swinging weapons, but Joseph Smith was able to fight them off and get back to his farm. Then a mob broke into the Smith house, looking for the golden plates, but Smith's wife hid them under the bricks of the fireplace. Another time, during a mob home invasion, the golden plates were placed next to a sleeping child under blankets to escape the rabble's scrutiny. I researched really deep into who else saw the golden plates, and there are a lot of witnesses. The first of which was Joseph Smith's wife. Do you want to hear what she wrote about the golden plates in her memoir from 1879?"

"Sure, Vicky, let me have it. I'm listening."

"Okay, here goes, this is what Smith's wife writes, 'The plates lay in a box under our bed for months and on the table in our home without any attempt at concealment, wrapped in a small linen tablecloth, which I had given him to fold them in. I once felt . . . the plates as they thus lay on the table, tracing their outline and shape. They seemed to be pliable like thick paper, and would rustle with a metallic sound when the edges were moved by the thumb, as one does sometimes thumb the edges of a book.'"

"Wow, tell me more."

"I found a lot of interesting history on the Mormons. In 1834, during the March of Zion's Camp, to Missouri, Joseph Smith, created a militia known as the Armies of Israel to protect his community. This group was also called the Danites. In 1838, the Latter-day Saint settlement of Far West, in Missouri, had Mormons organize into a paramilitary group known as the Danites, whose objective was to defend the community against persecution. The Danites were Joseph Smith's 'secret group of loyalists,' and they became the most legendarily feared band in frontier America. The Danites have been described as a consecrated, clandestine unit of divinely inspired assassins. They had a ritualized form of murder called blood atonement— providing the victim with eternal salvation by slitting the victim's throat with a knife."

"Holy shit, this information is worse than I thought. They have a ritual that has to do with slitting someone's throat? These are the people who are up here? Damn, wish me luck, Vicky."

"Hold on, Pete, it gets better. Listen to this, blood atonement was one of the doctrines that Mormons held 'most sacred,' and those who dared to flee Zion were hunted down and killed. There might have been large numbers of such atonements that occurred during the Mormon Reformation of 1856."

"I guess I better not stick my neck out on this one, eh, Vicky?"

"Ha-ha, definitely not, Pete, don't take chances with these guys. They believe in all this stuff, and that is bad for you if you're throwing a wrench in their wheel. You asked about the Destroying Angels. They were used extensively by the Mormon's second leader, Brigham Young. The Mormons were being persecuted from all corners, so they had to fight back or be killed. During Brigham Young's time, the number of Danites was over two thousand. Only twelve men were specially selected who were the most elite of all the Danite soldiers. This extraordinary squad was referred to as Destructives, or Destroying Angels, or sometimes Flying Angels. Their duty was to act as spies and to report directly to the Mormon presidency."

"There are no doubts then, the Destroying Angels are the

special forces of the fundamentalist Mormon Danite army," Pete said.

"This one guy written about in the history books, who was the personal bodyguard to Joseph Smith and Brigham Young, kept popping up on websites. His name was Orrin Porter Rockwell. He was also a US Marshal. Back in the 1800s, he showed up at Joseph Smith's house on Christmas after being in jail for some months. His hair and beard were long from being incarcerated for so long. At first, Joseph Smith didn't recognize him from across the room, but when he did, Joseph Smith told Porter Rockwell that he should never cut his hair or shave his beard, and for that, no harm would ever come to him. It was true, Porter Rockwell, the original Destroying Angel in the nineteenth century, never got hurt and lived to a ripe old age."

"Yes, that's why those bikers look like they do. They're Destroying Angels taking on the look of the original, Porter Rockwell. And the guy I had dinner with tonight, the detective, his name is Orrin. That's probably where his Mormon parents got his name from."

"Check this out, Pete. I was able to download the actual Destroying Angels oath that I found in the Mormon historical records. You want me to read it to you?"

"Sure, why not, I'll just add it to the rest of everything else on this crazy night," Pete said.

"'In the name of Jesus Christ, the Son of God, I do covenant and agree to support the first presidency of the Church of Jesus Christ of Latter-day Saints, in all things, right or wrong. I will faithfully guard them and report to them the acts of all men, as far as in my power lies; I will assist in executing all the decrees of the first president, patriarch, or president of the twelve; and that I will cause all who speak evil of the presidency, or heads of the church, to die the death of dissenters or apostates, unless they speedily confess and repent, for pestilence, persecution, and death shall follow the enemies of Zion. I will be a swift herald of salvation and messenger of peace to the saints, and I will never make known the secret purposes of this society, called the Destroying Angels, my life being the forfeiture in a fire of burning tar and brimstone. So help me God, and keep me steadfast.'"

"That's some crazy shit. Wow, scary stuff, it's no wonder the detective up here is afraid of these guys. What did you come up with on the FLDS?"

"The Fundamentalist Latter-day Saints believe in plural marriage, what's known as polygamy. They have lots of wives for one husband. The Church of Jesus Christ of Latter-day Saints, or the LDS, condemned the practice of polygamy by releasing the Manifesto in the year 1890. The FLDS home base is a two-town place called Short Creek on the Utah-Arizona border. One of the two towns is Hildale, Utah, the same place from where those motorcycles and the white van are from. At least that's according to the Utah license plates you had me run."

"Okay, Vicky, good work, thanks. The missing girl, Julia, called from a house up here in Palmyra. Those bikes and the van with the Utah plates are parked there. No doubt in my mind that she either was kidnapped by them or she hooked up with the FLDS and wants to become one of their wives. Hey, have you heard from Greg at all? He was supposed to call me hours ago after he went to the house on Canal Street. That house on Canal Street is probably filled with FLDS. They might not take too kindly to Greg snooping around, especially if Julia is in the mix."

"No, Pete, I haven't heard from Greg. I tried calling him on another matter, but his phone just goes to voicemail."

"Okay, Vicky, I'm going upstairs to my room at the Palmyra Inn to catch some z's. Speak to you tomorrow."

PRISONER GREG

"Is life so dear, or peace so sweet, as to be purchased at the price of chains and slavery? Forbid it, Almighty God! I know not what course others may take, but as for me, give me liberty or give me death!"

—**Patrick Henry**

T HE CHAIR WAS made of quarter-inch metal; it looked like custom-welded diamond-plate steel. The bottoms of the chair's legs were bolted to the concrete floor of the basement. Greg wasn't going anywhere. The heavy steel chain around his waist was an inch thick, and his wrists and ankles were duct taped to the chair. The hot air smelled like a familiar locker room, pungent human odor. The basement walls were gray cinder block, shadowy lit by bare bulbs. Things were coming into focus for Greg, and he noticed a ring on the cement basement floor. It was the CTR ring he gave to Julia! She was here! The pain of seeing the CTR ring was too much to bear for Greg. He struggled mightily against his tight bonds and flailed his body against the waist chain.

Greg overheard men talking as they stood out of view at the top of the basement steps.

"We'll meet again in Zion, my brother."

Greg couldn't see their faces but heard every word.

He looked towards the basement steps. Greg saw black metal-studded motorcycle boots, then jeans, and then the girth of a giant. He had long black hair and a red sunburned face that was covered with a black beard. He walked up to Greg's chair and stood next to the muscular guy who had originally answered the door. With his large right hand, the behemoth ripped off the duct tape that covered Greg's mouth.

"Fucking asshole! If I get out of this chair, I'm going to kick your ass!" Greg yelled.

The giant man and the muscular guy snickered.

"Listen up, you, what are you doing here in Palmyra? Why are you asking questions?" the big man asked.

"I'm not talking to you, asshole! Just let me out of this chair and I might forget about this and let you slide. Who the hell are you guys, anyway?"

"My name is Beast. This here is Jaguar. What are you really up to? You're not looking for a house, that's bullshit. Why did you come up to this house?"

"Hey, man, that's it, I'm looking for a house, and the next thing I know you guys kidnapped me. What's going on here? Why am I being held a prisoner?"

"Don't answer a question with a question. Tell us why you knocked on this door or you'll be sorry."

"I already told you, man. I'm looking for a house. My cousin lives on Main Street, and he's giving me a job. That's the whole story. I drove up from New York City to see the neighborhood. You fucking guys are fucking psychos!"

"Oh yeah, what's your cousin's name?" Jaguar asked.

"Timmy O'Donnell is my cousin's name. Now get me the fuck out of this chair!"

Beast drew a Bowie knife from a sheath on his belt. The blade looked massive. The steel curved edge and large, brass cross guard extended above the elk-antler handle.

"You see this? I'm going to cut you unless you start telling me the truth. The blood atonement will be the will of Thy Spirit if you lie to me."

Jaguar was going through Greg's leather wallet, dumping cards and pictures on the floor until he pulled out a driver's license and handed it to Beast.

"I told you fucking misfits everything. My name is Greg Rocco. I do plumbing work. There's nothing else to know."

Greg stared at the large knife in Beast's right hand. He held it low by his thigh. Beast occasionally tested its heft by twirling it or sweeping the air with the blade.

"I can tell when someone's lying, and you're lying. You're a good liar, but you're not fooling us. I'm going to ask you one more time, what were you doing coming up to our door?"

"Dude! I'm telling you the truth. Why are you guys so fucking paranoid? Now let me out of this fucking chair!"

When Greg yelled, Beast's eyes became wide. The knife came down on Greg's left ear, causing a swooshing sound of air as the destructive arc of the blade sliced through Greg's fleshy cartilage. Half of Greg's ear fell to the floor by the side of the chair.

"Ahhhhh! Motherfucker! You're going to be sorry, asshole!"

Blood flowed down the left side of Greg's neck.

"Start talking or things are going to get a lot worse," Beast said.

"Fuck you, asshole!"

I'll never tell them anything, ever, no matter what they do to me. They might as well kill me, because I'm not going to talk about Julia. These are the fucking psychos who kidnapped her, and if I get through this, then I'm going to get her back.

Beast commenced to slap Greg's face with his full hand and then backhanded Greg's cheeks with his knuckles. The blows stung. Greg became woozy, losing consciousness.

"Eh, just leave him here, Beast. We got to get going if you want to get a jump on what we were talking about. Besides, maybe this guy is who he says he is. There's not too much upstairs with this guy. Just leave him here. Let's get going," Jaguar said.

Greg stared at the two men with venom in his bloodshot eyes. His face started to swell. His lips were swollen and bloody. And the top half of his ear still lay on the floor.

They covered up Greg's mouth again with heavy silver duct tape and then walked up the basement steps. Jaguar turned around to face Greg.

"Looks like you're going to be here a long time. If no one finds you down here, well, at least you've got a comfortable seat," Jaguar said.

Both men laughed and closed the basement door.

Greg felt a hint of fear. He was usually impervious to anxiety and fear. How could anything bad happen to the Greg Man? Now, he was all alone, with no one to help him. He could die of thirst or hunger down in this basement. Despair started to set in. Julia had been taken away, maybe to a place called Zion. He had overheard the men say Zion to each other and Greg resolved that he was going there, no matter what. Zion was the place where he'd find Julia.

Maybe if I keep struggling, I'll loosen something up and get out of here . . . man, these freaks bolted this chair down to the concrete. They're fucking hard-core dudes who are also total assholes! Just wait until I get out of here, I'm going to fuck them up so bad!

ROOM 218

"I can't prove it scientifically, that there's a God, but I believe."

—**Billy Graham**

THE LONG TALK Pete had on his cell phone with his wife, Cathy, felt comforting at first but then raised his angst level. The conversation about what was going on in Palmyra, made him realize that he was getting himself mixed up with forces that were none of his business. So many things were going through Pete's mind as he walked through the motel's parking lot.

Maybe this was all a labor dispute between Orrin and his superior, Clayborn Taggert? And what happened to Greg's phone call to me? He probably found Julia and now they're off gallivanting in Niagara Falls. That guy rarely does what I tell him to. Wouldn't he know that I'd be concerned about him checking out a place with a motorcycle gang inside? There's also the possibility that those guys beat him to death and dumped him in the Erie Canal. If he found Julia, he should have called me so I can give a positive report to her parents and get the hell out of here. Whew, I'm too tired to worry about everything now. It's time for a short nap.

Pete walked into the lobby of the motel and past the young

blue-eyed, blonde-haired desk girl. She said hello with a bright smile before he took the elevator to the second floor. He entered the room and saw the open window. That was the last thing he remembered.

When he opened his eyes, he was lying on the bed, unable to move an inch. Ropes had been tied to his ankles and anchored to the bed's legs. Tight ligatures tied to the bed posts squeezed his wrists and caused his hands to turn blue. His left shirtsleeve was rolled up. Standing over him was a dark figure of a man. He wore thick-framed glasses, a black fedora brimmed hat, and a long black trench coat.

Pete thought to himself how life can change in an instant. Just like a sudden unexpected car accident. Here he was, strapped to the bed, frightened, not knowing who this person standing over him was. He had just finished a nice talk with his wife and now he was in his room, about to die. Pete saw his Detonics .45 placed up on the night table; he had been disarmed while he was unconscious. Thoughts of his wife and two sons flashed into his head. Pete prayed for a savior.

The man drew a large needle from a black nylon sheath on his wrist and held it in front of Pete's face. The large four-inch silver needle had a gold coil handle.

"This is an acupuncture hari that I had specially made just for you, and I know you're going to like it."

The sadistic figure slowly inserted the needle into Pete's left elbow. The pain that shot through Pete's skull was unlike anything he had ever felt before. He screamed, but his taped mouth prevented his screams from sounding like much of anything. Who can withstand such torture and remain sane? Pete was crazed with pain; delirium set in. His thought process was no longer coherent. The very soul of his existence was that of a man in the midst of physical torment. The tight ropes held him down to the bed, so all he could do was writhe in agony.

"I'm going to take the tape off your mouth. If you scream or say anything too loud, I'll kill you. Tell me where I can find the golden plates."

The pain from the needle in Pete's left elbow was so intense that he was going to pass out or do anything to stop the torment.

"Owwwweee, I'll tell you everything I know. Everything, whatever I know."

"Where are the golden plates?"

"They're on some hill. I don't know where they are! Ahhhhhh!"

Pain shot into Pete's entire body.

"I'm going to give you as much pain as you gave my left arm unless you tell me where the golden plates are. I want to know everything about the golden plates."

The black-clad man stuck the duct tape back over Pete's mouth and clamped a wire to the metal needle in Pete's arm. The wire was connected to what looked like an electrical capacitor the size of a soda can.

Pete screamed in pain, and his body shuddered on the bed, but his screams could not be heard. The device shot bolts of high-voltage current into Pete's elbow. The pain made his whole body jerk repeatedly like he was having an epileptic attack. He looked like a flopping fish struggling out of water.

The torturer's hawkish-looking face was now closely hovering over Pete's face. His thick, black-framed glasses made his eyes look abnormally large. Pete could feel his hot, putrid breath.

"I am with you in your suffering. Your pain is mine too. It's so bad, oh, and the hurt is so much more than we can stand. Do you want it to stop and never come back? Then tell me where

I can find the golden plates. Tell me the location and I will take this electrified needle out of your arm."

He disconnected the wire from the needle and ripped the tape from Pete's mouth again.

"No, no, no, no more, please. Who are you? What do you want?"

"Start talking. Where are the golden plates?" the voice rasped.

Pete shut his eyes tightly and prayed silently.

Dear God, I believe in You. I thank You for my children, my wife, and my good life. Please help me now in my time of need, for I will be forever grateful to You, God.

Pete saw the LED digital clock on the night table. Its red numbers lighted 12:08. He then looked at the bottom space between the floor and the door, and noticed two straight shadows caused by tall-heeled cowboy boots standing in the hallway outside the door.

Pete answered loudly.

"Ahhhh, please! Stop the pain and I'll tell you everything about the golden plates!"

A tremendous impact caused the room's door to fly open. Orrin stood silhouetted in the doorway, with his Colt Python in hand. He raised the gun and shot quickly, but the black-shadowed man moved too fast, and the .357 bullet hit the wall where the man had stood. Pete felt the needle in his arm suddenly come out. The black-clad man threw the steel needle across the room into Orrin's left eye.

"Ahhhhhh," Orrin screamed.

Orrin involuntarily fell back, and at the same time, the Python revolver roared with two more shots. Orrin stumbled back and sideways, into some empty coat hangers, falling onto a luggage bench. The Python blasted out two more thunderous shots as Orrin grabbed at the metal needle in his eye.

"Ahhhhhh! Satan, thou shall be destroyed!"

Orrin screamed as he pulled the needle out of his eye. It fell to the floor. He raised the Python again to let off a sixth shot at the attacker.

The black figure had athletically jumped through the large open window in the time it took to look away for a few seconds. He disappeared from the room just like a moving shadow. Orrin ran up to the window while swiftly ejecting the spent shells from the Python's cylinder and quickly snapping in a speed loader of six fresh .357 rounds. Orrin scanned the parking lot with his good eye, but it was empty. He didn't see the attacker at all.

"Damn! Where did that heathen go? Who from Satan's hell was that?" Orrin yelled.

"Orrin, please, untie me."

A stream of blood trickled down Orrin's face from his left eye.

"Ahhhhh, my eye! That guy blinded my eye. Ahhhh, he blinded me! I can only see through my right eye. Damn that hurts! Oh, my head, I need some water. What in blazes is going on here?" Orrin asked.

Pete's ears were still numb due to the concussive blasts from Orrin's revolver. Sounds were muffled. Pete hoped that no permanent damage had been done to his eardrums. The migraine in his head felt like a wood vice squeezing his temples.

"I don't know who the fuck that was, but he did say he wanted to give me as much pain in my arm as I gave him in his arm. I don't know what he meant by that. The only guy who might have ever wanted to say that to me is dead."

Orrin took out his pocket knife and cut Pete loose from the ropes that tied him to the bed.

Pete tried to hold back his scream when he moved his left arm, but the pain made him yell out.

"My eye hurts more than anything has ever hurt before. It's bleeding pretty badly too. I think my eye has deflated some."

Orrin used his knife to cut a straight white cloth strip from a bed sheet, which he then proceeded to wrap around his head and left eye.

"Hey, Orrin, thank you, I don't know what would've happened if you didn't show up. I can tell you now that I prayed to God, and He answered my prayers when you kicked the door in."

"Who was that guy? Did you recognize him?"

"No, he was in the shadows. He had a face like a hawk, with a curved-down nose. He wore these extra-thick glasses that hid a lot of his face, and his hat brim was turned down. Oh, and he wore a big, long black trench coat that wasn't buttoned. He was wearing black under that. I was in too much pain to think about anything."

"I wonder if it was one of the FLDS boys come to find out about the golden plates from you. The Danite army's Destroying Angels like to wear long duster coats to hide their sawed-off .44 pistols in their coat pockets. The coat also hides their big Bowie knives. I guess since you got half a look at this guy, especially his big glasses, we'll call him Four Eyes," Orrin said.

"Yes! He wanted me to tell him everything that I knew about the golden plates. He probably was one of those FLDS Destroying Angels you were talking about. I didn't tell him anything. Good thing you burst in just at the right time. The pain was so bad when he put the electricity into my elbow that I probably would have started making stuff up, just to say something, anything. Whatever the case, you saved me, thank you. We better get to the hospital and see what they can do for your eye."

"Unfortunately my eye is going to have to wait. That spawn from Satan blinded me, and that's that. I'll have to accept it. At least I got one good eye, my right aiming eye. Time is running out on us, and we need to do this now. Let's get out of here before Clayborn Taggert arrives with his boys. It's time to acquire the golden plates. How's your arm?"

"It's numb and weak, but I should have no problem pulling you out of that hole with my right arm and using my back as a belay point."

Orrin looked concerned.

"Chiseling the golden plates out of the rock shouldn't take too long. A few more perfect hits around the underside of the rock and they're out. Then I need you to pull me up. Are you sure you can do it? It's going to be my weight plus the weight of the golden plates."

"No problem. My left arm is feeling a little better as we speak. I was an Eagle Scout in the Boy Scouts. I remember how to do a mountain belay. I'll get you out of that hole as long as you don't get stuck on something."

"Okay, we only have two minutes until people start showing up here. Let's go and do what we need to do before Clayborn Taggert figures out where we might be. It's time to finally fulfill my vision, to acquire the golden plates of Mormon from Hill Cumorah."

"I'm right behind you, Orrin. Let's get your golden plates. Just keep that firing cannon of yours handy. I shouldn't be up in western New York doing this right now. I should be home in New York City, watching television. But I do want to help you fulfill your vision. You're a super-righteous guy. So I'll grit my teeth and help you out."

"Much appreciated there, Pete. I and the LDS Church won't ever forget this."

HILL CUMORAH

"On the west side of this hill, not far from the top, under a stone of considerable size, lay the plates, deposited in a stone box."

—**Joseph Smith**

ORRIN WALKED QUICKLY from the Palmyra Inn and jumped into his truck.

"We have to get to Hill Cumorah before the Destroying Angels and secure the golden plates! I think they've been following and watching every move I make," Orrin yelled.

Pete stepped up into Orrin's big pickup truck and they drove fast down Route 21. They soon came upon Hill Cumorah. The Hill Cumorah's top ridgeline was silhouetted against the sky and extended for a quarter mile from north to south. Orrin backed up his truck into an alcove of hanging trees to stay hidden from sight. The warm night was eerily quiet as they silently closed the doors of the truck and ran into the woods. Their panting breaths and the crunching brush under their feet were the only noises as they ran across woods and dirt through the spaces between the trees.

The ground was soft from the warm days of summer. Pete was completely out of shape. His pace slowed to a stumbling walk. The climb up the hill had been too much. He held on to a tree for a few seconds to catch his breath.

Orrin stopped and turned as Pete trudged up the hill, lagging behind.

"The golden plates have to be recovered before the Destroying Angels get here!"

Pete couldn't keep up with Orrin's fast stride as they ran up such a steep incline.

When extreme fatigue set in, delirium soon followed. Pete's mind started spinning blame on anything that he could think of. If it wasn't for that corrupt FLDS Police Lieutenant Clayborn Taggert, things would have gone easier for Pete. The case was supposed to be a simple teenage runaway, but now here he was, defending the Latter-day Saints' golden plates with his life, with just a promise of finding a runaway girl as his compensation.

It seemed to Pete that lately he was always taking one step forward and two steps back when it came to handling his cases. Why was he in these woods, following this guy, when religious fanatics with guns were going for the same prize that they were? He thought about turning around and saying "fuck it", but Pete pressed on, following Orrin up through the woods. Pete felt a weird sense of duty to people he was connected with; he couldn't just abandon Orrin out here, and Pete felt an obligation towards his friendship with this unique man.

Finally, Orrin stopped. He was breathing almost as hard as Pete was. The two men were near the top of the hill, more to the north side. The woods were quiet. There was no wind. The night was totally still.

"The golden plates are down this hole I've been digging for the past few years. All the metal-detector gizmos in the world couldn't find the golden plates because they would detect just this iron-ore rock here. The golden plates are under this giant rock in the ground," Orrin said.

Pete saw the silhouette of a large buried boulder barely

sticking out of the ground. It was about five inches above the surface and twenty-five feet long. Most of the massive tractor-trailer-sized rock looked like it was in the ground, below the surface.

"How far does this rock go down there?"

"Just about thirty feet or so, the golden plates are ensconced within it."

"Where the hell is this hole you dug? I don't see anything?"

Orrin stepped to the right, bent down, and put his hands in the ground. He pulled up a large piece of slate that had grass, leaves, and dirt on top. Orrin carefully placed the cover to the side of a small hole, barely wide enough for a man to crawl into. The light from Orrin's headlamp shined into the hole, and Pete saw a narrow ladder that went straight down into a dark abyss.

"I need to get down there and get the golden plates. There's a sideways tunnel I dug that goes right to the bottom of the rock where the golden plates are," Orrin said.

"You mean you're going to wiggle your way down in there?" Pete asked.

"It won't be a problem. Believe me. I'm long and lean. I learned to crawl through tunnels during the Vietnam War, fighting in the Cu Chi Tunnels. I know a thing or two about how to get around down there."

"How did you get out of the tunnel before?" Pete sounded incredulous.

"I was able to crawl backwards before, but I won't be able to get myself out while I'm holding the heavy golden plates. I'll tie this rope around my ankles. You just get ready to pull me out when I say so on this little walkie-talkie. I'll climb straight down using the ladder that's in the vertical hole, but then there's a right angle that goes for twenty feet under the rock to where the golden plates are. I set up a pulley, so you can pull from here and I'll slide up that horizontal diagonal hole on the way out with the golden plates. Then I'll use the ladder to help get myself up."

Orrin gave Pete a miniature two-way radio and clipped a second radio onto his shirt pocket.

He crawled head first into the small hole by using the narrow ladder. At the bottom of the vertical part, he grunted and pulled himself into the diagonal hole, disappearing, with just the faint light of his headlamp peaking up as he shimmied down the long, angled dirt hole.

Pete sat cross-legged in the darkness under a tree while slowly letting the rope play out as Orrin crawled under the giant rock.

The rope stopped moving, which meant that Orrin had reached the bottom of his tunnel.

"Oh, man! It's tight down here. Some dirt fell over the plates. I'm going to dig it out with my hands. Stand by," Orrin said, barely audible over the walkie-talkie. His voice was garbled.

"That sucks, Orrin. I thought you had them ready to go with just a few chisel hits," Pete said.

"You stay there. I'm extracting the golden plates loose from this rock. Just hold tight."

"Yeah, well, I hope you can do it quickly because I don't think my body will fit down there to rescue you," Pete said.

"It's going to take me ten minutes or so."

The seconds agonizingly ticked by.

Then he saw car headlights in the distance. There were three cars and a couple of motorcycles. They drove to the bottom of the hill and stopped. Their headlights turned off, and the night became very black again. Pete heard the slamming of car doors.

Oh no, here they are and I'm all alone! Shit! What the fuck is Orrin doing?

"Orrin, Orrin, come in, there are three cars and some motorcycles down below," Pete whispered.

No response on the radio.

From a distance, Pete heard the men walk into the woods. The sight of searching flashlights and the sounds of crunching ground were unnerving. At least six men were quickly walking towards Pete.

Holy Shit! Here comes trouble! Those guys are the Destroying Angels!

Pete surmised they would probably end up directly where he was within a few minutes.

Without further thought, Pete jumped into the hole and grabbed the round piece of sod to put on top of his head. He held on to the rungs of the ladder for dear life, in complete darkness. Dirt fell over his face, and a few specks got in his eyes. He dared not move.

Some minutes passed, and then suddenly he heard footsteps around the hole. It was the Destroying Angels, and they had walked up to his position. Pete's heart thumped like a speeding locomotive. He held on to the ladder in complete darkness, knowing the hole went down far enough to break his leg if he fell. He kept completely still, breathing as quietly as possible. The crunching of heavy boots above his head was loud. He wondered if any of them would suddenly realize that they had stepped on a piece of ground that was just a little too soft, raising suspicions of his hiding place.

After a few tense seconds that felt like an eternity, the footsteps subsided in the distance.

"Pete! Pete! Where are you?" the walkie-talkie cackled.

Orrin's sudden voice shocked Pete. He quickly turned the volume down and whispered into the radio.

"The Destroying Angels are on the hill, right above me.

I put the top hatch on and I'm hanging on to the ladder," Pete exclaimed.

"I figured this might happen. I've got about three minutes more of chiseling to get the golden plates out. I've got to work fast or get ready to die. Come farther down the ladder and stay still."

Pete went farther down into the narrow dirt hole using the rungs of the ladder. He was scared, but the alternative was to stay on the surface and confront the Destroying Angels.

The tense minutes dragged on too long. Pete heard Orrin's chisel working furiously, chipping away at the rock.

"I have them!" Orrin exclaimed. "Go up the ladder to the top and start pulling."

Pete was shrouded in blackness, but he could feel the rungs as he stepped up the ladder slowly to the top. He moved the camouflage cover up just an inch to look out. There was no one around. The forest was clear.

"Okay, I'm back on top. Get ready, I'm going to start pulling," Pete whispered into the walkie-talkie.

Pete wrapped the rope around the back of his waist and bent down. When he straightened out his legs, he tightened the rope around his back and pulled Orrin out a few feet. Then he bent again, letting the rope play out over the back of his waist, and stood up again, pulling Orrin another few feet. When Orrin went vertical, Pete grunted and pulled with all his might. Inch by inch, Orrin came up the hole. Finally, Pete grabbed his ankles and pulled him completely out.

"Here they are, behold, the golden plates!" Orrin loudly whispered.

Orrin brushed off some dirt, revealing in full tarnished splendor, the golden plates. They were a dull gold-metallic color, dark and light in different places. The hundreds of metallic pages were held together by three stout metal rings.

Pete was struck by a powerful feeling, deep in his body. The uncertainty of faith, with all of its jargon, was now factual, gleaming in his face. He was drawn to the golden plates and stepped closer to them. The soul of the Book of Mormon was now in front of him. Pete touched them with his right hand. The golden plates were real. He ran his hand along the edges' surface in the darkness, and they felt like thin metal pages.

In some places on the metal pages, the gold was very yellow and looked rich under the moonlight. Reformed hieroglyphics, Egyptian-type letters pressed into the gold, it looked just like a book made of metal. The hieroglyphics were incomprehensible to Pete but visually astounding. The Egyptian symbols were very detailed. The moment was dangerous and magnificent; the Destroying Angels were within striking distance of the precious golden plates of Mormon.

"Wow, okay, so what's the plan?" Pete asked.

Pete was still breathing hard from being overweight and out of shape. He was also nervous about the Destroying Angels lurking somewhere around their position. The anxiety constricted his chest.

"As soon as we can get out of here, I'm taking the golden plates into the Palmyra Temple, where they will be sunken into the inner sanctum sanctorum beneath the temple. The vault was just finished. No one will ever be able to get at the golden plates once they're secured there," Orrin said.

Orrin looked out over the edge of the hill and saw six men searching with flashlights, walking towards them.

"Pete, we have to go now. You ready to run? They're walking this way. Come on, let's go," Orrin whispered.

Pete followed close behind. It was obvious that Orrin was struggling with the weight of the golden plates as he tried to run.

"Here, let me help you with those," Pete whispered.

Pete grabbed a metal book-binding ring on one side of the golden plates while Orrin held another ring, and together they ran towards Orrin's pickup truck.

When Orrin slowly drove the truck out from the trees, Pete noticed a dark-blue Ford Crown Victoria parked about fifty yards away.

"That bad lieutenant you talked about is just down the road in that unmarked car," Pete said.

"Hey, Pete, you ever hear about a .357 bullet going right through a car's engine block."

"Yeah, but that's bullshit. The bullet can't go through an engine block."

"Minus your profanity, I agree with you. But you know, Pete, if you can hit the engine's belts and some other stuff just right, that car ain't goin' anywhere."

Orrin stopped the truck and jumped out with pistol in hand. He quickly got down on one knee and cocked back the hammer of his Colt Python while holding the revolver with both hands. The shot was startling in the dark night, and the flash lit up the area.

Orrin jumped back in the pickup truck and it lurched forward. The diesel engine bellowed as they sped down the road.

Orrin looked in his rearview mirror.

"Looks like Satan's child Clayborn Taggert can't start his car. I hit that engine just right. Put your seat belt on. We're gonna drive fast to the temple," Orrin said.

Orrin's pickup truck drove at breakneck speed up Route 21 with Pete nervously strapped in the passenger seat.

Suddenly three cars and a number of motorcycles were racing up behind them. After a furious drag-strip chase on the country road, a motorcyclist caught up to Pete's passenger side. Pete looked in the side mirror and saw a long-haired motorcyclist with a large snub-nosed revolver in his left hand. Two gunshots startled Pete, and Orrin's pickup truck lurched. Orrin turned the wheel, trying to keep control. The tires on Orrin's pickup truck were blown out and the rubber quickly shredded. The Destroying Angel had shot out the tires. Orrin raced the pickup on its rims as sparks flew behind the truck. Orrin swerved his truck back and forth across the road to block the motorcyclists from getting alongside the truck.

"Take the golden plates and run as fast as you can to the temple! You can see it all lit up from here. I'll meet you there soon! I'll take these guys out and catch up with you!"

Pete hefted the plates onto his lap in preparation to jump out the door when the truck stopped.

Orrin hit the brakes and turned the wheel hard to the left. The truck's rear end kicked out and then stopped. Pete jumped out the truck door and started running. The plates were heavy, probably more like sixty pounds. Loud pistol shots rang out. Orrin's .357 blasted again and again, hitting a Destroying Angel with every shot.

Pete was tired from carrying the weight of the golden plates after just a hundred yards. The lights of the Palmyra Temple made a glow in the night sky. Its radiance was a beacon directing him through the darkness. The temple's tall spire held the gold statue of the angel Moroni, a prominent image for rescue. It was a sign to show Pete an escape from the sheer evil behind him and embrace the welcoming arms of refuge inside the temple.

Even while he panicked and was almost out of breath, Pete thought about the strangeness of his present dilemma: chased by despicable men while holding the golden plates, the same circumstances that Joseph Smith experienced in 1827.

Pete could see the temple clearly now. He ran as fast as he could, but it seemed like he was moving in slow motion. The granite white steps of the temple were in front of him. He just kept moving, to get safe, no matter what.

I'm close to fainting, but I've got to keep it together long enough to just get inside the temple.

THE INNER SANCTUM SANCTORUM

"I want to see the temple built in a manner that it will endure through the Millennium. This is not the only temple we shall build; there will be hundreds of them built and dedicated to the Lord."

—**Brigham Young**

THE UNMISTAKABLE SOUND of Orrin's diesel pickup truck screeching on its rims rumbled through the temple parking lot. The truck braked hard on the asphalt and crunched to a halt. The truck's metal rims were heavy with white, hot smoke.

Pete stopped running, still clutching the golden plates, his chest heaving, his body totally exhausted.

"Quick, follow me!" Orrin yelled while motioning with the Colt Python in his hand.

The spotlights and street lamps around the manicured grounds surrounding the temple lighted their way. They both ran to the rear of the temple, around a building appendage made of thick white granite, a block that stuck out from the back of the temple. An electrified mesh fence protected the walls. The cube structure had a large basketball-sized black-globe security camera on its rooftop suspended by a robot arm.

"That's the outside of the vault room." Orrin pointed to the square, one-level, attached structure.

The weight of the golden plates felt heavy, but Pete was not going to quit. He would never lose his grip on them until Orrin told him to let them go.

They ran up to the front entrance of the temple. Stained artistic glass interlaced with iron-bar latticework and silver steel-framed double doors made the entrance look impenetrable. The outside of the temple appeared to be an art-deco angular design, a thick-walled granite fortress that would stand for a thousand years. The gold statue of the angel Moroni holding his trumpet towered above them, standing upon a fifty-foot-high pedestal. Orrin put his thumb on the side of the front entrance and a small hand-sized compartment door slid up, revealing a lit keypad. Orrin pushed a few buttons and the noticeable click of a lock was heard.

"When these doors close behind us, we should be okay. They're heavy-duty lead-lined glass and iron."

Crossing the threshold of the Palmyra Temple felt like entering a solemn place of security. The air inside smelled like fresh cut roses. The temple was a realm of comfort, a sanctuary from the wave of evil left behind outside.

Inside, the temple was all white, everything, from the drapes to the furniture. The vaulted ceiling looked twenty feet high. Large, alabaster tandem square pillars extended from floor to ceiling on either end of a white altar with a lace tablecloth.

"This is the Celestial Room," Orrin said.

The Celestial Room had a giant chandelier hanging from the middle of the ceiling and classic comfortable furniture. A ring of thick granite pillars encircled the space. Orrin and

Pete quickly crossed the Celestial Room and entered another chamber.

Pete couldn't hold the golden plates any longer; his strength was gone. He was just about to drop them when they finally arrived at the vault room. An enormous, circular, steel safe door was already open. The door looked about three feet thick. In the center of the vault was a thick glass cylinder on top of a cylindrical steel pedestal. Pete handed the golden plates to Orrin, who then placed the golden plates on a red pillow inside the middle of the glass cylinder. Orrin pushed a small button on a control panel and the glass cylinder sank into the steel pedestal. A metal camera-like aperture unfolded and closed the top of the pedestal, sealing the opening. Then the pedestal began to slowly descend into the steel floor. Orrin delivered a prayer:

"Oh, Heavenly Father, please may the Spirit protect this inner sanctum sanctorum for Thy most precious gift. As Thy had bestowed the golden plates to the prophet Joseph Smith, we now secure Thy most important writings to your Saints into this impenetrable sanctum sanctorum for our blessed Church. As Thy Word was given to Mormon, who gave the golden plates to his son Moroni, we honor and rejoice in gratitude that the golden plates of Mormon are now within the possession of the Church of Jesus Christ of Latter-day Saints for their study to bring us closer to the Heavenly Father and Jesus Christ. Amen."

The two men watched as the steel cylinder sank completely down into the hole. From in between the steel floor, a two-foot-thick steel trapdoor slid into place, flush with the floor, audibly hissing with an air lock and the clang of thick, closing steel bolts. Orrin tightly shut his eye and knelt in prayer, his arms crossed along his waist, his head bowed.

"Blessed is the name of the Lord and those who keep His commandments. These golden plates have been revealed by the power of God, and they have been translated by the power of God. The translation of them, which we have seen, is correct. I will bear record of what I have now seen and heard. Thank You, Heavenly Father, for bestowing the golden plates upon us."

A sudden sound made Orrin's right eye open.

Echoes of heavy marching boots reverberated through the halls of the building. Pete looked at Orrin, shocked at the prospect that the Destroying Angels had entered the building. Orrin stood up and quickly walked out of the vault and motioned for Pete to follow him. Orrin struggled to close the three-foot-thick bank-vault door, so Pete helped him by leaning his back into it. The deep metallic sound of the ten-ton steel door closing was the sign of ultimate security for the golden plates. Orrin spun the locking spindle and then the combination dial.

Pete and Orrin hid behind wide Romanesque-type pillars in the Endowment Room and then stealthily stepped into the large Celestial Room. They crouched low and hid behind two of the granite pillars that encircled the room.

"I thought you said that the outside was solid and that we were safe. Sounds to me like there's a fucking army coming our way," Pete whispered.

The Destroying Angels marched into the Celestial Room, loudly stomping their boots—large men, shoulder to shoulder, with an array of AR-15-type assault rifles and shotguns in their hands. They suddenly broke formation, quickly finding positions of cover around the room. A big man stepped forward in full police regalia. He wore a thick leather strap across his chest that supported a wide equipment belt and knee-high leather jackboots with steel-tipped toes. Four brass general stars were pinned on his collar. His official hat was loaded with gold braiding around the visor. The overly adorned policeman was Clayborn Taggert.

"Hey, Orrin, I know you two boys are hiding back there. Come on out now! You did a lot of damage back there, and you got to answer for that. And as the law here, I'm ordering you to step out and surrender. Your little buddy from New York City too. Come on now, let's see those hands. Step on out from there, the both of you. Just for your information, our former Palmyra police captain had a heart attack this afternoon, and that means I've officially taken over the department. Now come out of there before my patience wears thin and we just have to do things the hard way. If you boys don't step out from those pillars right now, I can guarantee there'll be a world of hurt coming your way soon."

"There's no way I'm stepping out of here, you FLDS terrorist! Taking little girls for your sister wives! That there is an affront to God, and I hereby arrest you, Clayborn Taggert, as being an accessory to kidnapping and child endangerment! Now tell your long-haired friends from Short Creek to lay down all that hardware, and I promise to bring you in all nice and peaceful like. Understand?"

Pete was scared. He was starting to accept the fact that Orrin was going to talk his way into a fight and these guys would lay into their positions with military-style rifles throwing some major calibers. He thought of his wife and his children. He wanted to just stand up and surrender. What the hell did he care if this crew stole the golden plates? Pete took out his Detonics .45, raked the slide, and held it low between his shaking knees.

Clayborn Taggert screamed.

"Arrrhhhhhhaaaa! You arrest me? I don't think so, Orrin! Now give me the golden plates or I must take your blood! Your attempts to change our way of life will not stand! Three wives is the minimum as ordered by the first prophet. Only we, the FLDS, are the true Mormon Church! That is why we must have the golden plates of Mormon and we must have them now. If you think they're worth dying over, then so be it!"

A shot rang out. Clayborn Taggert shot a nine-millimeter bullet right into one of the granite pillars. Two more quick shots by Taggert hit the granite pillar that Orrin hid behind.

"This is your last chance to surrender! Come out now or face certain death at the hands of my Destroying Angels!"

"You really want the golden plates that badly! Ye spawn of Satan! Have a piece of lead instead!"

Within a half a millisecond, too fast for the human eye to assimilate, Orrin had swung his revolver around the granite pillar and fired once. The .357 bullet went clean through Clayborn Taggert's neck, just above his bulletproof vest. He slumped instantly to the floor, a loose pile of a former person.

The shooting started and Pete crouched down. The fuselage of rifle fire shattered everything around him. The thick granite pillar was his only protection from the onslaught of high-velocity bullets shot his way. White dust clouds formed from the pulverized granite as hundreds of rifle bullets chipped away at the pillars. Pete prayed, to God, to help him live through this. He had prayed before in his life, and God had answered those prayers.

I promised long ago to You, God, that I believed You were real. You miraculously answered my prayers then. I pray to You now asking for help. Oh God, please help me. Please help me, God!.

Suddenly there was a thunderous explosion that shook the room, a bright flash, then another explosion that vibrated the floor, deafeningly loud, and another. Heat and shrapnel flew everywhere. Pete's ears were ringing. He looked to the side and saw bodies go flying after each explosion. He heard the screams of men as they went airborne from the force of the blasts rocking the entire room like an earthquake. Thinking that the cavalry had arrived, Pete peeked around the pillar, and much to his horror, he saw Four Eyes from the motel room. The human apparition was throwing hand grenades from behind the granite pillars, directed at the remaining Destroying Angels.

There were more screams as the Destroying Angels soared through the air, lifted by the powerful explosions of the grenades. Bodies lay smoking and motionless in the middle of the red carpet of the temple floor. The remaining Destroying Angels fired everything they had, AR-15 assault rifles and automatic shotguns. The bullets produced more clouds of dust as they ricocheted off the granite walls. Their directed fire was aimed at where they thought the hand grenades had been thrown from.

Pete and Orrin ducked closer down behind the granite pillars and looked at each other.

There was a momentary silence as the Destroying Angels tried to determine where their adversary was hiding. Then a sudden popping could be heard. A Destroying Angel ran out from cover onto the main floor and turned holding both short-barreled .44 pistols, one in each hand. He blasted at the shadow behind him, two full cylinders' worth of six bullets each at the same time. The high-powered revolvers looked like anti-aircraft pom-pom guns recoiling in the Destroying Angel's hands. Another small cap pistol crack echoed in the room and a hole formed on the Destroying Angel's forehead. He collapsed backwards, arms and legs akimbo.

One bearded man, who had been blown into the middle of the Celestial Room, struggled to stand up. Pete noticed that the man's body still smoldered from a grenade explosion. When the Destroying Angel gained an upright stance, he drew a large Bowie knife as he swayed back and forth, barely able to stand upright. Suddenly there appeared a figure, dressed in a black trench coat. It was Four Eyes. The Destroying Angel arched his Bowie knife blade down onto Four Eyes, striking his raised left arm. There was a clang of steel where there should have been flesh. Pete saw a flash of a silver blade and the Destroying Angel's right arm fell to the ground. Just as fast, the large man's neck was sliced through by the arching path of the blade wielded by Four Eyes. The Destroying Angel's head rolled off his shoulders and the body collapsed to the floor. Orrin took aim but not fast enough. In a mere quarter second, the elusive figure in black disappeared, maybe behind a chair or a granite pillar.

Pete was amazed at the ruthlessness of this psycho. He killed and vanished like magic. Painful memories were suddenly triggered by the present traumatic events. Pete tried to make sense of the sudden familiar fear, but it couldn't be him, the psycho in the Catskill forest! It couldn't be him because that man was lying dead in the woods with a hole in his head!

"Hey! Baranowski! I've got an extra grenade just for you and that fucking Howdy Doody cowboy you're with, unless you give me those golden plates. I'll let you walk if you give me the golden plates. Don't worry, I'll forgive the fact that I now have a metal arm and half a head 'cause of you," the man yelled from cover.

Orrin gave Pete a curious look. Pete shrugged his shoulders and shook his head in total amazement. It was him, the killer from the Catskill caper. Somehow, Four Eyes had lived through that fateful night in the forest.

But how did he get here? And how does he know about the golden plates?

"Listen, maybe we can work something out. How about I send you some money or something to compensate you for your arm? Just give me the address to send the money to and you got it. Anything you want," Pete yelled.

"What I want from you, Baranowski, is your fucking life! But come out with the golden plates and maybe I'll cut you some slack and have some mercy. You better come out with those fucking golden plates or I fucking swear to God, I'm going to toss this grenade right onto your fucking lap! Now give me those fucking golden plates! I'll give you sixty seconds to come out from behind there or I'm going to blow up both your sorry asses and take the golden plates for myself! Sixty seconds! That's it! Decide!"

Orrin made the sign of a gun with his hand, which Pete interpreted right away. Pete held up his Detonics 45.

Orrin whispered to Pete. "When I count to three and say now, you let loose with that whole magazine at that guy. Got it?"

Pete nodded, crouching even lower behind the granite pillar, clutching his compact .45 pistol in hand.

Orrin crouched behind another granite pillar as he crossed his arms in prayer. His eyes closed as he bent at the waist, whispering.

"Cry unto God for all thy support; yea, let all thy doings be unto the Lord, and whithersoever thou goest, let it be in the Lord; yea, let all thy thoughts be directed unto the Lord; yea, let the affections of thy heart be placed upon the Lord forever."

Orrin then slowly cocked back the hammer of the Python. He held his left hand up to Pete and signaled with one finger, then a second finger, and then a third. Orrin yelled, "Now!"

Pete pulled the trigger on his .45. The Detonics Combat Master fired rapidly and filled the room with six quick shots in succession in the direction of where he thought Four Eyes might be hiding. Simultaneously, Orrin took two long steps out from behind the granite pillar and jumped sideways, raising the Colt Python in the direction of Four Eyes, who was hiding behind a partition wall. Orrin shot his revolver as he flew horizontally in midair, with an exact angle to take aim at the hand holding the grenade. Orrin sent his .357 bullet at the center of the man's wrist, which was raised, about to throw a grenade. The bullet shattered his wrist bone, and the grenade dropped directly at the foot of Four Eyes. His wide-mouth scream directed at Orrin lasted only one second. The deadly explosion sent a concussive wave through the air and filled the entire room with orange flame. Orrin landed flat on the floor behind a pillar on the other side of the room, escaping the explosion and shrapnel.

Smoke and silence filled the room.

Pete was scared, and he huddled low. He was covered with white dust and sat frozen behind the pillar—the thought of standing was too frightening. There was so much death in front of his eyes, it was shocking.

Suddenly, after a period of two long minutes that felt like hours, he heard a voice.

"Pete . . . hey, Pete, you okay back there? Come on out, I got the guy. Everyone else here has passed," Orrin yelled.

Pete stood up and walked out from behind the granite pillar. Orrin emerged from the other side of the room. White dust covered both men. Pete looked around. He had a hard time mentally registering what he saw. The carnage was unbelievable: bodies were strewn everywhere, blood stained the walls. Just the head of a man lay on the floor.

Pete walked slowly over to Four Eyes, who was unrecognizable due to half of his face blown off. The body of Four Eyes was twisted and spread eagle on the far marble steps. He wore a black jumpsuit with a long black raincoat. Pete was relieved that he was finally dead.

"Who was that guy? He knew your name? Do you know something I don't?" Orrin asked.

Pete shook his head.

"It seems impossible, but whoever this man was, he should have been dead years ago. There was this case I handled in the Catskill forest where a gangster buried his treasure. I was hired by a client to assist in finding it. This murderous psycho was also going for the loot. Without delving into too much detail, he and I had a shootout, and luckily, I won. How he survived after being shot in the head, I'll never know. Even stranger, I never knew who he was, and I still don't know. It's a very long story. I'll fill you in another time. I don't have any idea how he got here or how he knew about the golden plates."

Orrin walked over to the lifeless body of Four Eyes and searched what was left of his pockets. The body was still smoking from the grenade's incendiary explosive.

"This man doesn't have any ID on him. He's just got a knife, a gun, a thick bulletproof vest, some broken-up circuit boards, and a metal left arm. And he's wearing some kind of Kevlar armored jumpsuit I've never seen before. This guy was like a one-man army. You were very fortunate to defeat him in that previous fight. Now that's a story I want to hear. There are mighty strange happenings surrounding you, my brother Pete . . . well, my brother, the Lord has permitted us the bounty of life, and we honor our Heavenly Father's decision, amen. Looks like all we have to do is mop up a bit, and by the goodness of our Heavenly Father and Jesus Christ, we have embraced the Spirit of good fortune. Amen."

"Orrin, I think I need your help with something in addition to finding the girl. My agent Greg was supposed to go to the house on Canal Street and see if he could find the girl there. He never called me back. We have to find my agent Greg. He hasn't answered his phone. I told him to go undercover and try to find the missing girl, Julia, and I've lost contact with him. The last time I spoke to him was on the cell phone yesterday. It's been too long since I heard from him, and his phone goes right to voicemail. He was supposed to call me right back after he did the job, but he never called. Can you come with me to the Canal Street house and see if something happened to him?"

"Of course, Pete, let's get on over there and find your boy. Come on, I'll drive. The church's security car is parked outside."

SALVATION

"You will never do anything in this world without courage. It is the greatest quality of the mind next to honor."

—Aristotle

PETE AND ORRIN drove fast to the Canal Street house. Pete jumped out of the car and knocked on the front door, but there was no response. He went around the house and peered into windows. The house looked empty. He banged on the door again, but there was still silence inside the house.

"Either no one is home or they're hiding." Pete said.

"My boot is about to land on that door. Stand to the side, my brother. I believe that some violent felonious activity is taking place inside this residence, and therefore I am obligated to act immediately."

Orrin lifted his leg, and his hard-heeled cowboy boot shot out like a battering ram. The door busted open. Orrin entered the house with his gun drawn. They searched the house, checking every room downstairs and upstairs. The house was empty, abandoned. There wasn't even any clothing lying around or garbage in wastebaskets.

"Let's take a peek down here in this basement. Looks like they put a padlock on the door," Orrin said.

With a couple of tugs of Orrin's pocket knife wedged into

the padlock, the metal latch came out from the door an inch. A couple more tugs loosened the latch enough for Orrin and Pete to force the door open. Orrin went through the door first, down the dark basement steps with his flashlight and Python in hand.

There was Greg, strapped to a chair, sitting in the darkness, bleeding from one side of his head. The top half of his ear had been sliced off. Pete flipped a wall switch and a string of lights along the cement walls turned on brightly. Greg's face looked pummeled. His swollen cheeks were bruised red, and his right eye was partially closed. There were a few mattresses on the floor and chairs scattered about the room. A group of people had been living in this basement for a long time by evidence of empty jugs of water lined up against a concrete wall and full garbage bags stacked up in the corner. Given the apparent dungeon like conditions, Pete thought that Greg was lucky to be alive.

"Holy shit, Greg, what the fuck happened here?"

Pete carefully took the tape off of Greg's mouth.

"Pete! Julia's CTR ring that I bought her is over there on the floor. They've got her. I know it! I overheard that they're taking her to a place called Zion."

"So they've kidnapped her? Or maybe she's hooked up with this crew? Just because we know that she was here doesn't mean that she was forcibly kidnapped. Maybe she wants to be with this motorcycle gang. But by the looks of you, we're dealing with some mighty rough customers. What the hell happened to you down here?"

"I'm telling you, Pete, these are bad dudes. A big-guy asshole who called himself Beast cut my ear off and slapped me around with his heavy hand. His bodybuilder friend who said his name was Jaguar had a shit-eating grin and tried to find out information from me. They definitely have kidnapped her. We have to go after her. Where the fuck is Zion? Isn't that a national park out West somewhere?"

Greg tried to wriggle his way out of the chair, but the chain around his waist was too tight. The thick chain was padlocked to the chair that was bolted to the floor.

Orrin used his knife to cut the tape around Greg's wrists and ankles.

"Thanks cowboy. Who might you be?" Greg asked.

"Detective Orrin Culver, Palmyra police department. Stay there just a bit young man, I'll be right back."

Orrin went outside to the church security car and brought back a bolt cutter, which he used to cut the lock, freeing Greg.

Greg jumped up out of the chair, took a few steps, and picked up the CTR ring off the floor.

"Look, you see this! It's the 'choose the right' ring I bought for Julia! It must have slipped off, or she left it for me so I'd know she was here! Julia was in this house. I've got to go after her. Where the fuck is Zion?"

Greg wiped the CTR ring off on his pants leg and put it in his pocket.

"According to the FLDS, that's a place on the Arizona-Utah border. Zion is what they call the two towns of Colorado City, Arizona, and Hildale, Utah. It's often just called Short Creek, but the FLDS agents of Satan call it Zion," Orrin said.

"Uh, Greg, buddy, you don't look too good. You need to get to the hospital. Come on, we'll drive you there now," Pete said.

"Sorry, boss, I'm getting in my car and driving straight to the airport and flying to Colorado City, Arizona, or Hildale, Utah, or Short Creek or Zion or whatever the hell those fucking bastards call it. I'm going to find Julia and get her out of there. And God help them if any of those big fucking freaks get in my way. I'll fucking kick their ass! One thing I got to say, Pete. I regret not following my heart, and not coming up here sooner to rescue her. It's something I should have done right away when we got the info that she might have been at this fucking house. No offense, boss, but the Greg Man has got to follow his own path now. I'm going out West to find her. That's my destiny."

"Okay, but listen up, Greg. We'll team up out there. Bring your radios out to Short Creek so we can coordinate. By my estimation, with us flying and them driving, we'll get to Short Creek a few hours before they do. Plus, we'll get paid for this trip because it's all part of the missing person case. Call me when you get out there, but wait for us. We'll be just a couple of hours behind you," Pete said.

Greg looked around the floor and found the top piece of his left ear that had been cut off. He went into a nearby rusty metal toolbox on a mildewed shelf and found a small roll of gray duct tape. Greg stood in front of a mirror that was over a slop sink and carefully taped the top half of his ear to what remained of the other half. He carefully wrapped a piece of white T-shirt cloth around his head, gently placing it over his left ear. Greg picked his baseball cap off the floor and covered most of his head bandage.

"Greg, maybe you should go to the hospital first and have a doctor look at your ear. Might help to get it stitched back together and save what's left of it. Also, they probably won't let you on the plane looking like that. You better get cleaned up," Pete said.

"Boss, no matter what, I have to do whatever it takes to save Julia. I can't waste any time here. I have to go where they took her so I can get her away from them. We promised each other that we'd become Mormons and get married, and that's what Big Greg is going to do. I'm keeping my promise to Julia, but first I have to rescue her from that fanatical religious motorcycle gang."

"Greg, why did you have to be such an asshole and put me in this position with the client?"

"I'm sorry, boss, you know how true love is. It's the real thing. I love her with all my heart. I'm Italian, so it's in me to become emotional. I'm telling you, Pete, this is the girl for me. But she's definitely kidnapped. Her ring on the floor means that she was here and taken out of this house by those big goons!"

"How do you know she was being forced? Do you know for sure that she was tied up here? Didn't she decide to meet with these guys before she ended up here?"

"Yeah, but, boss, she was supposed to meet with missionaries. These big guys with long hair are bad dudes, and they're not missionaries. I'm telling you, Pete, she'd never hook up with the likes of them. Julia is kidnapped and she needs our help. She was here, without a doubt, and those guys are taking her in the van to that place the cowboy here called Short Creek."

"So tell us in detail this time. What exactly happened down here?"

"After they knocked me out with maybe a stun gun or something, they led me down those steps. Then they threw me in the chair and chained me. When I looked down, I saw Julia's ring. My head was fuzzy from being knocked out but I definitely heard them say they were all meeting at Zion. Then that fucking big dude with the long hair cut part of my ear off and started slapping me. That fucking asshole! I'll hit him in the head with a fucking metal pipe."

"Are you sure they said Zion? How could you really know what they said after just becoming conscious again?"

"Listen, Pete, please, this is the ring I bought her. It must have come off of her finger while she was down here. Those dudes are skipping town and heading to Utah. That's the whole story."

"So when exactly did you hear them say Zion?" Pete asked.

"It was when they were standing at the top of the basement steps. The big dude said to someone, 'See you at Zion.' I definitely heard that."

"Okay, Greg, let's go find your love together. I'll fly out to Vegas and then drive to Short Creek. Please don't make any moves until I get there. Agreed?"

"All set, boss. I'll wait for you, but only if it helps me get to Julia sooner. If I see her, that's it, I'm getting her back on my own. I'm catching the first flight out of Rochester. But don't be late getting out there, because the Greg Man needs his woman. See you out there. I'll call you when I'm getting close, and then we'll talk about a meet-up point."

"Yeah, well hey there, hotshot, you really should take a couple hours' to get that ear stitched back on. Maybe you can save it. Why don't you listen to your boss, and do it before you go running off to Short Creek. Don't be in such a hurry to get shot by the Destroying Angels," Orrin said.

"Sorry there, cowboy, Big Greg has a mission and that's to rescue my true love and soul mate, Julia Olsen. Maybe you're the one who should go to the hospital. What's up with your eye patch?"

"Well, you got me there. We're just looking out for your welfare."

"You guys can go do whatever it is you're going to do. But I'm figuring on going right to Short Creek, so that's where I'm going. Boss, I need one big favor. What's the exact address of where those Utah plates were registered to?"

"I guess I'm going to give love a chance. Call Vicky at the office and ask her. She has that info."

"Thanks, boss, I won't forget this. I'll see you out there then."

Greg hefted on his brown leather jacket and walked up the steps of the basement and out the front door of the house. Pete and Orrin followed. They saw Greg run down the street to his parked car, jump in and make a U-turn in the opposite direction. Greg screeched his tires and revved his engine. Car exhaust blew out his car's tailpipe as he sped away down the street.

Orrin stood quietly beside Pete on the sidewalk in front of the Canal Street house and watched Greg's car in the distance, turn left and disappear.

"You know, Pete, with your man Greg there, some might say there's no cure for being headstrong. However, I admire his devotion and might give him credit for a thousand mistakes."

FORAY TO ZION

"Ignorance is preferable to error, and he is less remote from the truth who believes nothing than he who believes what is wrong."

—Thomas Jefferson

A s the morning sun rose over the Palmyra Temple, they sat on a bench and looked at each other. Pete broke into a spontaneous laugh and it infected Orrin, who started to giggle. Soon they were both slapping each other on the back while they uproariously chortled.

"Damn, Orrin, we're fortunate to have things work out like they did. Wouldn't you say?"

"Yes sir, Pete, everything came together last night. The prophecy of the golden plates has been completed. The sacred log of the Nephites is secure in the sanctum sanctorum forever."

"I would say let's go get drunk, but you don't drink," Pete said.

"No, no alcohol, no coffee either. Your personal good will is my reward and celebration. The Church is going to take care of you for this, Pete. We'll talk about your fee and I'll submit it to Church fiscal in Salt Lake."

"Orrin, there's still the matter of the girl. She's the only real reason I was up here in the first place. I got her parents waiting for my results, and now there's my rogue agent Greg flying to Short Creek, Utah. And who knows what trouble he's going to cause for me down there. If Greg finds her and then the parents somehow discover that my agent had sex with their daughter, or if by circumstance they're both held hostage in Short Creek, then, not so amusingly, I'm going to be up *shit's* creek!"

"Well, just tell them the truth and get some more business with them. You now have to go to Utah because that's where you think she is. I made a promise to you, that if you helped me with the golden plates, then I would help you get your runaway girl back. So I'm flying to Las Vegas with you, and then we'll drive to Short Creek from there."

"Thanks Orrin, I'm going to really need you out there. I'll get in touch with the parents and squeeze another check out of them. Let's meet after I take a shower at the motel, and then we'll drive to the airport. Are you going to stop at the hospital first and see what they can do for your eye?"

"Not just yet. Maybe I'll see a specialist when I get to Salt Lake. I'm looking forward to finally getting back to Utah. My mission here in Palmyra has been completed. Let's get ready to go west."

Orrin drove Pete back to the Palmyra Inn for a much-needed unwinding after the terrifying events. Pete picked up his phone and looked at it for a second, knowing that he would now have to twist the truth once again to Julia's parents. Sure, he'd keep legitimately looking for Julia; however, he'd have to leave out the fact that Greg and Julia were supposedly in love. He cued up the number for Mr. Olsen and took a breath before hitting the call button. Julia's father answered on the first ring with a gruff hello. Pete told him about how they had traced Julia from Palmyra, New York, to Arizona, where his daughter had been brainwashed by an overzealous religious sect. The father said that he would wire money to Pete's account to cover all expenses and also add a handsome $15,000 retainer for Pete and his staff. All he wanted was to find his daughter and bring her back safely to Michigan.

Pete called his wife and told her about going out to Utah. She didn't seem to mind after he assured her that the money was good and the trip was just for a couple of days. After freshening up and packing, Pete met Orrin in the lobby of the Palmyra Inn. Orrin had a black eye patch over his left eye that made him look like a pirate cowboy.

"I told the girl's parents about her going to Utah and they authorized my investigation to contact her. I'm ready to take a flight as soon as you are," Pete said.

"Okay, we're going to 'The Crick,' which is what the FLDS calls that place. That's definitely where they're taking your Julia. No doubt she's slated to become one of the sister wives of the FLDS leaders they call the seed masters."

"What's our flight plan?"

"Easiest way to get there is to land in Las Vegas, and rent a car for a three hour drive across the desert. There are just a few things I have to tie up first. Let's take a ride over to the Palmyra Temple. I want to check up on how things are going there," Orrin said.

Orrin and Pete stood in front of the Palmyra Temple and watched the cleanup crew work in relative silence. Church personnel flowed in and out of the temple, carrying out debris or bringing in construction materials. There were electricians, masons, carpet guys, cleaning women, and an amazing mass of people who seemed to appear from nowhere. Morticians wearing rubber aprons carried out the dead. Wayne County police cars were parked in the lot outside.

"Orrin, this is quite a surprising scene. I thought we would be in court for the next few years over this."

"My special Danite army folks from Salt Lake just arrived. They're all going to work in shifts around the clock."

Pete looked over at two men who had on all white suits and white ties. They were casual in attitude, lazily leaning against the doorframe of the vault room. Ivory-gripped pistols stuck out from their belts, 1911 Colt .45s in white leather cross-draw holsters that were visible to Pete by way of their open sport jackets. One of the men nodded to Pete; the other one smiled.

"Looks like you got the security end of things all tied up here, Orrin," Pete said.

Orrin looked at Pete with a wry smile.

"Wouldn't have it any other way, isn't that right, my brother?"

"So from what I see, I guess my worries are unfounded about being tied up in court in Palmyra?"

"No time for court, Pete. I made a promise to you, and I never break a promise. They're going to spin the story into a fight between rival fundamentalist religious sects who conflicted over use of the temple at the same time. It should be fifth-page news in some local paper next week. Then that's it."

"I guess you do have some official connections when you need them, eh, Orrin?"

"We've been fighting the FLDS all our lives, and we just won a big battle here. We're all very happy to clean up this situation. No one will ever say a word outside our circle."

"Okay, that's freaky, but I approve. After whatever happens

out West, I still have to get back to New York and keep making money. What time is our flight to Vegas?"

"Soon, we can drive to Rochester now," Orrin said.

"That's very good of you to honor your agreement to help me find the girl, but I know that you have to protect the golden plates, as that's your sacred vision. I don't want to impose on you, but I do welcome your assistance," Pete said.

"No worries there, Pete, the impenetrable inner sanctum sanctorum vault is three feet of solid steel and then another two feet of steel underground, so the golden plates will be safe forever."

The plane ride to Las Vegas was uneventful. Pete slept or looked out the window most of the way. Orrin used the flight time for reading of the scriptures. When they got to the Las Vegas airport, Orrin rented a Ford Mustang with a V8 engine. They drove fast across the desert, at ninety-mile-per-hour highway speeds.

During the drive, Orrin explained to Pete the details of Short Creek and how the place is a special location that the FLDS adopted. Also known as The Crick, the enclave is a Utah-Arizona border town that became a hotbed of FLDS activity. It was first settled by the FLDS in the 1930s. The people who live there are usually called "Crickers." Recently, the year 2002 brought on an ever-strong membership in The Crick; consequently, the illegal activity of child slavery and child marriage became rampant. The community is often just called Colorado City. Warren Jeffs, became the new leader, taking over as the FLDS prophet from his near-death father. The reports of his leadership were outrageous regarding the marriage of young teenagers to much older men.

After the mainstream Mormon LDS Church condemned the

practice of polygamy, fundamentalist Mormons who believed in the principle of plural marriage were excommunicated. The Fundamentalist Latter-day Saints, who believe in plural marriage, defend their practice of acquiring many "sister wives," young women who are promised to men. This practice was in direct conflict with the American way of life and consequently, the FLDS became withdrawn from the rest of society. They settled in Short Creek, a beautiful red-rock location that is very remote. In 1953, there was a big Utah government raid on the FLDS. The State government separated hundreds of children from their parents. Needless to say, this forced family separation was not a good thing to do politically, and the Utah government was shamed after the children were finally returned to their parents.

Pete and Orrin had arrived at Short Creek. The sight of the steep mountains behind the town was distinctive. It looked spectacular when the early-morning sun hit those mountains. How could so much evil lurk in a place that was so exceptionally scenic? The flat land in front of the jagged red-rock mountains was a dramatic backdrop to the picturesque desert town occupied by the FLDS. Although the natural beauty of Short Creek was outstanding, the ugly FLDS human element had dictatorship control over every facet of the two towns, including the mayor's office, the only supermarket, and the police.

Greg was parked on the side of a dirt road, just outside of town, sleeping in his car. As Orrin and Pete drove up, Greg propped up his car seat.

"Eh, boss, I got here a while ago and been catching up on some z's ever since."

The three men spoke briefly to verify their plan.

Both cars sped down the red dirt road, causing a plume of dust behind the fast-moving Mustang and Greg's compact two-door car. The sun was intensely bright, and if not for his dark sunglasses, Pete's eyes would be burned out from the light. They drove directly to the registrant address of the white van's Utah license plate.

The entire perimeter of the house was surrounded by a heavy corrugated-metal wall that was eight feet high. A hodgepodge of scrap metal acted as a movable gate that could be slid to the side. From a gap in the gate they saw a one acre dirt compound with a brown two-level house in the center. There were no vehicles at the house. It looked empty.

Pete asked Greg for one of his walkie-talkies and then told Orrin they'd wait at one end of the street while Greg waited around the corner.

The hot air caused blurred mountain mirages in the distance. An intense sun overhead baked the Ford Mustang. The car was turned off and Pete felt like he was sitting in an oven. The temperature was a hundred degrees inside the car. Their time was spent just watching and waiting. The hours dragged on. There were no assurances that these thugs were taking Julia to Short Creek and this western surveillance could turn out to be an enormous waste of time and money. If the targets showed up, there would be a frenzied maelstrom of activity. Decisions about what to do would have to be made in an instant. Pete wished he was relaxing on Jones Beach in Long Island instead of sitting in the desert.

There must be another way to live.

After a few hours of enduring the heat and monotony, they heard the sound of motorcycles in the distance.

"Here they come. Duck down," Pete said.

They watched three motorcycles and the white van drive into the compound.

"Pete, Pete, come in, you guys! That's the van from Palmyra!" the radio cackled.

"Ten four on that, Greg, let's hold tight and we'll talk about options."

After only about two minutes, the three motorcycles rode out of the compound and left the neighborhood.

"Let's hit it now," Orrin said.

"Go, Greg, now! Go to the house!" Pete yelled into the walkie-talkie.

The two cars drove fast to the address on Willow Road, right through the entrance to the compound. Both cars' braked fast on the dry dirt, causing a crescent of brown dust. Greg quickly jumped out of his car and forcefully knocked on the door. Pete and Orrin walked up behind Greg. When the door opened, there stood Greg's nemesis. At six foot six and three hundred pounds, with a square head of long hair and fully bearded jaw. The FLDS Destroying Angel known as Beast was standing directly in front of Greg.

Rage overtook Greg when he recognized Beast.

"Hey, buddy! Remember me?"

Greg sprang up from the doorway, using his powerful thighs. At the same time, he punched Beast directly in the face with a force that caused an audible smack.

Beast stumbled back a few steps and seemed slightly dazed by the shock of the punch.

"And you know something?" Greg yelled, as he advanced on Beast and punched him in the face a second time, making the giant man stumble back again, "you're a fucking asshole!"

Greg leaped straight forward with his fist extended and landed a square-knuckled punch directly on the point of Beast's broad jaw. The giant fell backwards and hit the floor with enough force to shake the entire house. Beast lay still, knocked out unconscious on the wood floor.

"Well now, I guess that boy had it comin' to him," Orrin said.

When they entered the house, it was empty, void of furniture, otherwise ordinary looking with the exception of a padlock on a wooden closet door.

Orrin placed the handle of his knife in the door latch and tugged hard. Then he forced his shoulder between the partially open door space and the metal latch broke off the wall. When he opened the door, a secret room was revealed under the stairway of the house. Orrin entered with a flashlight, and there in the small room stood four young women. They were all wearing the same one-piece white dress. The four women cautiously walked out from the hidden room into the bright light of the bare house.

Suddenly, there she was—Julia! After all this time and all these miles!

Her eyes lit up with glee when she saw Greg.

"My love is here! I prayed to God that you would rescue me!" she yelled.

Julia leaped at Greg and hugged him with all her might. They both started crying as they embraced, pouring tears, bodies shaking from their sobs. Greg and Julia kissed for a long time.

"I'm so sorry this happened to you, being held prisoner and all. It's horrible," Greg said.

The other three girls stood in the sunlit room. Their eyes squinted from the brightness.

When Pete looked towards the stairway, he saw two young guys wearing white shirts and paisley ties at the top of the stairs looking down. One of them was talking on a cordless phone held tightly to his ear.

"Hey, you two jerks on the stairs! Who are you calling? Fucking nerds! What's going on in this place here?" Pete yelled.

The two young men turned and ran back up the stairs and out of sight.

"Everyone, let's get in the cars. We need to get out of here quick! If these guy's friends get wind that we're here, then trouble is going to come, a lot more trouble than we can handle," Orrin said.

As the group ran out of the front entrance of the house, Greg stopped and turned to face Julia. He reached into his pocket and took out the CTR ring. Julia's face lit up when she saw the ring. Greg slowly slid the ring on her finger and kissed her lips. She emotionally hugged him tight. They ran to Greg's car, hand in hand.

The three young women got into the back seat of the Ford Mustang, and Julia jumped into the front seat of Greg's car. They sped out of the metal-walled compound and raced to the junction that would take them out of Short Creek. Both cars kicked up a cloud of brown dirt as they sped down the road to freedom. Pete was feeling elated. This was the end of the line. In just a few hours' time, he'd be on a jet plane back to New York City.

Joyous thoughts of home were suddenly dashed. Both cars had to slow down, creeping forward to a complete stop.

"Oh, Orrin, that doesn't look good. What's happening up ahead there?"

"FLDS, they're blocking us in."

About three hundred feet ahead, ten large pickup trucks blocked the road. The trucks were parked on a section of road that went over a dry creek bed. A man got out of one of the trucks holding a double-barreled shotgun. A few other men stepped out of their trucks, all of them wearing baseball caps, denim jackets, and jackboots, holding a variety of shotguns and rifles. A police-marked SUV with roof lights was in the line of vehicles. The Hildale marshal got out of his truck wearing a tall, tan cowboy hat. He stood in front of his SUV and spit on the ground. The FLDS marshal raked the slide action of a Remington 870 pump shotgun.

"Oh please, don't let anyone take us back to that hot room," one of the young ladies said, crying in the back seat of the Mustang.

Pete's nervous body heat caused moisture to form on the front windshield. He looked over at Greg's stopped car. Greg sat behind the steering wheel with a wide-mouthed expression of surprise.

"Hey, Orrin, what's your call here? We can't turn around . . . there are mountains behind us. Maybe we'll have to surrender this time. There are ten pickup trucks in front of us, and all those fanatics have guns. We're totally outnumbered," Pete said.

A thousand things ran through Pete's mind, visions of his wife, the kids, and his home in New York.

What does this life really mean? Is this the end? So it all came down to this moment, out here, in the middle of the desert. This guy Orrin is now going to start shooting again, but there's no fighting our way out of this situation. Oh, Greg and Julia and those poor girls. Oh, God, help us please, help us out of this. Please help us.

Orrin sat stoically, staring ahead at the line of pickup trucks and unsavory men. Orrin's eyes got watery and tears flowed down his cheeks. Pete became worried but didn't want to show his panic to the women in the back seat. The situation mandated that Pete surrender; he could think of no other way to avoid getting killed by the wall of steel and guns that were just three hundred feet ahead. Orrin's face was turning a shade of red, and Pete wondered if he was going to get out of the car and take a shot at the small army in front of them. Pete considered grabbing Orrin's arm if he started shooting, because he knew that it would be certain death to engage the FLDS militia. The car suddenly got intolerably hot, and Pete opened his window.

"The Lord shall reward the doer of evil according to his wickedness. I'm going to pray to the Archangel Michael. May he grant me the Spirit and defeat those who walk with Lucifer. The demons of hell are upon us!" Orrin said.

Orrin got out of the car, closed his door, and walked a few slow steps in front of the Mustang.

Pete also got out of the car and stood in the road.

"Hey, Orrin! What are you doing?"

Orrin dropped to his knees in the middle of the dirt road, crossed his arms, and bowed his head in prayer. The three young women in the Mustang's back seat stepped out and walked from the car, their white dresses blowing in the desert breeze as they all held hands and got on their knees together to pray. Greg and Julia also got out of their car and got on their knees in prayer. A sudden breeze started, whipping up the dirt all around them. Pete was overcome with the desperation of their situation. He had been through a lot in the past few days, but this state of affairs was the grand finale of misfortune. This was it. All he ever had or would ever have was dependent in this moment, and there was no actual help to be had anymore. They were done. Pete resolved that prayer was the only thing left to do. There were moments in the past that he prayed to God and his prayers were answered. He knew there was no other explanation that could have fit during those times of need other than that of a divine hand reaching in and saving him. Now Pete's pact with God must be summoned once again. He dropped to his knees and clasped his hands together.

Oh, God, please save us. I know I've asked for You're help in the past with the deal that if You saved me, I would always believe in You. Well You did save me, and more than once too. You are real, God. I acknowledge You, and I pray to Your total greatness. We need Your help now, just as much as I ever did in the past. Please help us, God. Please help us, God. Please help us, God.

Suddenly Pete heard Orrin's loud voice, higher pitched than normal and full of emotion. He was on his knees, and his torso rocked back and forth.

"And Michael, the seventh angel, even the archangel, shall gather together his armies, even the hosts of heaven. And the devil shall gather together his armies; even the hosts of hell, and shall come up to battle against Michael and his armies! And then cometh the battle of the great God; and the devil and his armies shall be cast away into their own place, that they shall not have power over the saints any more at all. For Michael shall fight their battles, and shall overcome him who seeketh the throne of him who sitteth upon the throne, even the Lamb!"

Pete stood up and noticed ominous dark clouds forming in the distance. A gray air nebula morphed and coagulated into a dark swirling storm. The black nimbus cloud quickly approached from a distance. The dark cloud swirled and congealed, about a quarter mile away. The sinister mass got larger. Bolts of blue lightning lit up the black clouds in strobe-like flashes, crooked bolts of lightning reached to the ground from the bottom of the clouds, and loud thunder soon followed. The wind picked up terrifically and blew at the white dresses of the three kneeling women. A turbid mist formed in the air. Pete looked up and saw light from a rainbow. It arched over him, but then the light transformed and became a patchwork of colors. The patchwork of light took on a human form, a one-hundred-foot-tall colossus man holding a sword. The glistening rainbow image was a multicolored glowing angel with wings on his back. A bright-yellow halo emanated from behind the angel's head. The angel raised his sword, which filled the sky with a bright-orange color. The blade itself was like a living, pulsing, solar deity, an orange-hot, glowing straight beam of light. Pete felt a rush of warm heat radiate from the blade. The enormous sword swooped down slowly over the pickup trucks.

The rainbow angel continued to stand over them as a bright prismatic sparkling body with changing colors and sun-filled yellow-golden hair. The angel glanced directly at Pete for a moment; the unmistakable eye contact sent a wave of emotion that consumed Pete and he spontaneously cried. The Spirit had entered his soul. The advent of this angel of God was too much to bear without expressing a loving response. Pete cried again and lifted both his arms to the angel while looking skyward. He prayed for God to save him so he could go back home to his wife and children in New York. Pete spread both his arms while looking skyward, surrendering himself to the angel and to God. Pete closed his eyes and silently prayed to the angel and to God to save the people he was with: Orrin, Greg, Julia, and the three women. The faces of his two children flashed in his mind.

Pete's face was wet with rain and tears. He looked up to the sky and cried out. "I will always believe!"

Then, just as suddenly as the rainbow angel had formed, the light dissipated and the image quickly evaporated. A bird's feather landed on the ground near Pete, a large black feather, about a foot long.

Pete heard something in the distance, a rumbling sound. A low-toned thunderous rushing noise. A great force vibrated the earth, and it shook the ground beneath where Pete was standing. Pebbles on the dirt road bounced and vibrated. The white noise became louder and louder. All of a sudden, a fuming tsunami of churning brown water broke into view, gushing through the canyon at forty miles per hour, an angry torrent of debris-filled water. The flash flood was a flowing death, a fast-moving force too powerful for anything to resist. The twenty-foot wave was inescapable, a rock-filled deluge flowing fast down the dry creek, heading straight for the line of pickup trucks. The dark wall of water roared as it hit the first pickup truck broadside. The tremendous hydraulic force pushed the pickup trucks all together. The surge flowed over them and enveloped them. The trucks flipped over one another as the multi-ton swirling mesh of steel vehicles and men were forced down river by the powerful flash flood.

A couple of minutes later, when the water subsided to a trickle, all of the FLDS pickup trucks and men had been washed hundreds of feet away. Human bodies and limbs looked broken and skewed as they remained motionless in the mud. Their trucks were ripped to pieces, blown tires and shredded car body parts were strewn everywhere.

By the grace of God, the span over the creek bed remained intact.

Pete stood in shock, not moving for a few seconds.

Orrin stood up and motioned with his arms.

"Okay now! Everyone back in the cars! It's time to get out of here! Let's go!"

Their two cars drove towards the bridge and sped over the creek bed as fast as their cars would go. Pete was too shocked to say anything. The three women in the back seat were silent too. Finally, after an hour, Pete spoke up.

"There were some amazing happenings back there. The Archangel Michael saved us. I know now that I have to believe in God and the power of good over evil. I could say that a scientifically plausible flash flood just happened at the exact time we needed the FLDS thugs to disappear. But it's obvious, God is for real and so are His angels."

"Amen to that, Brother Pete, amen to that," Orrin sighed.

SALT LAKE

"God has shown me that this is the spot to locate this people, and here is where they will prosper. . . . As the Saints gather here and get strong enough to possess the land, God will temper the climate and we shall build a city and a temple to the Most High God in this place. We will extend our settlements to the east and west, to the north and to the south, and we will build towns and cities by the hundreds, and thousands of Saints will gather in from the nations of the earth. This will become the great highway of nations."

—**Brigham Young**

THE SALT LAKE climate felt warm and dry, unlike the colder moist weather in Palmyra. Here out West, there was a certain beauty that Pete couldn't quite put his finger on. The Wasatch Mountains in the distance and the flat, clean city gave the atmosphere a surreal exquisiteness.

Pete drove the Mustang north on their way to Salt Lake City, as Orrin made phone calls to people he knew in his hometown. The three young women in back were smiling and talking with each another. The moroseness of imprisonment had fadded, and freedom brought a joyful glee to their faces. Greg and Julia followed Pete's car the whole way, close behind the Mustang.

Pete looked in the rearview mirror and saw that they were vivaciously talking with each other nonstop.

After a five-hour drive through the Utah countryside, they finally arrived at Salt Lake City. The people on the sidewalks were smiling at one another, which was something Pete was not used to seeing.

They drove into the center of the city and dropped off the three young women at a social-service help center. Orrin called ahead, and there were caring case workers waiting for the three women. Pete and Orrin drove on to a curved-shaped hotel with outside porches for every room. Pete and Orrin got out of the car and stretched. Greg and Julia pulled up behind and parked. They all stood in front of the hotel smiling at one another, each silently knowing what they all had been through.

"Well, Pete, our mission is complete here. I arranged a car to pick you up for the airport tomorrow. And Greg and Julia, I got you each a place to live, just a few miles south of here. It's a town called Provo."

"That sounds perfect!" Julia squealed.

"Julia, you'll be living in the BYU dormitory. For you, Greg, I got an on-campus apartment."

"Hey, Orrin, buddy, nice, you're really hooking me up. I'm going to owe you big time," Greg said.

"Okay, you can thank me by praying to our Heavenly Father and accomplishing the attainment of the Melchizedek Priesthood. Also, I got you a job as an assistant coach on the lacrosse team at BYU. But first, you and I are going to the hospital to get fixed up. They'll sew that ear back on. As for me, the local doctor said that I should be able to regain my full sight. To build your future, Julia, I got you a job in the campus cafeteria, where you'll work when you're not taking classes. You'll be enrolled as a full undergrad here at the Y on an open grant. I know a lot of people at BYU, and they unlocked their doors for us. I'm looking forward to hearing about your success. I'm going to live in Salt Lake from here on out, so if you guys need anything, I'll be right here. Oh and guess what? Right on time, here come my two friends now."

A brand-new late-model Ford pickup in pearl white drove up to where the group was standing outside the hotel. Two well-groomed suit-and-tie middle-aged men got out. Orrin shook each man's hand in peculiar ways, using their thumbs and grasping each other's shoulders. They obviously knew each other very well.

"This is Elder Bill Venck, one of our BYU lacrosse coaches, and Elder Lincoln Larson from the admissions office. Gentlemen, these are the two fine young people I spoke of, Julia Olsen and Greg Rocco. We just drove through the desert for a while, but I'm sure everyone will clean up real nice." Orrin smiled.

The two men spoke briefly with Greg and Julia. Smiles were all around, and it appeared that the lacrosse coach was impressed by Greg's varsity career at Marist. The admissions guy was cheerfully speaking to Julia. They all shook hands, and the two men got back in their white pickup and left.

"So it looks like you guys are going to be in their program?" Pete asked.

"We're a couple for life now, joined together by our covenant," Julia said.

"Don't you worry about us, boss," Greg said. "Me and Julia are going to be the best Mormons you ever saw. This whole setup is outrageously off the hook. Hey, Pete, are you going to come back to Utah next year for our wedding?"

"You send me an invitation, and I'll be there. But for now, I'm bidding you goodbye. I have to get some sleep and get back to New York City. Oh, Julia, I'll have to call your parents and tell them that you're here. I hope that's okay. They are my clients, you know."

Julia sighed, her shoulders slumped, and she looked down.

"Well, I guess if you have to. There's not much love between me and my parents, you know."

"You're out here with a whole spiritual family to support you and a loving fiancé who will do anything for you. I wouldn't sweat it. If they want to come out here just to talk with you, it will be fine. Now you can choose your faith and decide how to live, because it's your life, not theirs," Pete said.

Pete shook Greg's hand and hugged Julia goodbye.

Orrin's sinewy arms wrapped around Pete in a warm embrace that made Pete feel that this ultimate saga had come to an end. Pete was thankful and closed his eyes, trying to hold onto the euphoric feeling forever.

In the lofty room of the high-rise hotel, Pete looked out at the mountains and thought what an idyllic place this was. He tried to relax a little before calling Julia's parents. Once again, he felt the anguish of betrayal. He could inform them that Julia and Greg had taken a vow of chastity for a year before they would get married in the Salt Lake City Temple. Now it was time to decide how much truth to tell the parents.

After resting on the bed for an hour, transfixed in the moment of just gazing out at the mountainous scenery, he decided it was time to call the parents.

"Hello, Mr. Olsen, it's Pete Baranowski. I'm here in Salt Lake City, Utah, and I'm happy to report that I've found your daughter."

"Wait! Wait! Let me get Mrs. Olsen, hold on!"

A few moments later, Pete heard another telephone pick up.

"We're both on the phone, Pete. Tell us. Tell us where she

is? Is she okay? You're in Salt Lake City now? You're not in that town you said you were going to in Arizona?" the father asked.

"Sir, your daughter is safe and sound, here in Salt Lake City, Utah. Also, I'd like to tell you that my former agent Greg is going to stay in Utah and get a job."

"Greg? We met Greg. He's your investigator who told us that our Julia was up in that apartment. Does he have family in Salt Lake City? Is that why he's staying there?"

"Not exactly, but yes, you might say he has a new family. And I must tell you, sir that Greg and Julia have become somewhat of a couple. I did not know about their relationship until recently."

"This is strange news, Pete. What's going on here? I must tell you I'm very surprised, and a little upset," Mrs. Olsen said.

"What's this, Baranowski? Your agent, Greg, is cavorting with our Julia?" the father barked.

"I wouldn't use those words, sir. I would say that they love each other," Pete said.

"You mean my Julia and your investigator Greg are an item? He's a good-looking boy. They're not going to live together. Are they?" the mom asked.

"No, they won't be living together. I know that because they are both becoming Mormon and joining the Church of Jesus Christ of Latter-day Saints. They have to take an oath of chastity for a year prior to their marriage."

"They're becoming Mormons?" the father asked.

"Oh my god, what's going on? What's happening with our Julia?" The mother cried.

"I don't think it's a big deal, so the two of them found some religion. There could be worse things, you know. I have her address in case you want to write her or visit her."

"I don't know what to say, Baranowski. I'm grateful that you found my daughter, but it seems like finding her has come at a cost. What the hell is going on with all of you crazy people? Did you just say that our Julia is going to marry Greg? Is she totally out of that other business?"

"Yes, she is finished with that other business, forever. She's going to live permanently in Utah and go to BYU as an undergrad on a grant. I think this has all worked out well in the end. We all should be happy for Julia and Greg."

"I suppose you're right, Pete," Ms. Olsen chimed in. "Life and love. The world works in ways that are not predictable. Who would have thought that our baby would end up in Utah and become a Mormon? But as you say, there could be worse things."

"I think Julia and Greg have found true happiness through all of this. The cosmos has given love a chance and let those two find each other," Pete said.

"Sure, sure, Baranowski, now just tell us that address where Julia is staying and we'll take it from here. Go ahead, I have a pen."

Jet-plane rides gave Pete uninterrupted time to just think about the past, the future, and his everyday existence. The ever-present whir of the jet engines helped him contemplate what his next move in life was going to be. Some passengers liked to sleep; others liked to watch movies or work on their computers. Pete looked out the window and wondered about all the people living down below. What were their lives like? What did they do for a living? Were they happy where they were living, or would they rather live somewhere else? Did they believe in God?

The shock of everything that had happened over the past few

days still lingered in Pete's consciousness. He would never go back to Short Creek, the most beautiful and the most dangerous place in the world. Looking back, the despicable FLDS and their criminal human trafficking continued to give him a queasy feeling.

The golden plates were well protected, and Orrin was happy to get back to Salt Lake City now that his holy mission in Palmyra had been fulfilled. The bizarre trail that guided Pete to help Orrin was a path of events led by an omnipotent hand.

Three days later, Pete sat at his desk, taking care of the usual hassles for attorneys who wanted their cases done yesterday. That's when an unexpected FedEx envelope arrived. The return address read "Salt Lake City, Utah". Pete eagerly ripped open the envelope and looked inside. He saw a letter-sized white envelope, which contained a check from the Church of Jesus Christ of Latter-day Saints to Baranowski Investigations for $250,000. There was also a written note from Orrin Culver: "Thanks for all your help, Pete. Please find the enclosed check as payment for your much-needed investigation services."

Wow! The Church really does stand for truth and goodness! I guess that's what makes the Mormon faith so strong, its steadfast base of righteousness and brotherly love. These are qualities that are easy to become attached to.

Pete was elated over the large sum. He leaned back in his office chair and looked out the window at the hazy New York skyline.

Feelings of well-being and profound introspection filled Pete's soul as he daydreamed about the meaning of life.

Love is the greatest reality. The love between Greg and Julia has now changed their world completely. These last few days have shown me that faith is more important than fact and love is the greatest expression of faith. True love can be stronger than steel and hotter than the sun. Our faith in love is a Devine belief, locked inside our hearts forever.